BA

THE HOUSE OPPOSITE

BARBARA NOBLE was born in 1907. The author of six novels, she was also head of the UK office of Doubleday Books and responsible for the publication of thousands of further works by other writers.

Born in London, Barbara Noble was educated at home by her mother. Her first novel, *The Years that Take the Best Away*, was published to acclaim when she was only 22. After moving to London, and continuing to write and publish novels, she took a job with 20th Century Fox, eventually becoming story editor, buying and negotiating film rights for production.

In 1953 she became the UK editor for Doubleday, a job she held for 20 years. In this rôle, she published works by Margery Allingham, Daphne du Maurier, Olivia Manning and Ruth Rendell, among many others.

After retirement, Barbara Noble continued to work as an editor on a part-time basis into her eighties. She died in 2001.

NOVELS BY BARBARA NOBLE

The Years That Take the Best Away (1930)
The Wave Breaks (1932)
Down by the Salley Gardens (1935)
The House Opposite (1943)
Doreen (1946)
Another Man's Life (1952)

BARBARA NOBLE

THE HOUSE OPPOSITE

With an introduction by
Connie Willis

DEAN STREET PRESS

A Furrowed Middlebrow Book
FM36

Published by Dean Street Press 2019

First published in 1943 by William Heinemann

Cover by DSP

ISBN 978 1 913054 29 8

www.deanstreetpress.co.uk

To ENGIE
with my love and grateful thanks
for scoldings, exhortations and
encouragement.

INTRODUCTION

LET ME SAY right up front that I loved Barbara Noble's *The House Opposite*, and I am so happy that it's being introduced to a whole new generation of readers.

"Well, of course," you might say, "It's about the London Blitz." And it's true, anyone who knows anything about me knows I've been fascinated (some would say obsessed) by the Blitz ever since I first visited St. Paul's Cathedral years ago and saw the stone dedicated to the Blitz's fire watch. I've done research on it, read as many books about it as I could find, and have written about it repeatedly. So the assumption is that I'd love any novel that's Blitz-related.

But, actually, the opposite is true. I dislike most novels written about the Blitz. Most authors get the details, or worse, the attitudes of the time wrong, and the stories they tell are melodramatic and over-the-top, as if they concluded the Blitz wasn't dramatic enough on its own.

This is true not only of books written today but also those who experienced the Blitz first-hand, which proves that just because someone lives through something, it doesn't mean they know anything about it. In fact, the reverse is often true.

I can only think of two movies and two books which, till now, have gotten the particulars, the tone, and the story of the Blitz right. The movies are 1987's *Hope and Glory* and 2016's *Their Finest*, and the books are Rumer Godden's *An Episode of Sparrows* and Graham Greene's *The End of the Affair*. And now, *The House Opposite*.

Barbara Noble lived through the Blitz (though, as I said, that's no guarantee of anything) and her details of it--the makeshift ARP posts, the broken glass, the gutted houses, the tube station platforms covered with sleeping people, the tin helmets and searchlights and sirens and scent of charred wood and cordite--are spot on. But the tone of the book is spot-on, too. And so is the story she tells.

It centers on twenty-six-year-old Elizabeth Simpson, a secretary in a London office, and Owen Cathcart, the eighteen-year-old boy who lives in the house across the street from her. They're both right in the thick of the Blitz, and you'd think their primary concern would be staying alive. After all, not only are there nightly raids and fires and falling shrapnel in their neighborhood, but Elizabeth works in the constantly-bombed center of London, and Owen's waiting to be called up and looking at a future as an RAF pilot, a job with a life expectancy measured in months, if not weeks.

But they scarcely seem to think about those dangers. Instead they're consumed with personal fears and concerns--Elizabeth with the problematic affair she's having with her boss and Owen with the fear that his hero-worship of his cousin might mean he's gay--exactly the sorts of things Elizabeth and Owen's counterparts in far less dangerous eras would worry about.

This is true of all the characters in *The House Opposite*, and it's amazing how many of them we get to know in the course of this short book--Owen's kindly mother and mercenary father, Elizabeth's terrified mother and her irrepressible friend Joan, her boss's oblivious (and incredibly annoying) wife, Owen's cousin Derek, Elizabeth's soldier suitor, the vicar's daughter, the head air raid warden, an injured child at the hospital. And Elizabeth's father, an unassuming, seemingly ordinary man with surprising depths of empathy and compassion. We come to know them all, with their flaws and their virtues, their vulnerabilities and pettinesses and secret fears.

But the character we come to know best is the Blitz itself. Even though it's rarely addressed directly, it's always there, hovering over everyone and everything, a lurking, deadly presence which affects their every move, their every decision.

"If she stopped to wash her hands," Elizabeth thinks as she starts for the tube station after work, playing the game she plays with herself every night, "it might make all the difference to whether she was killed over not . . . If she waited for the escalator to carry her or walked down to the bottom, possibly catching an earlier train, it might make all the difference. This game pleased her very much. It added a perceptible spice to the general mixed flavour of life."

But the game's real, and so are the consequences. Accident and chance always play a part in our lives, but in wartime that part is magnified exponentially, and the Blitz was full of near-misses and deadly coincidences, of minor actions that took on cosmic importance.

Barbara Noble understood that perfectly. As I said, she lived through the Blitz. She was working in the city just like her heroine Elizabeth when the war started, a thirty-year-old who worked as a typist in the London office of Twentieth-Century Fox and in her spare time as a Red Cross nurse. After the war, she graduated to being a story editor, buying film rights for them, and then went on to become the UK editor for Doubleday, introducing novels by authors like Margery Allingham, Ruth Rendell, and Daphne DuMaurier to American readers and becoming one of the most respected figures in British publishing.

She also wrote novels of her own: *The Years that Take the Best Away, The Wave Breaks, Down by the Salley Gardens, Another Man's Life.* And two books set during the Blitz: *Doreen*, about a child who's evacuated to the country and is dealing with the conflicted loyalties of having two families and maneuvering between two classes of society, and *The House Opposite*, which is not only set in the Blitz, but is about the Blitz and what it was like to be an ordinary person living through an extraordinary time, working and eating and sleeping, making friends and growing up and experiencing heartbreak, while all the time waiting for the ax to fall.

Noble captured that feeling so perfectly that, as I read *The House Opposite*, I found my heart pounding during even the quietest of scenes: Elizabeth eating dinner in a restaurant with her lover, Owen walking through the park late at night, Elizabeth checking on a ward full of sleeping patients. Knowing that at any moment everyone--and everything--could be blown apart.

Which eventually happens. But not at all in the way you expect, and so casually that at first you don't realize it's happened—or how much damage was sustained.

All this might make *The House Opposite* sound like a depressing read, but Barbara Noble also understood that the Blitz wasn't unrelentingly grim, and that good things happened in it, too, and sometimes because of it—unlikely friendships and surprising acts of kindness, moments of hilarity and beauty and contentment. And the awareness and even wisdom that comes from living in such an extraordinary time:

"In between the sticky moments, we seem to have gone on much as usual," Elizabeth says, "being pleased or miserable about the same things, worrying about money and what our neighbors think of us, and getting a devil of a kick out of any sort of promotion or achievement. We're little people, and the big things have to be reduced in size or we can't handle them."

Indeed.

The House Opposite is a wonderful book, full of people we care about and rich with telling details and unexpected insights and indelible images. It's a book for any and all eras.

Particularly our own.

Connie Willis

* * * * *

CONNIE WILLIS is a multiple award-winning writer, a member of the Science Fiction Hall of Fame, and a Science Fiction Writers of America Grand Master. She's most famous for her novels about time-travelling historians from Oxford University who visit the Middle Ages, Victorian England—and the London Blitz, in works like her two-volume novel, *Blackout*-and-*All Clear*, and the novelette "Fire Watch," both of which won the Nebula and Hugo Awards.

CHAPTER I

CARTER CAME into Elizabeth Simpson's office at a quarter to six, ostensibly to borrow her paste-pot but actually because he hoped that the sight of him would recall to her mind the evening post. This stratagem was effective. She looked up at him over her typewriter, her hands resting on the keyboard, her forehead losing its frown of concentration.

"I expect you want to get off, Carter. I've done the envelopes for these last letters. You can stamp and enter them, and then cut along."

He thanked her, thinking she was not a bad sort, in spite of her strict ways. Miss Walsh was better fun but not so thoughtful as Mrs. Simpson. Now he could be on duty punctually at the Post.

Elizabeth had finished one letter, with the initials A.F./ E.S. in the bottom left-hand corner, and was inserting the carbon for another, when Joan Walsh came into her room, already dressed to leave. Her round face, always cheerful and unabashed, looked more child-like than ever framed in the hood of her camel-hair coat.

"Still at it? That man dictates too much. You ought to tell him."

"Don't interrupt me, there's a good girl. He's waiting for them."

She hoped that Joan would take the hint and go, but Joan was not much good at taking hints. She propped herself against the radiator and studied her make-up in a pocket mirror.

"I gather that Mr. Rowland has already left," Elizabeth said after a pause.

"Half an hour ago. Going to sit up all night holding wifie's hand and drinking cocoa, I bet."

Against her will, Elizabeth smiled. "Joan, you are a fool! Go home yourself, then."

"What's the attraction? Just the usual dreary party in the basement. Old Miss Dalrymple playing Patience, far too aristocratic to jump even when the roof falls in . . . Mrs. Henley knitting like a robot, the colour of cream cheese . . . Major Brett telling us what a hero he was in the last war and bobbing up and down the area steps all the evening, looking for incendiaries . . . and me manicuring my nails and wondering if the next lull will last long enough for me to get to the bathroom and wash stockings. It's dull as hell."

Elizabeth stopped trying to type and leant back in her chair. "'Dull as hell'. I wonder if that's the real horror of hell? That it's dull?"

"We shall all know soon enough if this sort of thing keeps up," Joan said cheerfully. "Well, I'll stop worrying you and go now."

But she did not go. The telephone bell rang and curiosity detained her. Elizabeth said:

"Who? . . . Why, Bob! Where are you? . . . This evening?" She hesitated. "I'm terribly sorry—if only you could have let me know you were getting this leave—I'm on duty at the hospital tonight . . . Of course I can't, silly. There's a war on. What about lunch tomorrow? . . . All right. Here, at the office—one o'clock. We'll decide where to go when we see what's standing. Where are you putting up? . . . Well, that sounds moderately safe. Don't do anything silly. Good-bye, Bob."

As she hung up the receiver, Joan said candidly:

"I didn't know you were on duty tonight. I should have thought all the patients were safely tucked in bed by the time you got there. What do you find to do?"

"Give 'em bed-pans," Elizabeth said shortly. "You're the most vulgarly inquisitive girl I know."

"Don't be cross with little Joannie. I might not be here in the morning and then you'd be sorry."

"That's cheating. All right, I forgive you—but for God's sake run along now and leave me in peace to finish these letters."

In ten minutes' time she had typed the linked initials on the last page and Carter had put the stamped envelopes on her desk and gone off whistling in happy anticipation of another night's death and destruction. Miss Lewis, the switchboard girl, left with him.

"I've put a line through to Mr. Foster's room," she said in parting. "Good night, Miss Simpson."

"Good night, Miss Lewis. Take care of yourself."

Mr. Foster was waiting to sign his letters, his feet on the desk, his chair tilted back, reading the evening paper. He did not look up when his secretary came into the room, but he murmured an acknowledgment when she placed it neatly-spaced, uncreased sheets of paper in front of him, swung down his legs and glanced through each letter before signing it. As Elizabeth waited, her glance went idly round the room, noting a boxful of filing to be done in the morning, a fresh cigarette burn on the edge of the desk, the headlines of the newspaper. When he had scrawled his name for the fourth time, he glanced up at her questioningly.

"Tonight?"

Her voice was carefully expressionless. "Bob Craven rang up."

"Craven? I thought he was at Aldershot or somewhere."

"He's got forty-eight hours' leave. He wanted me to have dinner with him."

"But you're not going to?" It was more statement than question.

"No. I told him I was on duty at the hospital."

Alex grinned. "That hospital would be surprised if it knew how many hours you put in there. Where are we going to eat? The concert will begin about seven o'clock, I suppose."

"Can't we have dinner at the flat?"

"A bit too soon, don't you think? The waiter so obviously recognised you last time. The Hungaria is nicely underground, but we're almost certain to run into people we know."

"Oh, I don't care where we go." Her voice was weary. "We'll try and find somewhere open in Soho. I don't want to be late home, anyhow. I didn't get much sleep last night."

"Noisy?"

"No. Uneasy thoughts. The noises didn't help, either, of course. I didn't hear anything come down, except shrapnel, but the guns were banging away and the 'planes went over in batches every half-hour or so. Probably *en route* to drop their bombs on you, I thought."

"I get a very strong impression that tonight you wouldn't much care if they did." He smiled, and she wondered, as often before, why his perfectly ordinary face, averagely good-looking, unremarkable in a crowd, should have the power to move her so profoundly. "Look, I've got a present for you. Open the parcel."

Inside the neat, brown-paper-covered box was a spray of orchids. At the sight of them, her heart lightened and her expression changed and lightened too. Alex laughed, pleased with her surprise.

"You didn't think I'd forgotten, did you? Our third anniversary. I believe you'd forgotten yourself."

"No, I hadn't. That's why I wouldn't go out with Bob." She was smiling herself now. "Women always remember anniversaries. We're the sentimental sex."

"That's not true, but I'll let it pass. Pin on your flowers. I'll go now and wait for you at the usual place."

"Very well, my lord and master."

Automatically, from long custom, she straightened his desk, covered over her own typewriter, sealed up the letters he had signed. Ten minutes had passed before she switched off the lights, closing up the office for the night, but in the main hall of the building she found Alex buttonholed by the tenant of another office, listening with false concern to a bomb story. He raised his hat as she passed.

"Good night, Miss Simpson."

"Good night, Mr. Foster."

That meant she would have to wait for him in the Sherry Bar. Outside in Soho Square it was not yet quite dark. A fine October night. Luvverly night for an air raid, as Carter would say. Not many people were about, even in Oxford Street, and those who were walked purposefully, all hurrying home to their little burrows—the inadequate protection of bricks and concrete, the far greater protection of dispersal, the law of averages and the anonymous ruling that many should be threatened but few harmed. Life was acquiring a large simplicity, all lesser insecurities swallowed up by that one enormous vulnerability. Time enough to worry tomorrow, when tomorrow might never come for you. Elizabeth glanced at the passers-by and some of them glanced back at her—each wondering, she imagined, if there went someone whose last night on earth this would be. But something—racial optimism, human egotism, youth—made her feel more pity and apprehension for those others than for herself. *She* was not going to be killed. Sudden and violent death was something that happened to those other people.

Alex joined her at the Sherry Bar five minutes later. He swore at the man who had detained him, ordered drinks. They talked easily, impersonally, about work and the current news. Once, he opened his pocket-book to show her a newspaper clipping and a snapshot fell out with it—one showing his two children in the garden of the country house to which his wife had taken them a year before. Elizabeth picked it up to look at, commented pleasantly, for once feeling neither pain nor guilt. But unconsciously, a moment later, she touched her spray of orchids. Their drinks finished, they walked slowly, for it was dark now, with only the dimmed headlamps of cars and the traffic lights to guide them, along Charing Cross Road and down one of the narrow streets which turned off it. Always sordid and dingy, Soho had now an appearance of infinite squalor. Fragments of dirty glass lay heaped in the blank windows of empty shops, mixed with a litter of display cards, torn and faded, and a miscellaneous refuse of no interest even to the lonely, self-absorbed figures who searched the dust-bins in the early morning hours. Here and there, the pungent smell of charred wood still clung to proud façades concealing nothingness. Only from basement doors inscribed by unskilled hands with the romantic-sounding names of clubs, new-born and soon to earn an epitaph in the police-court news, came a glint of light and the sound of dance music. The watchers at street corners were fewer now. The prostitutes had given their dogs a final exercise and taken themselves off to early business. Respectable Soho families, mainly Jewish and Italian, had gone to stake their pitches in the underground railway stations, burdened by strange bedding and a picnic basket. But here and there, faintly illuminated, the brave word "Open" signified a restaurant, still fashionable and even more expensive. Mr. Foster and his secretary went in at one such door.

They were known and welcomed. They would have been welcomed whether known or not, for there were few other people dining there that night; the architecture of Soho inspired little confidence. But the food was still excellent and the wine increasingly important. The majority of men dining were in uniform; officers on leave refusing to recognise the raids and their womenfolk too happy or too proud to make objections. Elizabeth wished, not for the first time, that Alex were in uniform; and then felt, as always, ashamed of herself. It was not his fault if he were in a reserved occupation. She stood to lose more than most women if he had eventually to go.

At eight o'clock precisely the sirens sounded. Neither of them commented. Nothing very much seemed to be happening as yet. It was probably the poor bloody East End getting it again. They could do nothing about it and it seemed in some way to be no concern of theirs.

At half-past eight Alex said: "Well, we might as well push on." The head waiter helped him into his coat. Alex asked him a question and he shrugged his shoulders mournfully. It was not the risk of staying open that they minded—it was that not enough customers came to make it pay.

"They want to go where there is dancing, a band to drown the noises, somewhere underground. It is natural. One understands. But after next week we shall only serve luncheons, I regret."

They went out into the street. A 'plane throbbed overhead, searchlights pursued it in slow, unhurrying curves and guns growled.

"Stand in a doorway while I find a taxi," Alex said.

"No. I won't be left. I might get frightened by myself."

"Come along, then."

They found a taxi fairly quickly. Alex was the kind of man who always found taxis quickly. With his arm about her, his hand warm and firm in hers, Elizabeth felt happy and absurdly secure driving through the dark streets, watching the gun flashes in the sky. Laughing gently, excited by proximity and the wine they had drunk, they amused themselves making up rhymes which seemed disproportionately funny.

"The guns in the park
Have a watchdog bark.
They answer to 'Rex'
And 'England expects.'

The guns on the shore . . ."

("That's the Embankment," Alex explained.)

"Make a threatening roar,
Like the roll of a drum
Or a gorilla beating his tum."

"That's not very good," Elizabeth complained. "It doesn't scan."

"Oh, what is man
That he should scan?" Alex chanted.
"So brief his span . . .
So brief his span."

"The repetition of the last line is intentionally poetic," he said quickly, too quickly.

But Elizabeth had turned her head and pressed her face against his shoulder. "'So brief his span . . . It's sad poetry. I don't like it."

The taxi drew up outside the block of service flats where Alex had lived since the outbreak of war. He tipped in full appreciation of the taxi-driver's enterprise. The hall-porter barely glanced up as they went in. He was listening to muted dance music on a radio set and reading an evening paper. Everything looked reassuringly ordinary, brightly lit, secure. They got into the lift and Alex pressed the button for the third floor. Two letters lay on the mat inside his front door. He glanced at them and put them unopened in his pocket. Without bothering to speak, Elizabeth went into the bedroom, where the black-out curtains had already been drawn. She unpinned her orchids and put them in the tooth-glass, hung up her coat and dress on hangers in the cupboard, washed her hands, touched up her make-up in front of the mirror. This was home. This was where her heart lived. For the next hour or so she would forget the war, the future and the past.

Overhead, another German 'plane chugged ponderously. A nearby gun spat up at it in impotent-seeming rage.

CHAPTER II

No one in Wordsworth Road saw Elizabeth Simpson come home that night except the Carthcart boy. It was past eleven o'clock and his parents supposed him in bed and asleep, but it was easy to get out of the window of his ground-floor room. Since the beginning of September he had slipped out for some part of almost every night. Once, he had nearly been hit by a fragment of shell and after that, for about a week, he had kept indoors. But the temptation was too great to resist. He knew that no real harm could come to him. He didn't really care if he lived or died (except just for that one moment when the hot, jagged lump of metal had whistled past his head, and his knees had turned to water and his heart had thumped); and that made him safer than the deepest shelter in the world.

It was exciting to stand concealed in a shop doorway at the end of the road, looking over the Common, and watch the fires burning in metropolitan London, the flashes of the guns and, sometimes even, the white glory of a flare, slowly consuming in its own heat. But he had to hurry back if it happened to be a night when Jerry decided to drop his stuff on Saffron Park. His mother could distinguish unerringly between the earth-shuddering thud of an exploding bomb and the loudest crash of gunfire. If a bomb dropped within earshot, she would always creep downstairs in bedroom slippers and softly, softly open his door, to listen to his breathing. Sometimes he was asleep, but at others he would murmur gently, instinctively anxious not to disturb his father: "Do you want me, Mother?"

Mostly she would murmur back: "No, dear. I just wondered if that big one had woken you up. I should go to sleep again, if you can." But every now and then, when the sinister double pulse of the German 'plane seemed hovering directly over the house and the guns crashed in a thunder that rattled the windows, she would come and sit on the edge of his bed and they would listen together.

"What's so odd," she would say, "is that it will seem so far away tomorrow morning. If anyone had told me five years ago . . . I wouldn't have been so surprised about the air raids, but I should never have believed that life could be so normal in between."

She said it to comfort herself, he thought, to remind herself of all the mornings when she had woken in a house still intact, with her son and husband still alive and unharmed. But she meant what she said, all the same. In the darkened room, he would sit up in bed and wrap his eiderdown around her shoulders, in spite of her protestations, and then presently he would fall asleep. He never knew how long she stayed with him on those occasions, but she was always gone and the eiderdown laid over him again when he next woke.

One night the near-by bomb would fall with no preliminary warning chug-chug of a German 'plane, and then his mother would creep in to find his bed empty. He knew the fear he risked inflicting on her; he loved her; but nevertheless tonight, like other nights, he stood in the doorway of the shop at the end of the road, and thus he saw Elizabeth Simpson come home.

She walked quite fast, though she carried no torch. There were stars in the sky and, for the moment, nothing else. An All Clear had gone about an hour ago, but there would almost certainly be another alarm before midnight. Where had she been? he wondered. He might step out of the doorway and say "Good evening". That would make her jump. He imagined her voice, heightened with apprehension, asking: "Who is it?" And he would answer, in a calm, sneering tone that she would hate: "Only that pansy Cathcart boy."

What would she say in reply to that? Would it make her feel ashamed, caught out? But he knew that he would never repeat those words aloud to anyone—least of all, perhaps, to her. They had caused him the bitterest pain he had had to endure in his eighteen years.

At first he had been only angry—angry, and hurt with the pang any sensitive human being must feel at the chance discovery that he is held in contempt by an acquaintance, someone he has never criticised even in thought, who has not mattered until now.

Five casual words, casually overheard. It sounded melodramatic to tell himself that they had changed his whole life, yet that was a fact. They had awakened a dread in his heart that had not slept since. They had splashed him with a foul stain which now he must for ever finger in secret loathing. He should have been able to dismiss them with the healthy derision of a small boy sticking out his tongue. He could not so dismiss them. He had begun to believe that the thing they implied was true.

Perhaps nothing existed fully until it had been named. "In the beginning was the Word." Words created, they did not merely act as interpreters between men and their emotions. Perhaps he had not been a pansy boy until Elizabeth Simpson had called him one. But now the cheap, slangy phrase, verdict of an age upon its own standards, had brought something to life within him. Incidents, impulses, imaginings which he had never before analysed or questioned took on suddenly a new and terrifying aspect. He saw himself and his life up till the present in a distorting glare of revelation. Everything was changed and different. Everything was smirched and poisoned. He hated her for that. But most of all he hated her for shadowing his thoughts and memories of Derek.

At school, he realised now, he had been unusually happy. He had been accepted without criticism as an amiable sort of chap, inoffensively brainy, pretty useless at games but not unsporting. It was significant that people had rarely mentioned his name without adding, as identification, "You know, Hammond's cousin". There had never been any need for him to carve his own footholds. Derek had mounted steadily and pulled him up behind him. Everything came easily to Derek—it was natural to find him in the van. Not consciously but with a pure contentment Owen had forgone his separate existence. Let Derek be the substance, he the shadow. But now the substance had departed and the shadow had resolved itself into a moody, aimless boy, kicking his heels between two worlds. In another six months he would be called up, but in the meantime there seemed nothing for him to do—nothing to do but walk the streets by night and in the daytime haunt the Public Library, to search out books which must be read in secret and which made him more utterly miserable the better informed he became.

Derek would think him completely crazy, of course. To begin with, Derek didn't read books except as a means to an end—an exam to be passed or time to kill. He had a simple and direct mind and a quality of good nature which amounted to tenderness. Very few boys of fifteen, in their second year at a Public School, would have taken for granted that a newcomer a year younger, a relative barely known till now, must be protected and encouraged in defiance of all tradition and at the risk of personal unpopularity. Because it had been Derek, no one had resented it for long. Terms passed, and it became accepted that where went Hammond, there went Cathcart too. And then there were the holidays as well. The Hammonds lived in Oxfordshire and Derek was the only son, fourth to a trio of adoring sisters. It was the obvious thing to invite Owen down to spend a part of every holiday, since Derek liked him, seemed to prefer his company to that of any other of his schoolfellows. The Hammonds thought it very right and proper that the cousins should be friends, that Owen should so obviously hero-worship Derek. Sometimes the two of them went off for long week-ends on walking tours. More occasionally, Derek came to stay with Owen at Saffron Park, to do the round of London theatres. Thus, with a firm and gentle pressure, unconscious but unremitting, the stamp of Derek's stronger personality bore down upon the soft clay of Owen's mind and heart. Derek, for Owen, was the pivot on which the world turned. Life held nothing better than to play David to his Jonathan.

But now Derek was in the Air Force, training to be a pilot, and Owen was lonely for him beyond the actual physical separation. His letters grew scantier and vaguer, full of new names and unfamiliar jokes and slang. Ashamed, Owen was yet bitterly jealous; yes, and envious too. He imagined himself in Derek's place and knew that he could never achieve the same success. He imagined the popularity which Derek would always command and his easy, unconscious assumption of leadership. To Derek, he must seem still a schoolboy, still thought of with affection but no longer of particular importance. The reflection filled him with an anguish out of all proportion to the actual facts. He was terrified of what he might become apart from Derek. Derek was the fever and its antidote combined, the sword-thrust and the shield. Derek would protect him from the sharp eyes and hard voices of young women, cruel in their intolerance and vicious in their scorn of what excluded them. With Derek beside him, he would be happy enough not to care what Elizabeth Simpson thought of him. But tonight there was no Derek and he cared very much.

It was cold in the doorway of the shop. He had just decided to walk up to the edge of the Common and back, to warm himself, when the mounting wail of the siren broke the frosty silence. A warden walked past with a tread as deliberate as a policeman's. Unwilling to attract attention, Owen waited until he had gone by. Then, swiftly, he hurried back to the open window of his bedroom, climbed in over the sill, undressed and slipped into bed. Five minutes later, the guns on the Common broke out into a thunder of aggression and half a mile away a stick of bombs fell, killing seven people and injuring another twelve. But Owen was asleep already and he slept on undisturbed.

The air-raid warden from whom Owen had concealed himself continued on his way towards a concrete dolls' house built on the verge of the park which gave the suburb its name. Through force of habit, as he walked along, he looked for chinks of light from improperly blacked-out windows, but domestically all was darkness. He felt the tremor of the ground under his feet when the bombs fell, and paused a moment in his deliberate walk, looking back and calculating distances.

While he stood there, a fire engine drove along the main road out of sight, its bell ringing urgently. Then the noise died out of hearing and he walked on faster.

Inside the post, one man was speaking on the telephone, another lay back in a deck-chair. He looked tired, a middle-aged man with a bald head and a ginger moustache, who glanced up now with an expression of pleasure and relief.

"Good old Simpson! I might have known you'd be on the tick. It's very decent of you to take over from me. You're on tomorrow too, aren't you?"

"Yes, but it's Friday and I only work half day on Saturday. You were on all last night, weren't you?"

"Johnson's ill, that's the trouble. Makes us short-handed. Poor devil, he was operated on yesterday. I'd be scared stiff to be in a hospital now. He said to me before he went in: 'only hope to God they haven't got a Red Cross painted on the roof.'"

The man at the telephone rang off.

"'Evening, Simpson. Hear that stick come down?"

"Yes. Have you any idea where they fell?"

"Pratt's gone off to try and find out. Somewhere over by the Reservoir, by the sound of it. The police'll be round presently—they'll know."

"I heard the fire-engine go by, as I came along."

"I don't think that's a local call. I heard earlier on that there's some big fires started up West, from the lot that came down before ten o'clock. Someone else's spot of bother. I can't say I'm sorry. I don't like fires around this time of night, lighting up the place for miles."

Buckley, the man with the ginger moustache, had put on his overcoat and muffler and his tin hat.

"So long," he said. "Hope it keeps fine for you. Take a land-mine to wake me tonight, once I'm in bed. Did you get any sleep before you came on, Simpson?"

"A couple of hours. Enough to rest my eyes."

"Well, thanks again. Good night, Thorne."

"'Night, Buckley."

Thorne, a full-time warden and acknowledged leader of the part-time men, was glad that it was Simpson who had come on. He was one of the quiet kind and nothing shook him. Buckley had been a bit jumpy this evening. Over-tired, probably. He wrote up his log-book and then stood and stretched himself, looking enormous within the narrow wall-space.

"Well, that's that, for the moment. Seems to be a lull."

"Famous last words," Simpson smiled. He sat down in the deck-chair, still warm from Buckley's thick-set body. "What's happened to everybody?"

"O'Neal and Miss Plummer are going the round of the shelters. Mrs. Brown and Calverly are patrolling. Quite a good turn-out, considering how many hours everyone has had to put in lately. I don't know how some of you people do it, working all through the day as well."

"We nod a bit, round about lunch-time. But we catch up at the week-ends. I slept the clock round last Sunday."

There seemed nothing else to say at the moment. Thorne picked up a magazine and Henry Simpson opened the book he had brought with him, "The Spirit and Structure of German Fascism". But after a few pages he found that reading made his eyes ache and it was an effort to keep them open. He supposed that he would have to smoke to keep awake, and already he smoked far too much during the day.

When he had closed his book and lit a cigarette, he began thinking about Elizabeth. She ought not to come home so late when there were raids on. He admired her for ignoring them as she did; he would have been very much disappointed if she had reacted otherwise; but there was such a thing as reasonable precaution. It worried her mother—worried him too, if it came to that. One of these days she would miss the last train and nowadays no taxi-driver would bring her out as far as Saffron Park. It would be better if she were to arrange to spend the night with her friends, as he had suggested to her this evening. But one had a superstitious dread these days of urging any particular course of action. And in any case—what right had he to advise the younger generation?

At the thought, it was as if his mind gave a click and slipped into a grooved track. Now the wheels would start revolving and carry his tired brain along the worn, inevitable route. It meant going back to the last war, his own feelings in 1918, the economic depression, the lethargy of exhausted men and the crime of lazy ones. He wished, whole-heartedly, that he could casually shrug the burden of individual responsibility off his own shoulders and on to those of a vague entity called "the Government" or, more spaciously, "the Nazis". That was what almost everyone else he met seemed able to do, with no slightest twinge of self-doubt. Was he alone in feeling a personal guilt for the deaths of young men in the sky and on the sea, for the suffocation of women and children trapped under the smouldering refuse of their homes? Were there no other men and women of his generation who woke in the night and saw blind faces that accused them inasmuch as they had had eyes to see and had deliberately closed them? He had not even the excuse of ignorance or stupidity. There had been leaders—he had recognised them—but he had not followed them. It had not remotely occurred to him to be himself a leader. Cowardice and self-distrust had kept him a prisoner in his narrow world, paying timid lip-service to the gaolers of complacency and popular belief. Now, even now, he could be only physically brave. He could share without flinching the ordeal of aerial bombardment, but he would not take the risk of boring or antagonising people with his own convictions.

From these unhappy, self-accusing thoughts, it was a relief to be interrupted by Thorne. He had gone to the door to look out and now he called to Simpson to join him.

"Come and look at the fires up West."

They stood together in the narrow passage entrance and stared above the trees of the park at the angry flush in the night sky.

"Beautiful, isn't it?" Thorne said. "There's a lot in this war that's beautiful, I often think—the black-out, and searchlights, and balloons."

"And men baling out with parachutes from blue skies," Henry agreed. He felt closer to Thorne at that moment than ever before. "But the thud of an exploding bomb is an obscene sound and the siren is a wail from hell."

"Funny thing—I don't mind old Mona, except when she wakes me up. Must be very unmusical. Some chap ought to compose a symphony after the war, bringing in the Warning and the All Clear."

"What would he call it? 'Inferno, 1940'?"

Thorne hunched his shoulders against the cold. "You hate every minute of this war, don't you, Simpson? Oh, I don't mean you *mind* the bombing, in a personal way," he added hastily. "But you think a lot about the causes, and what's going to happen to the world afterwards? I've noticed the kind of books you read and things you've said sometimes."

"Yes." Simpson hesitated. "I feel rather . . . responsible. I mean—our generation. We went through the last war. We ought to have been on the watch. But we just wanted to forget about it and put it behind us. That makes us partially guilty of what's happening now, to my way of thinking."

"Well, frankly, I can't see that," Thorne said amiably. "I grant you we ought to have picked our governments better these last twenty years. But it's my belief that we'll always have to fight the Germans every second generation. There'll never be any peace in Europe till we've finished them off. But I tell you this, Simpson—I wouldn't say it to everyone, but you'll understand even though you don't agree—I've been happier this last two months than I've been since 1918."

Henry nodded, without surprise. "You like the action—the comradeship—the feeling that you're doing a good job to the best of your ability."

"That's it," Thorne agreed eagerly. "There's plenty feel like me—I'm an ordinary sort of bloke. I was twenty-five when the last war ended. I've been right through it. I'd never had a good job before I joined up and I've never had one since. I stopped being ambitious a long time ago, and three pounds a week, plus my army pension, seemed a sound proposition to me. All through the first year it was pretty deadly, with everybody hating your guts for pulling them up over the black-out and rather giving the impression that they thought you were taking government money on false pretences; once or twice I nearly chucked it up; but now it all seems worth it. All these raids—they've justified us. They make me feel that I count for something again—that I'm pulling my weight—even, well, serving my country, if you like."

"If I like," Henry thought, with a wry smile to himself in the darkness. (The darkness—that was it. People talked more freely when their faces could not be seen.) I like it very well—I like you, Thorne. Here is a chance to explain my point of view, perhaps to make a convert of it. But I shall say nothing, or nothing that matters, because you are a likable honest man and I have neither the heart nor the courage to tell you that just your kind of easy-going acceptance of the world's injustices have brought you and the world to such a pass as this.

He said aloud: "I know exactly how you feel. But there's something wrong with things when a man can't find an opportunity to serve the community until high explosive bombs are raining on his neighbours' heads."

"The community!" Thorne laughed with genuine amusement. "Don't tell me you're a ruddy Communist! You're already under a bit of suspicion, you know. You can take it from me—we shall have to fight the Bolshies when we've finished off the Huns."

"God forbid. I hold no brief for the Russo-German pact, but I certainly don't want to fight the Russians." He shivered suddenly. "It's cold out here. Let's get inside again."

The sickly smell of the oil-stove and the stale smell of tobacco greeted them. Blinking in the light, they were strangers again, and it was a relief when the patrolling wardens returned, clamouring for tea to be made. Miss Plummer, a tough-looking little woman in her late thirties, was voluble about the trench shelters in the park.

"God, how they smell! I wouldn't sleep in one unless an angel with a flaming sword appeared to warn me personally that it was my only chance. They're full right up, tonight. Nearly everyone asleep, too, except in No. 3. There's a baby there, yelling its head off. Murmurs of 'Shame!' and 'She ought to take it to the country' going all along the line. They all looked at me as if they thought I ought to be able to do something about it. Me! Never handled a baby in my life. You should add gripe water to the Post equipment, Thorne."

"Maybe I ought to go over," Mrs. Brown murmured. She was motherly and conscientious.

"Nonsense, Brown," Miss Plummer said briskly. "Let it yell. You drink your tea."

In the middle of the tea-drinking, Pratt arrived back—a keen young man who would soon be called up for the Army. He was breathless and excited, after his first view of an incident at close quarters.

"It was a stick of five and they fell in a line from Hampton Road to Buckingham Avenue."

"That's B.5," Thorne interjected.

"As far as they can make out, three direct hits on houses, one in a garden and one plumb in the middle of Margaret Road. Very hard surface and all the fronts of the houses fell in either side. But they don't think there are any serious casualties there. The principal mess is in Buckingham Avenue—some people certainly killed and others trapped. They said they didn't want any help from us, but it all seems a horrible confusion. Pitch dark, of course, and everybody tumbling over everybody else— wardens, police, ambulances, rescue parties . . . I helped to calm down a poor old dear who rushed out in her nightgown from a perfectly undamaged house in Hampton Road, and then I thought I wasn't doing much good, butting in, so I came away."

"I know some people in Buckingham Avenue," Henry said uneasily.

"Bad luck. Well, it's a long road."

Unnoticed by anyone but Henry, he flushed, realising that his attempt at consolation had sounded only callous. Henry smiled at him in understanding, and Pratt smiled back apologetically, thinking that Simpson was a nice old stick, rather handsome in his clean-shaven, legal-looking way.

The rest of the night passed uneventfully and slowly. Henry took his turn at patrolling in the pattering shrapnel. A number of 'planes went over and the barrage remained spasmodically heavy, but no more bombs fell within earshot. At four a.m. an All Clear sounded and everyone except Thorne and Calverly and himself went off duty. Till six o'clock, when somebody came to relieve him, he dozed uneasily in his deck-chair. All the way home he thought of nothing but a hot bath, breakfast and bed tomorrow afternoon. The victims of the incident in Buckingham Avenue, the progress of the war as a whole, seemed, in comparison, of little consequence.

CHAPTER III

DURING THE NIGHT, somewhere between Saffron Park and the place where the railway line ducked its head and went underground, a bomb had fallen. No trains were running and Elizabeth had to go to work by 'bus. Her season ticket was accepted as fare and she was rather pleased to be travelling above ground. In common with everyone else, she looked around her for bomb damage, but there was not much fresh to be seen, though at one place the 'bus made a wide detour and the man sitting next to her grunted: "Caught a packet there last night."

"Many casualties?"

"A good few, I heard."

"They dropped some on Saffron Park about midnight—seven people killed and twelve injured. My father's a warden there."

"Ah." He sounded pleased, not, Elizabeth knew, from callousness, but because it was satisfactory to have some well-authenticated information to pass on during the course of the day.

Getting off the 'bus at Oxford Circus, she bought a newspaper. The papers never reached Saffron Park nowadays until after she had started for the office. In the Stop Press the night's raid was described officially as "sharp", which to Londoners implied a very unpleasant night but to their friends in the country apparently nothing at all. Soho Square, she saw with relief, was unharmed. She was not worried about Alex, because she had phoned him from a call box at Saffron Park station. Mercifully, the lines were intact.

Although she was a quarter of an hour late at the office no one else had yet arrived. But it was stupid to get panicky about that, she told herself. They couldn't all be dead, residing in totally different parts of London. Probably it only meant a general breakdown in transport, or oversleeping after a disturbed night. Mechanically, she caught up with her filing, listening with a tenseness of which she was unaware for the sound of a footstep in the passage. No post had been delivered, so there was no mail to open. At ten o'clock she tried to telephone Joan Walsh's rooms, but the exchange was out of order, the operator said. Neither Miss Lewis nor Carter was on the 'phone.

A few minutes later they all three arrived almost simultaneously and greeted her excitedly, competing for her attention . . . "My dear, the bombs just *hurtled* down, *all* round me, *all* night long . . ." "A terrible blaze, Miss Simpson, only two roads away from us—incendiaries on a furniture repository. They say there wasn't even a night watchman on duty . . ." "Chap at our Post got knocked out by a lump of paving-stone. Came clean over the roofs of two rows of houses. Got a fractured skull, he has."

Even allowing for Joan's habitual exaggeration, Miss Lewis's melancholy pleasure in bad tidings and Carter's astonishing nose for news, Elizabeth felt that they all had far more to contribute than she had herself.

"Carter, if you want me alive at lunch-time, for pity's sake take the thermos and fetch some coffee," Joan entreated dramatically.

She took off her hooded coat but made no pretence of starting work. "I don't suppose Roly-Poly will be in before twelve o'clock. If the line from Hatch End is out of commission, it would never occur to him to get a lift by road, or anything sensible. Besides, I don't suppose darling wifie wants to be left alone after her terrible ordeal."

"You really are absurd," Elizabeth laughed. "You've never even seen that poor woman and you make up the most libellous fables about her."

"I know what sort of woman Roly-Poly would marry," Joan said darkly. "She must be wet, or she'd never have accepted him. Elizabeth, you would have screamed last night. There was the most God-awful row going on about half-past nine, before that first All Clear, and we were all sitting in the basement pretending we didn't hear it and Miss Dalrymple was telling an incredibly boring story about a Swiss alp she'd climbed in the 'sixties, when suddenly, whoosh! down came a thousand-pounder, I should say, about a couple of yards away—or that's what it felt like, anyhow. The poor old house just rocked and the sideboard leant forward and bowed in a polite way and then went back again. I fell on my stomach and hit my head against the Major's— he'd had the same idea. Mrs. Henley let out a sort of strangled squeak, and Miss Dalrymple shot forward off her chair and then climbed back again in the most dignified way and said in just the same prim little voice: 'I used to pick a lot of gentian and press it between the covers of a book. Such a lovely blue!' Honestly, I have to hand it to the old girl."

"What did you reply?"

"Oh, I'm honest. I just said: 'Holy smoke, that was a near one!' The Major took out a handkerchief and wiped his forehead and Mrs. Henley scuttled out of the room. A close shave like that is as good as a dose of opening medicine to her."

"I can't imagine what you'll find to talk about after the war," Elizabeth chuckled.

"Oh, I'll bore my grandchildren with bomb stories for generations. Besides, I can always find something to talk about," Joan said confidently.

When the swing door opened, Elizabeth looked up expectantly, hoping it was Alex, but it was only Carter, holding aloft the thermos flask and slowly shaking his head.

"No coffee!" Joan exclaimed, outraged.

"No gas, Miss Walsh. They got a main last night. It's still burning, they say."

Elizabeth thought privately that Carter's next errand would undoubtedly take him in a direction to see for himself.

"But I got the mail," he added helpfully.

The business of the day at last began. Joan's Mr. Rowland rang through to say he would be late and would she look out all the invoices for the Koehner, Lee account, and Alex came striding through the reception-room, with a brief greeting to Miss Lewis at the switchboard, and immediately rang for Elizabeth on the house telephone.

When the door closed behind her, he looked up and smiled. "Thank you for ringing up. I was worried last night, when that second alarm went, as to whether you'd get home in time."

"Yes. It was all right."

After all, they did not speak of personal things at all. It was a rule between them never to risk arousing suspicion in office hours. There was Rowland, Alex's partner, to consider, and—far more dangerous—Joan Walsh.

At half-past twelve, with a guilty start, Elizabeth remembered Bob Craven. He was coming to take her out to lunch at one o'clock. Seeing her glance at her watch, Joan remembered also and offered to cut her own lunch hour in order that Elizabeth could have longer.

"Is he nice?" she asked with frank curiosity.

"You can decide for yourself when he comes."

"Is he the one who's in the Army, who took you out on his last leave?"

"That's the one."

"You are a secretive old devil! I suppose one day you'll suddenly spring it on us that you're getting married next morning and then we shall all have to whip round frantically and give you a travelling clock."

Elizabeth smiled, without commenting. Conversation on these lines troubled her conscience, not on account of Joan Walsh but on account of Bob. She knew very well she was using him as a screen, both here at the office and at home to her parents. Up to a point she had been honest with him, but not entirely. Quite deliberately, she had left him a loophole for his natural optimism. She told herself that he deserved it, for being just a shade complacent, but she knew that this was not the truth. She was being unfair to him and to the hypothetical girl with whom he would console himself. But he was too useful to forgo. He was not only an alibi for her—he protected Alex too.

There were times when she felt no inclination to protect Alex, when her brain and her heart turned cold and she saw their relationship, the central motive of her life for the past three years, as no more than a dirty little liaison—one of the cheapest and most ordinary in the world. She could find no pleasure or excitement in the technique of intrigue. She disliked Alex's wife in a quite honestly impersonal way and did not lie to herself in thinking that she would have found her tiresome and small-minded in any circumstances; but that was not sufficient to acquit her conscience on Naomi's account. She had been brought up to a scrupulous observance of other people's rights and possessions and no generalised, acquired conviction on the limits of material or personal ownership could overcome entirely the weight of that taboo. On the score of the children she felt no guilt. She had not robbed them of harmony between their parents, for that had not existed for more years than she had known Alex. It was they who had robbed her. They were the part of Alex in which she could have no share. They had achieved existence at the expense of the children whom she might herself have borne him.

It gave her pleasure and comfort to be Alex's secretary. The extent of his reliance on her, the hours of work she devoted to his interests, supplied at least an illusion of that stability and interdependence to be found in successful marriages. It pared down some of the ugly edge on the word "mistress". When their relationship had first changed, had become personal and emotional, he had suggested that it might be easier for her to resign her post. But she refused, and not only from the purely instinctive wish to be with him. There was a real tranquillity to be found in working side by side, sharing a part of their lives that had nothing to do with love. She was a very good secretary and she took pride in her efficiency.

Punctually at one o'clock, Bob arrived to take her out to lunch. He had been commissioned since his last leave and he looked consequently smarter and more attractive. He had booked a table at the Carlton Grill, he told her with some pride, and after that he proposed to hire a taxi and drive round to have a look at what they'd done to poor old London. She would come with him, of course. Well, why couldn't she come with him? All this talk of work to do was absurd. When a man had forty-eight hours' leave, he expected a girl to fall in with his plans.

Elizabeth was glad that he was in this sort of mood. Cheerful and self-confident, he was harder to handle but less of a concern. She enjoyed her lunch, an enjoyment not detracted from in the least by the sounding of an air-raid alarm as they were walking down the Haymarket. The thin, curling trails of vapour high up above them, signatures of death and endeavour, seemed too remote to be real. Like so many other Londoners she had grown callous with the permissible callousness of those who share an equivalent hazard.

Over coffee and liqueurs, Bob became painfully sincere. He said, and Elizabeth was forced to believe him, that he was miserable at the thought of her in London. Last night had been an eye-opener to him. He had been in a cold sweat, had hardly slept at all. Each time he had seen a bombed house, he had imagined her beneath the debris. He wanted her to marry him and get away to safety. "Almost anywhere the Army is, is safe," he finished bitterly.

"Oh, Bob, we've been over this so often before," Elizabeth protested unhappily.

"Sometimes I think you're lying to me and there's somebody else," he said disconcertingly.

"Why do you think that?" she parried.

"I don't know . . . Or perhaps I do. You can usually tell. Most girls, even the type who aren't come-hither, are a bit self-conscious and—well—showing-off with a man when they know he admires them. But when they really fall in love with one man, it's as if they turned off the lights for all the others. I've noticed it often."

"Bob Craven on Women," she said lightly. "You make yourself out to be rather disgracefully experienced."

He did not join in the joke. She realised uneasily that to him it was no joking matter.

"If I really believed there was someone else—" he spoke with a kind of earnest belligerence—"I'd . . . I'd punch his head off. Because if he was the right type, you'd be engaged to him. That's how I've worked it out."

She hesitated, but only for a moment. He had uttered a threat to her secret life and it must be dealt with promptly.

"Well, there isn't anyone else, so you needn't bother."

The lie was so palpable to herself that she was astonished when his dogged, almost fierce expression changed into a smile of relief.

"In that case, I shall just keep on trying," he said almost buoyantly. "I shall stick to the trail like a faithful bloodhound. You'll get so sick of saying no that one day you'll say yes from sheer fatigue, and then I'll rush you to a church before you've time to change your mind."

"Oh, Bob, don't jump to conclusions," she pleaded. "I'm very fond of you—you know that—but it doesn't mean I'll ever be in love with you."

"I can wait," he said confidently. "I'm the patient kind. In the meanwhile, you'll have dinner with me tonight, of course."

"That's impossible, I'm afraid. Father goes on duty at the Post at six o'clock and I can't leave Mother alone in the house during the raids. Come home with me and spend the night. You know they'll love to have you." A guilty conscience made her put more warmth into the invitation than she had intended.

He looked pleased but hesitated politely. "I mustn't eat your rations."

"Oh, Mother can easily open a tin of something. She's a very good manager. We always seem to have plenty to eat."

Occupied with very different thoughts, they walked back to the office in silence. The All Clear had sounded, apparently, for the policemen were wearing their respirators at the back again. Arrived at the square, Bob hailed a taxi and began a lengthy conversation with the driver about the best route for bomb damage. Elizabeth returned to work.

She had hoped that Alex would not mention Bob, but at the end of the afternoon, when he was leaving to catch a train to spend the week-end with Naomi and the children, he broke their rule.

"Did Craven ask you to marry him again? No, don't tell me. It only makes me feel more of a cad than usual."

"Don't be a fool," she whispered. And furtively, fleetingly, she kissed his hand.

He sighed. "Oh, Lord. I don't want to go down there. I wish . . ."

She interrupted him. "Have you remembered the things from Fortnum's?"

"The perfect secretary." His tone was bitter. "Yes, I've remembered. I'd never have heard the last of it if I'd forgotten."

"Sweets for the children?"

"Yes, damn you. There's a moon tonight, isn't there?"

"I believe so."

"I wish you'd sleep somewhere a bit safer than that gimcrack little house."

"What a way to talk of Saffron Park's desirable residential property!" she mocked him, suddenly gay and happy again. "Don't worry—'what will be, will be'. Either I'm safe there or I'd not be safe on the platform of Leicester Square tube station."

"You honestly believe that, don't you? It must be very comforting. But it doesn't comfort me." He glanced at his watch and picked up his suit-case. "Good night, Miss Simpson."

"Good night, Mr. Foster."

They exchanged a long, steady look. Then Alex turned abruptly and walked quickly out of the room and out of the office.

Earlier in the afternoon, Elizabeth had 'phoned home to tell her mother that she was bringing Bob to dinner and to spend the night. Mrs. Simpson hurried out to the shops, in the hope that the tale of a soldier on leave might procure some valuable rarity. Walking up the High Street, she mentally transferred him to the Air Force, as likely to arouse more sentiment.

She met her neighbour Mrs. Cathcart in the grocer's. They exchanged the conventional remarks about the shortage of various foodstuffs. Mrs. Cathcart liked Mrs. Simpson, since it never occurred to her to dislike anyone except on direct provocation, but Mrs. Simpson did not like Mrs. Cathcart, because it equally never occurred to her to like anyone who had not been of positive use to her. She admired Mr. Cathcart's rather boisterous good humour, which made her own husband seem dull and unsociable by comparison, but she thought Owen Cathcart a pale-faced, sulky-looking boy with no life in him. Nevertheless, she enquired after him with apparent interest.

"It's a problem what to do with boys, between the time they leave school and their call-up," Mrs. Cathcart sighed. "My husband has arranged now for Owen to be coached in mathematics every morning—he wants to get into the Air Force and his maths are weak. He misses his cousin, you know—they were almost like brothers. And how is your daughter?" she reciprocated politely.

Mrs. Simpson was pleased at this opportunity. "Tiresome girl—she's just rung up from the office to say that she's bringing a friend of hers home for dinner and to spend the night. He's on forty-eight hours' leave. I've come out to try and find something to buy. I always think Friday is the most difficult night in the week."

"Have you had any luck?" Mrs. Cathcart asked sympathetically.

"None so far." Mrs. Simpson shot a look of barely disguised hatred at the grocery assistant which, automatically and unconsciously, Mrs. Cathcart tried to palliate with a smile.

"Then, my dear, you must just come straight home with me and raid my store-cupboard. I laid in a really good supply before the war, that time when we were asked to do so, and I do feel that nothing is too much to do for our men in the Services. Is he in the Air Force?"

Remembering in time that Mrs. Cathcart would very likely see him, Mrs. Simpson said no, the Royal Engineers. But really she wouldn't dream of depriving . . .

"It would be a pleasure," Mrs. Cathcart said sincerely. "I feel so sorry for the poor soldiers—so unfortunate in France and now with nothing to do. I mean, nothing spectacular, like the Navy and the R.A.F. No, really, I insist."

Mrs. Simpson gave in, not over graciously. She hated to feel under an obligation. On the other hand, it would be nice to be able to spoil Bob, for whom she had a genuine affection, and she had always wanted to see inside the Cathcarts' home.

Mrs. Cathcart apologised for the untidiness of the sitting-room. They used it as a dining-room, too, she explained, since the raids began. They had moved Owen's bed into the dining-room, because everyone said it was a little safer to sleep on the ground floor. Owen himself got up politely when they came in, slipping the book he had been reading down the side of his chair, but Mrs. Simpson thought as usual that he was an unattractive boy, who never smiled when he shook hands. She couldn't imagine him in the R.A.F.

When the two women had gone through into the kitchen, Owen drew a breath of relief. But he did not risk opening his book again. Mrs. Simpson was a nosy sort of woman, he thought. Instead, he crossed to the window and stared out disconsolately at the uniform suburban road. It might be a good idea to go and see a film—there was one about West Point Military Academy which could be interesting. But most films were full of girls and nowadays he had a horror of love stories. Up to a few months ago they had only bored him; he had even taken pride in the fact; but now they made him uncomfortable and miserably conscious of his loneliness. It seemed that the whole world walked in step except himself. He had almost grown to believe that people, glancing at him, saw the difference, wondered sarcastically what interest the basic Hollywood plot of boy-meets-girl could have for him. The contempt in Elizabeth Simpson's voice expressed the contempt of the major part of mankind. "Pansy boy . . . pansy boy . . ." the voices sneered. Their murmur in his brain tormented him. There could be only one thing worse—to hear the taunt transformed into an invitation. For although it was frightening and wretched to feel an outcast in the world of ordinary people, it would be sheerest terror to be claimed as kin by other outcasts.

In the kitchen Mrs. Cathcart said smilingly: "Owen's got a schoolboy appetite, though he wouldn't like to hear me say so, for he thinks himself quite grown up now." She looked with satisfaction at Mrs. Simpson's shopping-basket. "There! I don't really think you'll need to worry any more. I don't really like to take the money, but I know that it will only worry you to try to replace the tins."

"I'm sure Elizabeth will want to thank you herself," Mrs. Simpson said almost graciously.

"Are we going to hear of an engagement?" Mrs. Cathcart asked with an interest too kindly to be resented.

"Well, they don't call it that, but I suppose they'll be getting married one day. Young people nowadays are so odd about such things. Elizabeth talks a lot of nonsense about her work, but it doesn't seem to be so important as all that, particularly in war-time, when anything might happen. Her father and I are very fond of Bob. I don't think she could do better, myself."

"How nice for you—that you like him, I mean! It must be such a comfort. And remember, if you want a little celebration some time, you must call on me again."

She came to the door to speed Mrs. Simpson across the road, full of the good will felt by those who have done a kindness towards the recipient. Owen ducked back from the window. Why on earth must Mother get friendly with the Simpsons, of all people? It seemed disloyal of her.

Sensing his disapproval, without understanding the reason for it, Mrs. Cathcart explained apologetically:

"Elizabeth Simpson's young man is coming on leave and I've let Mrs. Simpson have some tins, to help out."

"Oh. Well, you'll be sorry when the invasion comes and your only son is starving," he teased her gloomily.

"Owen! Don't say that, even in fun."

"I don't like the Simpsons."

"Why ever not? They're very harmless, ordinary people."

"I just don't. And Father won't be pleased, either, if he hears you've been so lavish."

A shadow fell across Mrs. Cathcart's pleasant, still attractive face.

"I don't think I'll tell your father. He does have funny little prejudices . . ." Her tone was unconsciously apologetic.

"All right. I'll keep your guilty secret." He put an arm round her shoulders and gave her a brief hug. Then he yawned and stretched himself. "Oh, Lord—maths on Monday."

She regarded him critically.

"Darling, need you go about looking quite so untidy? That dreadful old pullover—and a tie like a piece of string! You used to take so much care of your appearance."

"I used to do a lot of silly things," he muttered defensively.

"Well, I like to see you well turned out. Even when you were quite a little boy, you were always very neat and you liked your ties and socks to match. It's only recently you've grown so slovenly. And don't tell me there's a war on. That's no excuse at all."

"People think it's stupid for men to fuss about their clothes," he said almost desperately. "I'd rather leave that to the girls. They fuss enough for two. I'll look all right in uniform."

"I suppose so." Unconsciously she sighed.

He had an uneasy feeling that she was going to ask him some question which he would not want to answer. He moved towards the door, anxious to be away but unwilling to give the appearance of a rebuff. Hesitant, reluctant, he avoided meeting her eyes. But all that Daisy said was:

"Don't let your father see you looking like that when he comes home."

CHAPTER IV

DAISY CATHCART, though she did not know it, was the ideal citizen to whom all radio talks were addressed, at whom all newspaper propaganda was directed. She was simple enough to need explanation and amenable enough to accept it. At one time she had believed implicitly in Mr. Chamberlain; with no awareness of disparity she now believed implicitly in Mr. Churchill. Food rationing she accepted uncomplainingly, though she was too gentle-minded to berate the grumblers, and she conscientiously tried out the economic recipes in all the Women's pages. She worshipped her son, but it did not occur to her that he had any choice but to become a fighter pilot at the age of twenty. If he should be killed she would not put the blame on God or even Hitler. She knew already that the blame would lie on her. It would be a punishment for her sin.

In all her forty-eight years she had only committed one real sin, as far as she knew, but that one was heinous. She had given her husband's name to a son who was not his own. On Sunday mornings, lingering after the service at St. Matthew's to talk to her friends in the congregation, a wave of guilt would sometimes engulf her, stiffening the smile on her face and confusing her speech. All these admirable people, secure in the conviction of their blameless lives, what would they think if they knew her as she really was? She felt apologetic for contaminating them. But she couldn't cease going to church. God resided at St. Matthew's and she must talk to Him at least once a week. She must pray to be forgiven. It was, she knew, at best only a secondary act of repentance. Her real retribution lay in confession to her husband, and she would never have courage enough for that.

Any woman might shrink from an acknowledgment of infidelity, but Daisy Cathcart was afraid of the man she had married on more counts than that. She respected Lionel but she felt no reliance on him. After twenty-four years, she was still bewildered by his moods and uncertain of his motives. A guilty conscience had made of her a model wife, but she had never been a happy one. She did not understand how a man could be so consistently jovial in society and so often morose and irritable at home. Surely it was more enjoyable to be good-tempered all the time? You loved your own family best, didn't you? Then why couldn't Lionel sometimes show himself conversational and cheerful in private life too?

She asked herself these questions, although she believed, dreading her belief, that she knew the answer. It must be because he knew or at least suspected that Owen was not his son.

Well, he had kept silent, then, for twenty years. The only person except herself who could have told him had been on the other side of the world for as long as that. There had been moments when she had longed for Lionel to accuse her, when pent-up hysteria had clamoured for relief from the pressure of unspecified resentment. Those moments had passed. There was scarcely any price she would not pay now for his continued silence. For supposing Owen were to find out also?

It was not that he was particularly devoted to his supposed father. She knew very well that his devotion was all for her—and for Derek, of course. But she dared not imagine the effect on him of learning that his mother was (she took a mental gulp before the word) an adulteress and he the seed of a man he did not even know existed. Owen was so sensitive. He took things to heart and brooded over them. She knew very well that he had been unhappy ever since he had left school, though she could not find out the reason. It was no use questioning him. Derek was the only person he would be likely to confide in. She wished she could consult Derek herself. He never gave away Owen's confidences but he often used to discuss him with her in a kind, elder-brotherly way. Lionel was always so impatient with Owen. He didn't understand him and he certainly did not try to. His easily aroused resentment against Owen was chief among the things which made her fear he guessed the truth.

Mercifully, Owen himself appeared to take it for granted. He had never known him any different and it did not seem to occur to him that other fathers were more loving. Derek's father had died too long ago to supply any standard of comparison. Daisy sighed in passing for her brother, whom she had loved very much. John had never wanted her to marry Lionel. But that was an old, old story. Now it was 1940 and there was another war on and it was silly to worry a great deal when they might all be bombed in their beds that very night. There was so much suffering in the world, one ought not to fuss about one's own small affairs. That was what the Vicar had said last Sunday. Think of the terrible suffering in the Nazi-oppressed countries, he had said, think of the poor homeless East-Enders . . . But human egotism, tough and unabashed, kept deflecting one's better resolves. So Mrs. Cathcart thought of Owen's gloom and her husband's irritability and even—how to tell her daily servant, who was easily offended, that she did not properly clean the bath.

That evening she also thought, with pleasure and satisfaction, of the kindness she had been able to do her neighbour, Mrs. Simpson.

"You will have to slip across and thank Mrs. Cathcart, Elizabeth," Mrs. Simpson said, over dinner.

"I ought to do that, really," Bob remarked.

Alice Simpson smiled fondly, as though he had made a particularly amusing joke, and Elizabeth thought impatiently: Really, Mother is positively silly about Bob: I don't believe she'd bother about my feelings in the matter if she had the chance to acquire him as a son-in-law. Bob himself seemed determined to behave as a son-in-law. He insisted on clearing the table and stacking the plates ready to be washed up in the morning, and he took on the job of mending the switch of Mrs. Simpson's reading-lamp. For the first night since London had been raided, Mrs. Simpson heard the 'planes and gunfires with something approaching equanimity. Subconsciously she felt that the presence of a young and active man, bearing the King's commission, must prove a safeguard. Besides which, Bob's candid admiration for her civilian courage made her feel ten times braver than the maddening disregard for danger shown by Henry and Elizabeth. There had been nights—bad nights when the flimsy little house had rocked on its foundations from the impact of descending bombs—when she had actively hated her husband

and daughter. One of their most maddening traits was their insistence on the relative immunity of Saffron Park. What did it matter to her that Stepney and Bow, Chelsea and Westminster, had suffered far worse? It did nothing to lessen the suspense of listening, night after night, to the monotonous droning of the German bombers, piloted by grim-faced, pitiless young men who had only to flex a finger to hurl down death for Alice Simpson. They lived too near to the guns on the Common. They ought to move—only, one heard such tales of people who had left supposedly dangerous areas to be killed immediately in neighbourhoods remote from any possible target. The really sensible people had long ago evacuated to the country. Even if Henry couldn't leave his work, there was no need for Elizabeth to keep on her job. It was her plain duty to take her mother to a place of safety. Other people saw that; friends in reception areas were always writing letters urging her to join them; but her own family was hopelessly selfish. It did not seem remotely to occur to them that she ought not to be expected to remain in London, and she was much too proud to point it out herself. That was why Bob's praise and admiration were so sweet. She hoped that he might open Elizabeth's eyes a little. When Bob was with her, she could almost dispense with thinking about Peter. In fact, Bob might even become Peter, if Elizabeth would only have the elementary sense to marry him.

Peter said: "Mother, I won't have another word of protest out of you—you're going down to Aunt Lucy's tomorrow and you're not coming back to London till the war's over." Peter said: "I think Mother's grand, the way she's stuck the raids and managed so wonderfully with ration-books and the black-out." Peter said: "I don't believe you two appreciate what Mother's had to go through."

But Peter had never been born.

"There! That's fixed it." Bob switched on the reading-lamp. He raised his voice slightly above a particularly heavy burst of gunfire. "Got any more jobs for me? Must make some use of the Army, you know. A chap said the other day that we ought to be knitting for the brave civilians."

He's very sore about the Army's inaction, Elizabeth thought. He keeps harping on it. She felt sympathetic towards him and smiled on him so warmly that he was misleadingly encouraged.

"Don't be idiotic. Who do you suppose is firing those guns? Go on, hit him!" she applauded a thunderous roar that rumbled on and on into the vastness of the night sky.

But the German 'plane continued its deliberate-sounding chug-chug.

"He didn't, you see," Bob said gloomily.

"Well, never mind, he probably will next time."

And bring down a burning 'plane on top of the house, Mrs. Simpson reflected bitterly.

"Let's amuse ourselves by imagining where we'd like best to be at the moment," Elizabeth suggested.

"In a bomber over Berlin," Bob said promptly.

"In America," Mrs. Simpson confessed.

"Anywhere where Alex is," Elizabeth thought but did not say. "I rather agree with Bob," she contributed at random.

"You know, we came down in the tube tonight," Bob addressed Mrs. Simpson. "I'd not travelled on them since they were turned into dormitories. Most extraordinary sight. Whole families—and everybody seemed to know each other. I thought they seemed very cheerful on the whole. It's a wonder to me, though, that the children don't fall on the rails and get electrocuted. Of course they're supposed to stay behind that white line but you can't keep kids from running about. You'd think it was a most unhealthy life for them, but they don't look much the worse for it."

"Elizabeth says the conditions are very insanitary," Mrs. Simpson said rather primly.

"There's a horrible smell in the mornings," Elizabeth corroborated bluntly. "Chiefly stale urine. There'll be a typhoid epidemic if they don't improve the lavatory conditions. I'm almost sure I'd rather die than spend a night down there."

"And yet any amount of those people have Anderson shelters," Mrs. Simpson lamented, anxious to change the subject.

(Elizabeth ought not to talk like that in front of Bob. What would he think of her?)

"Yes, but they're not as safe, whatever the government may say, and they lack the attractions of propinquity. People feel much braver when there's a lot of them together. It's a natural primitive reaction, and we're all getting very primitive nowadays."

"I know I've got a very primitive thirst," Bob remarked tactfully, observing that Mrs. Simpson was not enjoying the conversation. "Would Father Simpson mind if I opened a bottle of his beer?"

"Of course not. Go and help yourself. And bring me a glass. This is decidedly one of those occasions when malt does more than Milton can to justify God's ways to man." And now I've said the wrong thing again, Elizabeth told herself recklessly. Who cares?

Bob returned with the beer and three glasses on a tray. He put it on the table and then winked at Elizabeth in a conspiratorial way.

"Does your nearest pub keep open in the raids?"

"I think so. Why?"

"Wait and see. I'll be back in a minute."

In a short while he had returned with a half-bottle of rum.

"Beer and rum is a very good mixture," he announced. "That's one of the few really useful things I've learnt in the Army. Come on, Mrs. Simpson—just a short one. It's patriotic to drink rum— Nelson's blood, you know."

She protested, but not very much. More stimulating than alcohol was the flattery of Bob's insistence. They toasted Churchill, a speedy victory, the Merchant Navy, death to Hitler, bombs on Berlin and the Royal Engineers. Mrs. Simpson got no further than the Merchant Navy, but that was far enough to banish all fears. Even the high-pitched whine of three bombs passing over the house to explode on the Common (missing the gun positions but excavating neat pits in the soft ground) left her unmoved. Tonight she knew that she was invulnerable. Protected by Bob and Nelson, the silly Jerries in their tin-pot 'planes were powerless to harm her.

"You've made Mother tight," Elizabeth giggled, by no means unaffected herself.

"That's what I meant to do," Bob grinned back. "Damn good notion. You're looking a bit bright about the eyes yourself."

"Can you respect a woman when she's under the influence of alcohol?" she asked, pronouncing her words a shade too carefully.

"When you're the woman, certainly. Nothing you did would make any difference to me."

They were sitting side by side on the sofa. Elizabeth looked across at her mother and saw that she had nodded off in her chair. To her surprise and dismay, she heard herself say: "Dear Bob." Her head had somehow come to rest on his shoulder and his arm was round her. This is all wrong, she thought in a confused, remote way; this is most unfair. But she was much too comfortable to move.

"Darling." Bob's arm tightened around her. "You do like me quite a bit, don't you?"

She made an enormous effort. "Of course I like you. But this doesn't mean a thing, you know. I'm drunk."

"Never mind. *'In vino veritas!'*" Bob quoted triumphantly.

Oh, poor lamb, *in vino* nothing, she thought dreamily. But why be mean about it? She submitted to being kissed with a very good grace and even exerted herself to kiss back occasionally, from some vague notion of give and take. What a good thing Bob was stationed such a long way off. With so much rum about . . .

Time passed comfortably and tranquilly for all three of them. Round about midnight the All Clear, that usually welcome clarion, roused them reluctantly to an awareness of the hour and the advisability of going to bed. Elizabeth powdered her nose and avoided meeting Bob's determined gaze. She was feeling ashamed on a dual account. But Bob and Mrs. Simpson, for different reasons, were very well pleased with the evening's events.

CHAPTER V

ALL THROUGH September they had taken the day raids very seriously at the office. The dingy old-fashioned house held three other firms besides their own and when the sirens sounded most of the personnel of all four would walk or run, as their temperaments directed, down to a basement room which had, by the addition of a little timber, been converted into a shelter. Each small group occupied a separate corner and had provided their own chairs or benches. Some attempt was made to carry on work. Carter staggered up and down with Elizabeth's typewriter, but there were too many people in a confined space for much mental concentration to be possible. Joan frankly enjoyed the opportunity to slack and read a novel. Carter had to be perpetually restrained from darting out into the square to report on the dog-fights overhead. Miss Lewis had a habit of "turning faint", which necessitated opening the first-aid satchel to administer sal volatile and caused a lot of enjoyable flap among the rest of the shelterers. She and Mr. Rowland, Elizabeth decided, were genuinely nervous. Alex was only bored. He would have remained in his office throughout the raids if Elizabeth had not blackmailed him to come below by the threat of remaining with him. When there were no letters to be dictated and no forms to fill in, he would produce a draughts board and play with Rowland to occupy his partner's mind. Sometimes there were three alarms during the day, lasting an average of an hour apiece, and evening would find them with no mail ready to despatch and no work completed. A murmur arose from the ranks of even the laziest and most timid. This was "playing Hitler's game". After a formal, rather absurd meeting of the whole staff of Foster and Rowland, Exporters, it was decided to chance the raids, remain in their office on the third floor and get on with the job of earning American dollars to support the British war effort.

Although a few daylight bombs fell thereafter sufficiently near to cause excitement and a brief uneasiness, the decision to ignore the Luftwaffe until after dark became so much a habit that in a week it was hard to remember at any moment of the day whether the last siren had sounded a warning or a reassurance. Even the little restaurants where the female personnel lunched inadequately for eighteen-pence abandoned their habit of closing down in mid-meal and turning their hungry and indignant customers into the street. Each day that found one still alive, still domiciled in the same place and working in the same office, brought with it a certain highly-strung gaiety which overcame fatigue and anxiety. Early in the morning, with several hours of work to be got through, the night seemed a long way off. There was encouragement and comfort in every gesture of the daily routine—opening the mail, filling the inkwells, taking down shorthand and typing it back, balancing the Petty Cash and writing up the stamp-book. Only Miss Lewis at the switchboard found it hard to forget the war, when so many numbers were unobtainable either because the lines were damaged or because telephone bells were ringing aimlessly and eerily in buildings hastily vacated to accommodate a time-bomb.

There was still shopping to be done. A new hat, Joan Walsh decided, would cheer her up a lot. Elizabeth wanted to buy a wedding present at Heal's. But you couldn't get down Tottenham Court Road now, could you, except by making a wide detour? Yes, if you took an obscure turning that ran behind Frascati's and then walked down along two planks set at right angles over the low wall of a shattered warehouse and picked your way across the rubble out into an alley opposite Great Russell Street. But you must hold your nose because the smell was so appalling that your stomach heaved. A fractured drain or buried corpses? No one seemed to know.

Quiet and desolate, the roped-off area of shabby, squalid Tottenham Court Road had acquired a cloistered calm, a mournful grandeur beneath its mantle of grey dust. Only a few yards off, the traffic of Oxford Street rumbled by as usual, symbolic of the life that had departed, for the moment, from these bombed and blasted houses. Death brought dignity even to a contraceptive chemist's. Hard to believe a year ago that you would ever look with awe and sorrow on the Tottenham Court Road.

So Elizabeth thought, and to cheer herself up invited Joan to accompany her to the lunch-time Ballet at the Arts Club. The Marie Rambert dancers were doing "Peter and the Wolf" today. The performance ran for an hour from 1.15. They could eat sandwiches in the bar-lounge and come back to the office only a little late. Ballet was heaven in war-time—the perfect escape.

Sitting beside Joan in the stalls, enjoying grace, beauty and humour for the price of one shilling, it occurred to Elizabeth that she had become very fond of this absurd young woman. Joan had guts. She might be lazy, casual and irreverent, but her good qualities were of the kind which mattered in war-time— physical courage, a sense of proportion and the capacity to laugh in trying circumstances. The office without her these last two months would have been hell. You got to know what people were really like in times like these, Elizabeth thought . . . or did you? With a slight feeling of shock she realised that actually she knew very little about Joan Walsh, except the superficial things—her parents in Suffolk, her brother in the Navy, her "steady" in the B.B.C. at Bristol who turned up every now and then to take her out. In fact, she knew just as much about Joan as Joan knew about her, and that was nothing. It was so easy and so flattering to the ego to suppose that you alone had the monopoly of a secret, hidden life. "The heart knoweth its own bitterness," it said in the Bible. It didn't stipulate any particular make of heart.

"Lovely," Joan said as they pushed their way out past the impatient people gathered for the next performance. "I hadn't seen any ballet since before the war. I'd forgotten what fun it is."

"We'll go again, if they don't get bombed. Or we don't."

"It's extraordinary that Soho Square has escaped so far," Joan mused. "All right—I've got my fingers crossed. Only a few windows gone from that smash-up in Dean Street—we've been amazingly lucky. Supposing we come up one morning and find the poor old office nothing but a heap of rubble—what shall we do?"

"Start digging for the safe," Elizabeth suggested.

"Oh, that! Well, Rowland takes most of the most important files home with him every night, anyhow. I was thinking of my bread and butter. I suppose I could go home for a few days to recover from the shock, and then I think I'd join the Wrens. They're about the most exclusive of the women's services and I'm nothing if not exclusive. Look out!" She broke off to guide Elizabeth along the pavement. "All this broken glass is very dangerous. I've become very glass-conscious since the raids. I'd no idea there was so much of the stuff till it started to throw itself about. If we want to be rich after the war, we'd better marry glaziers."

"How does one get to know a glazier?"

"We might advertise. Oh Lord, that's a horrible mess where the Fire Station was. It gives me the pip to look at it. I think on the whole I'd prefer to marry a fireman, if there are any left, and try to provide him with a beautiful home life in compensation."

Yes, Joan talked a lot of nonsense, but nonsense had its value at the moment. There was something very touching in the good-humour of tired Londoners. Travelling home on the tube in rush hours, for instance—with bodies jammed so tightly together that it was difficult not to become involved in an almost indecent embrace, your arms pinioned to your sides, and the hard rim of a tin hat, worn slung through the strap of a respirator, digging painfully into your ribs. At each station, as the doors slid open, the people nearest the platform were subjected to a terrifying pressure from the desperate, determined newcomers trying to squeeze inside. Strap-hangers teetered on their toes, striving to maintain their balance, and some unfortunate, imprisoned down the far end of the car, would start a crushing counter-surge in struggling to alight. Red in the face, perspiring, weary from lack of sleep and nervous strain, the patient British public doggedly endured. And one irrepressible humourist with a weak joke about sardines or Hitler could send a ripple of genuine cheerfulness down the packed ranks, re-illuminating the flickering spirit of fellowship and bringing smiles to faces forced into lover-like but most unwilling nearness.

Yes, you could love your countrymen and women in the tube at rush hours. But it was highly preferable to travel earlier in the day.

"Back to the treadmill," Joan sighed at the door of the office. "The Satin Soap representative has got an appointment to see one of the boys at three o'clock—if he turns up. Your Foster's in a very grim mood today, isn't he? I wouldn't care to be his secretary. When I first came I envied you the young and handsome partner. Rowland's such an old sheep. But I've come to the conclusion since that I've got the better man, from my point of view. I wouldn't be good enough for Foster, anyhow. He wants enthusiasm and efficiency, and I don't possess either—at least, only about half an ounce to the pint."

Elizabeth knew why Alex was in a grim mood. They had spent the night before together and he was suffering from a mental hangover. Not that they had quarrelled, but he had taken his unhappiness and apprehension and disquiet and dropped them into her lap for her to dispose of. Well, she hadn't succeeded in doing so. Personal affairs could no longer be arranged by the persons concerned. The war was a length of clanking chain that impeded one's slightest movement. Thus their relationship, always tortuous and difficult, had become more difficult than ever and did not look like getting any simpler. In the office they must meet as servant and employer, and outside the office they could rarely meet at all.

Lying in his arms when they had gone back after dinner to the flat, she found herself having to plan ways and means as though she were his secretary still, looking up trains for him to catch or fixing appointments. She didn't like that. Sex without spontaneity was surely rewarded by a particularly terrible inferno. It was curious that the aerial bombardment of London, which had ennobled so much that was normally sordid, should only debase a love affair between two people who had managed for three years to overcome the threat to their relations implicit in all such. To die together would be simple. It would not be so simple to be dug out still alive from the same collapsed building.

"This sort of thing is absolute hell," Alex groaned. "We can't go on with it. I'm used to feeling like a cad but now I feel like an assassin too. If only you hadn't gone to live in that goddamn suburb! It wouldn't be so bad if I could take you home by taxi as I used to. But dashing through the shrapnel to catch the last train and then going back alone to wonder if you reached home alive . . . It's unendurable."

"Darling." She rubbed her cheek against the smooth skin of his shoulder in a lazy caress. "If I'd stayed in Chelsea I'd probably be dead by now. Besides, we've gone over that before. I went back to live at home again because of Father. He honestly believed that London would be razed to the ground in the first weeks of the war. I've spent a year regretting it, but I can't do anything about it now. Least of all now. I feel guilty enough as it is when he has to go on duty and my mother is left alone in the house. She's nervous of the raids."

"Well, I'm nervous of the raids," Alex grumbled gently. "The only time I'm not nervous is when I'm in bed with you. So what are you going to do about that?"

"I'll come and spend next Sunday with you," she promised. "The whole day—from breakfast on. And quite soon we'll go away together for a week-end somewhere. Everybody says the raids are bound to slack off in the winter months. We'll choose a week-end when there isn't any moon and stay at some country pub—if we can find one not choked up with Londoners in flight."

And probably run into someone you know—some business friend who recognised me as your secretary or a woman who has met your wife, she added in her mind. She hated going away with him for week-ends. They were both of them secretly apprehensive all the time.

"Supposing Naomi decided one day to come up to town and give you a lovely surprise," she said, voicing an old fear.

"Don't worry about that. There was a certain amount of risk before the blitz began but she'd never take the chance of being bombed."

"She might be worried about you and come to see if you were all right."

"Naomi doesn't worry about anything except my money-making capacities," he said bitterly. "As long as my signature's good on a cheque and I put in a sufficiently regular appearance to uphold her prestige as a married woman, she'll lose no sleep on my account. And when I'm with her, she doesn't lose any sleep either. You know that, don't you, darling?"

Yes, she knew it, but she could never be told it too often. It was the foundation stone on which their relationship was built. Let Naomi have the cachet and the children and the inalienable rights of legal possession—none of that mattered in comparison with the fact that as a lover he belonged only to her, Elizabeth. Nor was that something which she had stolen. Naomi and he had been physically as well as mentally estranged since the birth of the second child, he said, a whole year before Elizabeth had become his mistress. Naomi wasn't amused by that side of marriage. She had made it abundantly clear, and no man of any sensitivity would inflict himself on an unwilling wife. Elizabeth found this hard to understand when the man was Alex, but she knew that a great many women felt like that. It was her good fortune that Naomi should be one of them.

"Why don't you answer?" he demanded rather brusquely.

"I was just thinking. Nothing disagreeable. I've never suspected you of running a harem, darling."

He laughed with more amusement than the joke seemed to deserve.

"No beautiful Circassia in a flat at Tooting Bec? Perhaps you're right."

It was at that moment that the Molotov bread-basket fell. The contents scattered effectively and a small number of incendiaries landed on the roof of the flats. Overhead, there was a sudden stampede of feet and a few seconds later someone hammered on Alex's door.

"Foster, are you there? Stirrup-pump wanted upstairs."

Alex was already struggling into the necessary minimum of clothing. He swore fluently.

"I don't suppose it's anything much, but you'd better get dressed and go downstairs. I'll meet you there."

It seemed silly to say "Take care", so she didn't say it.

Dressed completely, even to her coat and hat, she avoided using the lift and walked down to the hall. Quite a number of people were apparently sleeping on mattresses in the corridors outside their rooms, but no one had as yet retired to bed there. In the hall itself, a group of women, most of them in slacks or siren-suits, were gathered in varying attitudes of indecision. News of the incendiaries on the roof seemed to have travelled fast.

"We'll be an absolute *target*," a raddled little woman sitting on a large suitcase lamented. "Only ten o'clock—hours to go before it's daylight."

"There's nothing to be afraid of about incendiaries as long as they're detected quickly," another woman argued rather belligerently. "It was the greatest good fortune that Mr. Green went up to that empty top flat to keep an eye on things. There's not the slightest danger of the fire getting a hold." She produced her knitting, to underline her point.

Most people apparently agreeing with her, they had leisure to observe Elizabeth, with poorly concealed curiosity. Not a resident. Came down the stairs, so she must be a guest. Whose?

Perhaps I'd better go back to the flat, Elizabeth thought. She was afraid that Alex would come to collect her clad only in trousers, shoes and pullover. But while she still hesitated, half listening to the conversation around her, half to the usual raid noises outside, he appeared. He had obviously gone back to the flat and finished dressing. His manner was formally polite.

"All over, ladies. We doused the lot. I'm sorry, Miss Simpson, to have bundled you out like that, but we can go back and finish now. I don't think you ought to leave the building just yet."

"No, I think I'd better wait till it's a little quieter," she murmured.

Interested glances followed them up the stairs.

Inside the flat, Alex started swearing again. It just wasn't possible now to have a private life, when any moment this sort of interruption was likely to occur. And these flats—one no longer felt as if one were living in London, where people minded their own business. Everybody in the place—the handful that were left—knew everybody else. All sleeping end to end in corridors, huddling together in fantastic costumes, swopping life stories in the stress of mutual funk . . . One might as well be in a boarding-house. The national character was changing, and decidedly for the worse.

He was so earnest in his rage that Elizabeth began to laugh.

"Pipe down, my love, and give me a drink. And then I'll have to go, whatever the Luftwaffe's doing, or I shall miss my last train."

Still grumbling, he poured out whiskies and sodas.

"What happened on the roof?" she asked.

"Oh, Green had already dealt with two or three, just emptying a bucket of sand on them. One burned through into a top flat, but they'd removed the furniture, so it didn't make much mess. We put that out with the stirrup-pump. Another one exploded and one man was slightly injured. It was all over in a few minutes. Not a bit exciting."

"Well, that's one bomb story I shan't be able to tell."

Suddenly she was very tired. The evening's events had illustrated their argument far too well. Alex was right. There wasn't any private life left. If we were married, she thought, I would wash up the glasses and change into slacks and lie down on the bed again with Alex. Even if we couldn't sleep, even if we were frightened, we could lie there together all night. In the morning I would meet those women in the hall, on my way out to collect the rations, and they would congratulate me on the splendid way my husband had behaved . . . She felt very sorry for herself and her eyes filled with tears.

Alex mustn't see them. She put down her empty glass.

"Come on. We might just as well go now as wait for one of those dangerously deceptive 'lulls'."

He handed her his tin hat and she put it on without arguing. She would give it him back at the entrance to the tube station. It was the ritual. They had only about a hundred yards to go and they covered them without incident. The smell of not very clean people herded together underground rose up from the bottom of the escalator to sicken her. But there was nothing to do but go down and meet it. For a moment she clung to Alex in an embrace as desperate as if she knew it to be final. Then, without looking back, they separated.

CHAPTER VI

OCTOBER PASSED and November passed. A number of Londoners met violent death in the night, a still larger number suffered varying degrees of injury, the largest number of all suffered nothing more than inconvenience and nervous strain. London had adapted herself. With a mixture of chivalry and vanity, she even worried about the fate of the big provincial towns, which sometimes filled her place as victim No. 1. Better, surely, that the largest member of the family should take the most punishment? A little wryly, she received the congratulations of the western world. "Some have greatness thrust upon them," Joan Walsh snorted. "Nobody's offered me any alternative to being a heroine."

In their private lives, people who remained unaffected by such upheavals as the call-up or an alarmingly compulsory change of residence marked time. The immediate future was so uncertain that few cared to make a change for change's sake. Governmental spokesmen uttered warnings of invasion in the spring, but practically nobody believed them. With sublime smugness, the vast bulk of the population of Britain listened to the message of their bones. And their bones assured them that nobody ever invaded England and that England always won her wars, in time. Bones were obviously more reliable than politicians, though great respect was accorded to every word uttered by Mr. Churchill, however full of admonition. It was only to be hoped that he took sufficient precautions for his own safety. Probably not, the nation thought, and pitied, with a grin, those entrusted with his guardianship.

But nerves became a little taut and Londoners had scant sympathy for skulkers. "I'm sick of people who talk as though the alternative to being bombed were immortality," Elizabeth Simpson said. "If they'd ever seen anyone with cancer of the bladder, they'd realise that there are worse things than sudden death."

People losing everything except their lives in the time that it took for a noise like an express train rushing through a way-side station to culminate in blinding shock, the crash of masonry and terrifying darkness, reacted with a semi-hysterical gaiety which endured for several days. A primitive exultation upheld them, all values merged into the single one of relief in self-preservation. Afterwards they shed tears for upright pianos recently paid for on the hire purchase system and the destruction of almost everything that proved their past to them. All the evidence they had collected over years that they were themselves and no other, that people had written them love-letters, remembered them at Christmas and owed them bills, had vanished in an instant. So Daisy Cathcart prayed nightly that her home might not be destroyed, and expended a special part of her all-embracing kindness on the bombed-out.

The very young, impatient of their elders' sympathy, were brave without much effort, congratulating themselves on their good fortune in being born at such an active period. Competition and jealousy entered into the collection of war-trophies and the silken cord of a land-mine parachute outweighed a ton of shrapnel. Owen Cathcart, extinguishing an incendiary bomb on the Common one night, forgot entirely that he had recently and most unfortunately discovered the works of Marcel Proust. At the cost of smarting finger-tips, he carried home the tail-fin in triumph.

Out in the Atlantic Ocean, men sank choking under the crests of reared-up waves and swam, blackened like negroes, through a field of blazing oil and died of scalding in their punctured boiler-rooms. Henry Simpson read the figures of shipping losses and saw each numeral change into the rictus of a corpse. On duty at the Post he became more and more silent, except on one occasion when he seemed deliberately to lash himself into a temper and quarrelled bitterly with Calverly about the future of the Party system. Thorne, concerned for him and for the smooth running of the Post, tipped the wink to keep off politics when Simpson was about.

A well-aimed high explosive having damaged a small power station, the residents of Saffron Park were without electric light for ten days. Alice Simpson, fortunate in the possession of an oil lamp, knitted furiously in the semi-gloom and brooded on her wrongs. Resentment and grievance merged within her mind into a cold, implacable hatred of the enemy. She took comfort in devising tortures which a year before she would have been shocked and embarrassed to find herself capable of imagining. In particular, she felt contempt and loathing for the ordinary German who submitted to such leadership, unaware that, but for an accident of birth, she would herself have been ideal material for Nazi doctrine. But more representative members of the race, unable to adapt themselves to modern war conditions, still greeted baled-out Jerries with a pitchfork and a cup of tea.

In the reception areas, a wave of generous sympathy swept away the irritation felt for town evacuees in days before the raids. Naomi Foster knew herself to be justified in having taken her children out of London and conveniently forgot that it had been at her husband's insistence. The country did not seem so boring viewed as an alternative to being bombed. At week-ends, she wanted to take Alex visiting in the village, an interesting exhibit from the front line. But Alex made excuses and was very poor company, preferring to amuse the children in the mornings and sleep in the afternoons. Also, he forgot their eighth wedding anniversary.

"I suppose you'll say your secretary ought to have reminded you," Naomi gibed, extremely put out.

It might have been rather tactless of her, considering how tired he seemed to be, but need he have lost his temper so completely?

In spite of various statements to the contrary, the cost of living rose and almost everyone became increasingly aware of shrunken incomes. Lionel Cathcart joined, with laudable good humour, in the general lamentations. Which was discreet of him, in view of the fact that, in a banking account held in quite another name, he was rapidly accumulating more money than he had ever possessed in his life before.

So November passed and December passed, and it was Christmas 1940. The office in Soho Square closed for the holiday. And Elizabeth went on duty at the local hospital from 8 a.m. to 1 p.m. on Boxing Day.

It was a matter of luck to which ward you were directed. You had simply to take the first on the list where you signed your name. Today, Elizabeth was relieved to find, it was Men's Medical. That was easy. The sister would ignore her, but in a pleasant way; the nurses, not too overworked, were friendly. There would be sputum mugs to empty, which made her retch, but nothing else that could not be easily borne.

Although there were twenty-four beds in the ward, only fifteen of them were occupied—mostly by young men, which seemed surprising until she realised that they were soldiers, bronchitis and pleurisy cases. Old Grandpa was still in his corner. He would be there till he died. The depressed man with the gastric ulcer had gone. Someone was behind screens. She saw all this at first glance, and after that was very busy for the next two hours, making beds, cleansing lockers, carbolising rubber sheets. It was a dull ward, really, with no dressings to watch, but the morning passed gradually. The new gastric ulcer had to be wheeled down for an X ray; there were inhalants to administer. Presently she found herself out in the sluice-room, pretending to tidy up, while she watched Nurse Dove test urine and listened to her conversation with Nurse Jones.

"That Corporal Lees has a cheek," Nurse Dove said, boiling the contents of a glass tube over a spirit lamp. "You have to watch what you say to him. He was silly-assing about just now when I rubbed his chest—'You'll get me into trouble with Sister,' I said. 'I'd love to get you into trouble,' he said—with such a *look*. I couldn't think of anything to answer."

"Well, I'd rather be here than in Sister Fuller's ward," Jones said feelingly. "All those air-raid cases—they give me the pip. At least it's cheerful up here, when the boys get convalescent. And Sister Webster doesn't nag you all the time."

"Write down for me, dear," Dove interrupted, "Henderson—118—acid—sugar plus."

"I can't stop and do that now. Nurse here will help you, won't you, Nurse?" she asked kindly.

"Love to," Elizabeth said with a genuine relief at having something to do.

When she had watched for a little while, she asked if she might do the testing herself. Nurse Dove agreed amiably, enjoying her role as instructress. Cleaning up afterwards, she became even more friendly, asking personal questions with a disarmingly frank curiosity that reminded Elizabeth of Joan Walsh. But compared with this girl of about the same age, Joan, for all her rattle, seemed level-headed and mature. The world of hospital and the psychology of nurses fascinated Elizabeth. Within walls which more than any other held a microcosm of human suffering, there existed a community fundamentally non-adult. She had never felt further removed from the realities of life than in the company of nurses. It was not merely that they were mostly young; middle-aged sisters, beneath their necessary dignity of authority, were just as obviously the victims of their environment. The very best nurses, nurses by vocation, were stamped with the simplicity of nuns. Nearly all ordinary nurses were stamped with the jejuneness of the boarding school. In the hourly combat with bodily sickness, they had developed an occupational disease of their own. They had not been able to grow up.

No doubt for some the work had its rewards, but it seemed to Elizabeth, in spite of the poor terms she had herself closed with in life, the saddest job on earth. The price paid for the courage to face blood and stench and fear and agony was more than weariness and social exile and a dubious chance of comfort in old age; it was the smooth glaze of professional callousness, the mother-of-pearl crust which the oyster grows to protect itself from the grit in its vitals, the easy acceptance of other people's suffering which hardens the soul.

Casual ministrants to pain, visitors like herself from the real world outside, could afford to be kinder and more sympathetic. The burden they had temporarily assumed, the burden of participation in suffering and fear, could be exchanged at the end of the day, with a clear conscience, for the lesser burden of individual living. But if you could never escape from the shadow of that towering mound, the accumulated tragedy of man's pathetic indignity in physical decay, would you attempt to shoulder that? The great majority, unconscious and instinctive, chose rather to ignore it or to make a joke of it. They joked as children, for they had turned their backs on death and they were shut outside the life of ordinary women.

"I've got to go on nights at the end of this month," Dove confided gloomily. She was small and sallow, with large dark eyes.

"Oh, bad luck."

"I wouldn't mind if it was here, but it'll be Women's Surgical, for sure. Some of the patients get so frightened in the raids. There's one thing—you're kept too busy to feel scared yourself. Not that I mind them all that. I'm always so tired by the end of the day that I sleep through anything. But I don't like to hear about all the hospitals that get bombed. How long do you think the war's going to last? I never seem to have time to read the papers."

"I don't think you'd know the answer to that one if you did read the papers. Another couple of years, perhaps."

"As long as that? I hope I don't get stuck here all that time. I'd rather be a Land Girl. I was brought up on a farm."

"It would be a terrible waste of your training, wouldn't it?"

"Oh, they won't let me, anyhow—I know that. But I wish I hadn't ever taken up nursing."

"What made you?" Elizabeth decided that two could play at personal questions.

"Oh, I don't know." Her voice went flat and vague.

But I think I know, Elizabeth told herself. You lived on the farm and you wanted to get away. There was no money to train you as a shorthand-typist and none of the girls you knew had done that, anyhow. Nursing was a step above serving in a shop and you had romantic ideas about tending a handsome young man with money who breathed a proposal of marriage while you stroked his fevered brow. And now your feet swell and you can't stop your hands from chapping and all the young men have girl friends who visit them on Sundays wearing smarter clothes than you can possibly afford. You get two hours off a day which you spend at the cinema with one of the other nurses, because you don't know anyone outside the hospital, and when your fortnight's holiday comes round you go back to the farm, because you haven't enough money to put up at a seaside place where you might make some new contacts. In fact, it's a hell of a life—and then people wonder why so few girls want to take up nursing nowadays.

She said, apparently at random: "Did you finish that green jumper you were knitting last time I was on?" And was rewarded by seeing Nurse Dove's face light up.

"I've only got the second sleeve to do now. I ran out of wool in the middle. I'd have done it long ago, if it hadn't been for that."

Nurse Jones put her head round the door. "Now then, you two, don't stand there gassing. It's time to lay the lockers for dinner."

The man behind the screens was dying of pneumonia. Sister Webster had been with him most of the morning and the House Physician had stayed a long time. Even the exuberant young soldiers, still celebrating Christmas, were a little subdued when the news reached them by the subtle, jungle telegraph system which exists in hospital wards. They questioned Elizabeth, calculating that she would be less professionally adept at evading them.

"Nurse, that chap behind the screens, he's pretty bad, isn't he?"

"Oh, he'll be all right presently. You're never very happy when you've got pneumonia. What have you done with your table napkin?"

"They're giving him oxygen, aren't they?"

"That doesn't mean anything. They always do that. How long has he been in?"

"Came in Christmas Eve. We never even saw him. He's had the screens round him all the time. Grandpa reckons he'll pop off tomorrow morning, early."

Elizabeth laughed. "Grandpa knows everything, of course. He practically runs this hospital."

She rather liked Grandpa, though he had dirty habits which included taking out his false teeth and hiding them under the pillow. He looked at her suspiciously when she laid his locker for dinner and criticised her arrangement of the utensils. On visiting days, the nurses said, his meek little wife always left him in tears, shed for herself, not for him.

"What's for dinner today, Nurse?" the cheeky corporal asked.

"Sorry—I don't know yet."

"Well, we had a damn good feed yesterday, anyhow, and presents and crackers and all. Like my paper cap, Nurse? Think it suits me?"

"You'd look wonderful in anything," Elizabeth riposted easily.

"There!" He turned to the grinning man in the next bed.

"Nurse says I'm beautiful. D'you think I'm better-looking than Clark Gable?"

"Your ears are flatter," Elizabeth said judiciously.

But she broke off hurriedly and moved on as Nurse Jones approached them. She had found that the professional nurses did not like the part-time volunteers to be on too good terms with the patients, especially the male ones. Their jealousy was easily aroused. Which was understandable enough, Elizabeth thought. Since their contacts with the world outside were so circumscribed, they might at least be allowed to reign unassailed in their own little world. But it was sometimes rather bad luck on the patients, who liked the stimulus of an unaccustomed face and personality.

Holding plates while Sister served in the ward kitchen, she ventured to ask about the pneumonia case.

"Not much hope," Sister said briefly. "He was brought in too late. One of those shelter cases—we're always having them now.

He'd been lying in about a foot of water, as far as I can make out. He's just as much a raid casualty as if he'd been bombed."

Sister Webster did not fit into either of Elizabeth's pigeon-holes of nun or schoolgirl. She was nearer the type of a woman doctor. She went her own way, with serenity and good breeding, and was said to be cordially disliked by the Matron. Elizabeth, who had not thought of Alex once since she came on duty, suddenly thought of him now. What advice would Sister Webster give her in the matter? she wondered. And she wondered, too, if she had had many death-bed confidences.

By one o'clock the dinner had been served, eaten and cleared away. Intensely weary, Elizabeth presented her book to be initialled by Sister, was graciously but curtly thanked and took her leave. She hoped very much that in the past five hours she had made a useful contribution to the war effort, but it seemed unlikely. She had thrown a sop to her conscience. It probably didn't amount to any more than that.

CHAPTER VII

THE DAY AFTER the big City raid on Sunday, December 29th, Owen received a telegram from Derek: "Ten days' leave from Wednesday. Going home. Please come." He felt so happy that he could only appear enormously matter of fact and casual about it. Ten days with Derek at Lampton! He hadn't believed that such things could happen any longer. And then, with a quiet perceptible drop of his heart, he remembered: the raids: Mother. The moment he turned his back on the house, removed the protection of his invulnerability, it was almost certain to be bombed.

But Daisy brushed aside his objections with unaccustomed vigour and decision. The glow of the fires the night before, visible for miles, and the news of the damage which began to trickle through during the day, strengthened her anxiety to get Owen, even temporarily, away from London. Derek's leave seemed

heaven-sent to her. Of course Owen must go! She started immediately to pack his bag, as if to get a good start in a race with
the Luftwaffe. Owen himself, without mentioning it, packed the
tail-fin of his incendiary in the satchel in which he carried his
gas-mask. He wouldn't produce it if there were any competition,
but he didn't think there would be, at Lampton.

Fortunately for Daisy's peace of mind, there were no Alerts
the two succeeding nights. With infinite relief she watched her
son set off. It would mean a break in his coaching, of course, but
even Lionel had made no objection to that.

Crossing London on top of a 'bus, Owen tried to imagine how
it would look to his aunt and cousins, who had not been up since
the summer. They would mind the shattered houses far more
than the loss of a Wren church they had passed without notic-
ing. Poor mutilated houses, surgically exposed to view, forced to
display the mediocrity of ordinary people's taste in wall-paper,
their cheap crockery still standing on its shelves, their photographs still strung along the mantelpiece. The 'bus-top gazers
stared out with sober faces. No one commented. Your turn
today—mine tomorrow, perhaps. The 'bus took unaccustomed
routes, travelling down quiet streets which never before had had
their upper windows overlooked. Policemen guarded wooden
barricades with unexploded bomb notices, and argued with the
light of heart who *knew* that it was safe for them to risk it. A
fire-engine trailer went by, full of exhausted-looking men with
dirty faces. If one had not been English, one would have given
them a cheer.

Owen's train ran late, which was to be expected, but he
arrived at the house in time for tea.

Derek was home but had gone down the village, Aunt Susan
said. They hadn't known what time exactly to expect Owen. Only
two of his cousins were there: Lorna, with her baby, and Harriet,
called Harry, whom he liked the least. She did good works and
took care of her mother. His favourite, Cynthia, was now a Waaf
and stationed in the north. He was sorry to miss Cynthia and yet
sneakingly, meanly glad as well. She was Derek's favourite too,

and they would probably have talked shop all the time and made him feel a little out of it.

"Why don't you walk down the lane and meet Derek?" Aunt Susan suggested kindly. "You can't miss him. He's only gone to try and get some cigarettes. He said he would be back before dusk, to help me with the black-out. We've done it very badly, I'm afraid—it's still a case of climbing on chairs and sticking in drawing-pins."

"Is he in uniform?" Owen asked—absurdly, as if he wouldn't recognise him unless forewarned.

"Yes. He said he'd give the village a treat this evening. But he's going to wear mufti for the rest of his leave—he's promised me."

Poor Aunt Susan, Owen thought compassionately. She does hate Derek being in the Air Force.

He had forgotten how beautiful it was in the country, even now, when the trees were bare and the ground was sodden with rain. This was the place he loved best in the world. He would have a house here when he was middle-aged and had retired. There would be a wood at the bottom of the garden with a stream running through it, and kingcups, and primroses, and wild orchids. The house would be furnished exactly like Aunt Susan's, comfortable and shabby; secretly, for it was disloyal even to think it, he didn't care for the furniture at home. But who would live in the house, except himself and someone to cook the meals, he couldn't imagine.

He hadn't gone far along the village before he met Derek. He was talking to a girl, Owen saw with quick jealousy, but was relieved, a moment later, to recognise Ann Parsons, the Vicar's daughter, whom they had both known since they were children together. Derek looked very well in his uniform. Ann and he were laughing. She saw Owen before Derek did and he believed he detected a fleeting disappointment cross her face. Perhaps it was because Derek himself showed such obvious pleasure that even Owen was assuaged. There was only a third of his attention left for Ann now, and she knew it. A third was a poor exchange for the whole. Philosophically, she turned in at the gate of the vicarage and left the cousins to walk home alone.

"Let's see what the blitz has done to you," Derek demanded. "H'm, a little peaky. I bet you don't take any exercise, now I'm not there to keep you up to the mark. You always were the laziest hound."

"Too many parlour games and not enough outdoor sports," Owen misquoted a slogan of their school-days. "You look disgustingly fit."

"Have to be. No alternative. You wait till it's your turn to do P.T. in shorts at six o'clock in the morning! How are the maths going?"

"Not so bad. The man who's coaching me is a local schoolmaster with a watery blue eye. I think he drinks. But he knows his stuff and he says I ought to pass all right."

"It would be marvellous if you were posted to our place. I'll have been transferred by then, of course, but I could teach you all the ropes and put in a word for you with some of the boys. They're wizard types."

"It will be funny to go back to school without you," Owen said a little breathlessly.

"I know. I couldn't think what was missing when I first joined up. Then I thought, Good Heavens, it's old Tudor! I'd got so used to having you to chivvy around and haul out of the soup!" He laughed without a trace of embarrassment at his own expression of affection.

Owen's heart soared and he kicked a stone into the ditch by the side of the road to demonstrate his happiness. What a fool he had been—what a bloody fool!

"I'll be glad when the next six months are over," he confessed. "Hanging about at home—waiting—with not enough to do—it's getting me down."

"I gathered from your letters that you were taking rather a dim view of things," Derek said solicitously. "You read too much—that's half your trouble. And air raids—they can't be much fun, really."

"Oh, the raids aren't so bad. I feel better when there's a raid on. Oh, I know that sounds like bravado but it's true. They take you out of yourself. But I wish I could be doing something useful.

I wanted to join the A.F.S. as a messenger, or something, but Father put his foot down. He said I'd far better swot up mathematics and make sure of getting into the R.A.F."

"I think he's right," Derek said judiciously. "We need all the men we can get. Don't pass this on to Mother, but there's a lot of chaps crash in training. Seems a lousy way to go, doesn't it? There's some sense in being shot down. They'll put you in Bomber Command, if they know what they're doing. You're the steady, reliable type, although you're such a dreamy idiot. I'm rash and silly, so I'll be a Fighter Boy. If I get my wings," he added hastily, crossing his fingers.

"You'll do that all right," Owen reassured him sincerely. Hadn't Derek always won what he set out for? "You'll probably get the D.F.C. as well, and then you can go down to the dear old school on Speech Day and present the prizes, with all the juniors trotting at your heels and all the seniors envying your guts."

They had reached the house, and now, with a good grace, Owen must step down from his position at Derek's shoulder. It was easy to do, for he was feeling happy and secure. How generous and ungrasping you could be when you felt secure! So much of what was accounted merit in one's character was only a lucky accident of environment.

Derek changed into mufti for dinner and talked no more about his work. It was impossible to keep the conversation off the war, but everyone tried to dwell on its lighter aspects. The really extraordinary behaviour of the evacuees—"poor things"—was much discussed. But some of them were quite nice—Mrs. Foster and her two children, for instance. Her husband worked in London, in some reserved occupation, and came down every other week-end.

"How's Michael?" Owen remembered to ask Lorna.

"All right, thank you, Owen. He had a week's leave in November. He's a full-blown captain now."

"Brown type," Derek muttered with a mocking grimace at his sister.

"Less of your lip, young Derek. A couple of years ago and you were offering to polish his buttons."

"I know. What an ass I was! I've learnt better now."

"I suppose I'll be introduced to the baby in the morning," Owen persevered.

"Susan to you. After Mother. Don't sound so depressed about it, darling. I won't expect you to nurse her, though Derek does it beautifully. He's very avuncular."

"Yes, I've got the hang of it now. She banks a bit, but the thing you've got to be really careful of is her *in*tractable undercarriage. She soaked me to the skin this afternoon."

Everybody laughed, even Harriet. Harry was nicer since the war, Owen decided. She ran the First Aid Post in the village and was a keen supporter of the knitting circle and felt useful and responsible. Her blond severity was tempered now by a little animation. She wasn't bad-looking, Owen thought, really seeing her for the first time. She ought to get married—that would probably improve her still further. But she would never be placid and shrewd and kind, like Lorna, or gay and sceptical and quick-witted, like Cynthia. He asked after Cynthia.

"She's got herself engaged, to a Flight Lieutenant. Derek thinks it's just to help him on in his career," Lorna answered.

"What's he like?" Owen asked, his besetting sin of jealousy sharpening his tone. That was the end of the old comradeship with Cynthia.

"We haven't met him yet," Aunt Susan said. "They hope to arrange their next leaves together, so that she can bring him home. He sounds very nice."

"We're all irresistible," Derek said blithely.

And then, because his mother looked uneasy, he changed the subject and they all talked of local things again until dinner was over and Owen and he went off to play darts in the study.

"What a contrast those boys make," Mrs. Hammond remarked, when they had left the room ". . . Derek so fair and Owen so dark. Owen doesn't look well, does he? It must be a great strain, living in London now. But he's broadening out nicely. You'd never think, would you, that he was a premature baby?"

She spoke in good faith, with auntly affection, entirely unaware of how her sister-in-law would have winced in shame to hear her.

It was nearly midnight before Owen went to bed, but for a long while he could not sleep. He found himself listening for the siren, wondering what was happening at Saffron Park. He must wake up in time to hear the eight o'clock news, he thought. In spite of Derek's uniform and everything that had been said and left unsaid that evening, the war seemed a long way off down here. He almost missed the lullaby of gunfire. But finally he fell asleep imagining what he would do tomorrow. Derek had said they might walk over to the heronry. Harry had said you could still get pear-drops at the post office. And there were nine more days. . . .

It was on the sixth day that Elizabeth Simpson came down to Lampton.

Alex had joined his family for Christmas and had almost immediately contracted a chill. Since it annoyed him to be ill, he had neglected it and it had turned into bronchitis. The new year found him still in bed, morose and miserable. He was worried about the office, he told Naomi. Rowland was such a fool. Twice, against doctor's orders, he had gone downstairs in a dressing-gown to speak to Elizabeth on the 'phone and give her instructions. The second time, his temperature shot up alarmingly.

"You'd better have your precious Miss Simpson down for the day and dictate some letters to her," Naomi finally suggested, thoroughly exasperated.

Alex had hesitated, then agreed. It was arranged that she should spend the night—it was too far to come and go back the same evening. Naomi herself rang up Elizabeth to make the arrangement.

"She didn't sound too pleased with the idea," she reported to Alex afterwards. "You've probably upset a date with her boy friend."

"He's in the Army," Alex grunted.

"Well, he might have leave, mightn't he?"

Naomi was not very pleased herself. She did not like Miss Simpson and it was a bore having to cater for an extra person.

All the way down in the train, Elizabeth argued with two voices. One of them said: "You're going to see Alex, whom you love, who is ill." The other said: "God damn Alex for having let you in for this." The second voice clamoured loudly in her ear when Naomi met the train with the car to drive her to the house, but in the moment that she saw Alex, looking thin and strangely helpless, she heard only the first voice, as urgent, as insistent as her quickened pulses.

"Hullo, Miss Simpson," he said with a wan, rather silly smile. "Nice of you to come."

"I'm afraid you don't look very well, Mr. Foster." Her voice was conventionally solicitous, but it came out of a dry mouth. "You mustn't try to get through too much work at once. I've brought my portable typewriter and some of the more important correspondence. And there's a letter for you from Mr. Rowland."

"I thought we might make a start after lunch. You'd like to wash now, and park your suitcase, I expect."

He was dressed and downstairs for only the second time, Naomi told Elizabeth as she took her to her room. Silly of him to attempt to work so soon, but you know what men are. Here is your room and I hope you'll find everything you want. The bathroom is across the landing and lunch at 1.15.

The first thing Elizabeth did when she was alone was to cross to the dressing-table and look at her reflection in the mirror for a full minute. Not a tell-tale face. Pale, slightly Mongolian, a little sulky in repose—handsome, but not by everybody's standards. The mouth, full and sensuous, was a giveaway to the discerning, but fortunately there were not many of them. Not for the first time she wondered, with genuine surprise and humility, what Alex saw when he looked at her which had commanded his fidelity through three years of strain and frustration. But it was a fruitless conjecture. What, for the matter of that, did she see when she looked at him? A tall, bulky, blond young man (though older than her by eight years), whose hair already receded a little in front and who would be stout in middle age. His hands were the best thing about him, well shaped and agreeable. But you didn't fall in love with a man because of his hands. It's just propinquity, she told herself with a show of dispassion. "Whether or not we find what we are seeking is idle, biologically speaking." In the meantime, she had better unpack her bag.

At lunch, Naomi handled the conversation and was gracious, as to a social inferior who must not be made to feel at all awkward or out of place. Elizabeth played up to this with a becoming meekness. She did so principally in order to embarrass Alex, who was responsible for the situation. Feeling angry with Naomi, it was natural that she should avenge herself on Naomi's husband. But compunction pricked her at the sight of his pallor and the fined-down contour of his face. She was glad for his sake when the children appeared with the coffee and made a diversion.

Sally was six and Donald four years of age. Sally had a neat, small head, dark curly hair and blue eyes, like her mother; Donald was like Alex, fair, grey-eyed and fresh-complexioned. They appeared to be fonder of their father than of Naomi, but that might be only that he had the charm of novelty and also must be made a fuss of, because he had been ill. Naomi was a little jealous, Elizabeth thought. She scolded them for both trying to climb on Alex's knee at once. With Elizabeth they were shy, curious and polite. Rather pleasant children, Elizabeth told herself, trying to pretend she had no personal interest in them.

"I thought we might work in here this afternoon, when the table's cleared," Alex said.

"Only till tea-time," Naomi commanded. "Don't you agree with me, Miss Simpson? I'm sure that's enough for the first day."

Miss Simpson thought that she was perfectly right.

The moment she was alone with Alex, he said quickly, as if to forestall her:

"You're angry with me, aren't you?"

"Yes, I think I am. It's so totally unnecessary. There's nothing I can do down here which couldn't have been handled perfectly well from the office for another week or so."

"I know. But I wanted to see you, and to get you out of London, even for one night."

She was not to be appeased as easily as that. In every argument between them he sought to disarm her by a trick of naïveté, an ingenious confession of self-interest which was hard to withstand by anyone who loved him. But he had not reckoned with her pride, which had endured much but had a limit to its immolation. Inevitably, it was Naomi who made her most aware of all that was precarious and ignominious in her situation. To be forced to be her guest, to lie to her with every unspoken word, was infinitely galling and humiliating. Her reason told her that there was no difference between using her position as Alex's secretary in London to cover up the fact that she was his mistress or in doing the same thing here, but her instinct told her there was all the difference in the world.

"It was unfair of you," she said in a low voice, "unfair to me—and to her. You should have thought of that."

"Aren't you being rather illogical, darling?"

"Perhaps I am. But some things go deeper than logic. How do you suppose I feel, in this house?"

"It's my house," he said sulkily.

"Don't be childish. The fact that you pay the rent has nothing to do with it."

"All right. I apologise. I've behaved very badly. And where do we go from here? Are you planning to catch the next train back?"

"You know damned well I can't. Oh, Lord!" She sighed and opened her notebook. "It's no pleasure to me to be angry with you, as you're perfectly aware. But I'm not going to throw myself on your neck and thank you for having given me an opportunity to see you. My conscience isn't so easy that it welcomes a good rub on the raw."

"In fact, I'm a blunderer as well as a sinner." His voice was taut with nervous strain and she was reminded again that he had been ill. "I've said I'm sorry. What more do you want me to do?"

"Nothing. Let's forget it. We shall just have to go through with it as gracefully as possible. This is a dangerous conversation, in any case. Read your letters and dictate me some replies."

They worked till four o'clock and for the next hour and a half, refusing to stop for tea, Elizabeth typed back her shorthand. When Alex had signed his letters, she said that she would take them to the post office in the village. No, she could find her way alone—it was a clear evening and she would take a torch; it would be pleasant to get a little country air before the long, blacked-out night.

The centre of the village was built around a green with a stream running through it, crossed in two places by low stone bridges. The post office, a general store as well, was shut, but Elizabeth dropped her letters in the box in the wall and then hesitated, wondering how far she could explore without getting lost. Inside the closed shop, someone turned on the radio for the six o'clock news and she waited to hear the summary— things still seemed to be going well in Libya—there had been no bombs dropped on London the night before. While she stood there listening, a young man appeared out of the thick dusk and flashed a torch on the wall as he dropped in a letter. For an instant she was caught in the beam of light and she was conscious of being stared at. Here's an excitement for Lampton—a new face, she thought idly. Then she became aware that it was very cold, and darker than she had realised. If she went for a walk now, she would probably fall in the stream. She clicked on her own torch and walked as fast as she could up the lane to the house. The young man walked the same way. If she had been of an apprehensive temperament, she might have thought that he was following her.

"The children are having their supper. They'd like you to say good night to them, Miss Simpson," Naomi said as she came in.

Elizabeth went upstairs to the nursery. The Fosters had rented the house unfurnished and there was nothing makeshift in their manner of living. Miss Glover, the nursery-governess, greeted her with an air of smiling conspiracy, as another superior employee of the family's. Elizabeth was not very fluent with children, but they made it quite easy for her, innocently showing off. Sally was half protective, half patronising in her attitude to Donald. Her two years' seniority made him seem a very little boy. His clear skin flushed with excitement and his voice rose to an eager shout as he struggled with a still inadequate vocabulary. He was so like Alex that Elizabeth felt a little sick.

"Just like his father, isn't he?" Miss Glover said, as if she had guessed her thoughts.

"Yes."

"And Sally's the image of Mrs. Foster. Donnie, don't make such a noise. Miss Simpson will look at your train in a minute. It's done them the world of good, living in the country. Everybody says I'm lucky, getting away from London when I did, but it makes you feel kind of out of it. The raids must be awful, though."

"They're slackening off a bit now. We do get quite a lot of nights when nothing alarming happens. But I agree with you about feeling out of it. There'll be two distinct races of people after this war—those who were bombed and those who weren't."

"It won't be as simple as that," Miss Glover said shrewdly. "There's a lot of people in these parts who think they have been bombed—just because one lone 'plane jettisoned a couple of high explosives three miles away. They're never really going to believe that anyone has suffered any worse than them."

"Aren't they?" Elizabeth said grimly. "Then the government had better arrange motor-coach tours of the East End after the war."

The conversation was pursued no further because Donald's bid for attention became overwhelming. Sally insisted on reciting her two-times table and Alex appeared to say good night to the children and to tell Elizabeth that there was a glass of sherry waiting for her downstairs.

She did not stay to watch him with the children. She knew his feelings towards them and there was no need to add to her pain by seeing him demonstrate them. Word for word she remembered what he had said three years ago:

"I can't leave Naomi, because of the children. I begot them and I'm responsible for them. I wouldn't trust her to bring them up without me. Unless she goes off with another man and gives me the custody—and I think that is very unlikely to happen—I can't ever marry you. So think very well what you're doing."

A small, dispassionate part of her brain sometimes suggested to her that he might have reminded himself of all that before making love to her. As it was, he had simply noted down figures on a slate and left her the responsibility of chalking in the total. And then, more telling than any defence he could make himself, she would supply the counter-charge: Yes, it's true that he's a very imperfect human being, full of weaknesses and self-deceptions, but are you so wonderfully fine yourself? You were twenty-five. You went into it with your eyes wide open. It's all of a piece with the rest of your conduct in life. You've always been secretive, self-sufficient, hard. You would like to resemble your father, wouldn't you? You love and admire his idealism, his self-lessness. But in fact you are much more like your mother, for whom you feel sympathy but no respect. Alex and you are both second-grade people, but at least you love each other more than a good many married couples. You bring out the best in each other. So what the hell?

"Alex says there won't be any sherry left in England in a year's time, if the war's still on," Naomi lamented.

Elizabeth saw from the label on the bottle that it was the brand she and Alex usually drank at the Sherry Bar two or three nights a week. Nothing very strange in that, but it gave her a slight distaste for the drink. She refused a second glass on impulse and then regretted it. She would need all the help available to get through this evening.

"It's bitterly cold out, cold enough for snow," she remarked, making conversation.

"That's just what I'm dreading. It was terrible here, the first winter of the war. We were completely snowed up for a week. The children loved it, of course."

"What did the children love?" Alex's voice interrupted them.

But neither of them bothered to answer him, for the gong sounded for dinner and they went in without waiting for Miss Glover, who joined them half-way through the soup, breathless and needlessly apologetic. Her presence made the meal easier than lunch had been.

It was obviously the routine for the nursery-governess to retire to the nursery after dinner, but tonight Naomi invited her into the drawing-room, rather to Elizabeth's amusement. She felt sure that her hostess would really have preferred to pack her off upstairs with Miss Glover. Alex, looking tired and white, refused irritably to go to bed before the nine o'clock news and the evening passed slowly and flatly, Naomi and Miss Glover knitting and listening to the radio, Alex and Elizabeth pretending to read. They were both very much aware that they had quarrelled and would have no possible chance of making it up before morning. And so it proved to be.

CHAPTER VIII

WHEN OWEN flashed his torch towards the wall of the village post office and its beam illumined Elizabeth Simpson's face, he received the most unpleasant shock of his life. The coincidence was so unlooked-for that it seemed to him there must be some dire fatality in it. Already he had fallen into the way of personifying in her the dark preoccupation which had made a misery of the last few months; now, more than ever, he was forced to believe that the illusion of escape he had felt since this visit to Lampton was false. You couldn't escape from your own nature. Intangibly in your dreams, tangibly in the figure of your accuser, it caught up with you, denounced you, condemned you.

He was overwhelmed once more with all the symptoms of acute neurosis which had tormented him so recently—self-disgust, terrified and terrifying ignorance, above all, a loneliness of spirit which made him sometimes want to beat his head against a wall. Everyone but himself, and an unnumbered, faceless, untouchable horde of others like himself, walked in light and fellowship; only he and his kind crawled miserably in darkness and despair. His mind could evoke nothing but images of separation, which cut him off from ordinary, normal people, the fortunate ones, the well-beloved. Most of all, he knew, he was cut off from Derek. Derek would not understand at all. He would be incredulous, embarrassed, concerned and utterly uncomprehending if Owen were ever to try to explain. Cornered, he might admit reluctantly that he loved Owen, that it was probable that Owen loved him—if you must put such things into distasteful, sentimental words. But he would certainly refuse to believe that his cousin could be serious in supposing that his share of the bond between them went beyond what was reasonable, natural and laudable. Where did you pick up a bloody silly idea like that? he would demand. With difficulty, Owen imagined himself replying: From a girl who lives in the house opposite, who spoke about me as "that pansy Cathcart boy". Put like that, it did sound rather silly. In the same circumstances, Derek would only have laughed. But then—how to explain to him that no one ever *could* say that about him, on however slight an acquaintance? That was the kernel of the whole affair. An accusation must possess some element of truth before it has the power to wound. He might perhaps have gone on for years unaware of any difference between himself and other men, inoculated against danger by the fortunate chance that it was Derek whom he loved. But one day, when Derek was married, settled down, with children possibly (for he was very fond of children), one day he would encounter someone else, less safe and sane. And then, if he had any sense, he would put an end to an uneasy life.

In the meanwhile, there didn't seem much point in doing that, when a bomb might oblige any night. Besides, he was going to join the R.A.F. and there was a very fair chance of being shot down in the air—a far more satisfactory death. No one need ever know then. His mother would look upon him as a hero, and even Elizabeth Simpson might be sorry for what she had said.

He had followed Elizabeth back to the house from the post office and made a careful note of its name. At dinner he asked as casually as possible:

"Who lives in that house called Downside?"

"Evacuees," Aunt Susan answered. "Quite nice people called Foster—husband and wife and two children. Mr. Foster works in

London and only appears at week-ends, but I heard in the village to-day that he has been ill ever since Christmas. We ought to go and enquire, Harriet. I've been meaning to drop in, anyhow. I promised Mrs. Foster our recipe for wartime marmalade."

"There's rather a nice-looking nursery-governess," Lorna broke in. "I expect Owen has seen her and wants to get to know her."

"Good Lord, no," Owen exclaimed with too much fervour, imagining himself brought face to face with Elizabeth Simpson. She couldn't be the nursery-governess, could she? No, he was certain that she was a secretary or something and worked in an office in the West End. She must just know these Fosters and be staying with them.

Derek, who had not been listening to the conversation, said: "I believe it's going to snow tonight. That'll be wizard. We can get out the old toboggan, Owen, and make a run down the blackberry field."

It snowed all night and all the following morning. The boys spent till lunch-time tinkering with the sledge in the garage. In the dazzlingly clear light reflected from the snow, Owen's fears and scruples seemed to shrink. It was impossible not to feel invigorated and content in such an atmosphere. He looked lovingly at the pied trees, each twig supporting its soft, irregular trail of whiteness and with a deep, thick wedge tucked in the angle of the boughs. He listened with delight to the squeaking sound the snow made under his feet as he walked along the garden paths, childishly stamping the imprint of his rubber-soled shoes on the untouched patches. Inside the garage, Derek pirouetted to keep himself warm and swore without rancour when a nail tore the woollen mittens which his mother had insisted on his wearing. Owen threw down bacon rind, for the sake of seeing the delicate tracery left by the delicate-stepping birds. He quoted:

> "'The way a crow shook down on me
> The dust of snow from a hemlock tree
> Has given my heart a change of mood
> And saved some part of a day I had rued.'"

"That's nice," Derek commented, surprised at his own liking. "Say it again."

Owen repeated it.

"Who wrote that?"

"Robert Frost—an American."

"Jolly suitable name. I never knew Americans wrote poetry."

"You are a fool," Owen chuckled. "What's your idea of what Americans do write?"

"Oh, magazines like 'Esquire' and wonderful ads., telling you you've probably got a loathsome foot disease and that you ought to drink more tinned soups."

Far, far away seemed the terrors of the night.

Immediately after lunch, before setting out with the sledge, they took spades and cleared a path from the door to the gate.

"What a blessing that you boys are here just now," Mrs. Hammond said.

She watched from the window as they walked up the hill carrying the sledge between them, stumbling into drifts, exchanging salvos of snowballs, talking in clear voices that were borne a long way in the purified atmosphere. They seemed so very young. Her eyes filled with tears.

"Look! Look! Boys sliding down the snow!" Sally shrieked.

The children were out for a walk with Miss Glover and Elizabeth. After all, Alex had decided at breakfast, Miss Simpson had better not go home till next day—they still had a lot of work to get through and it also seemed rather inhuman to turn someone out into snow. So Elizabeth had 'phoned the office and 'phoned home. She had made no public demur, but she had intended when alone with Alex to make a private protest. It was Naomi, unconsciously, who stopped her.

Waiting in the dining-room for Alex to join her and begin work, she saw him come downstairs and go into the drawing-room where Naomi was sitting. Both doors were slightly ajar and she heard the murmur of their voices. She sat very still, not listening deliberately, drawing a pattern on the cover of her notebook. Then Naomi's voice rose sharply, in a tone of irritation.

"My fault? You know perfectly well that it's yours. I warned you, didn't I?"

Alex replied inaudibly, but Naomi's voice came through clearly once again.

"It's always self with you. I'm sick of it. Your first reaction always is to wonder how anything is going to affect *you!*"

Someone, presumably Alex, shut the drawing-room door with a sharp click. Elizabeth stared at the pattern she had drawn. A certain fastidiousness prevented her from puzzling over the meaning of the fragment of conversation she had heard, but she could not fail to understand the tone of voice in which it had been spoken. Querulous, bad-tempered, discontented. . . . It was no wonder this marriage had foundered. Perhaps Naomi had a genuine grievance. Perhaps she had a genuine grievance herself. But it would be impossible now to add to that recital of complaints. To be nagged by wife and mistress on the same morning was more than one would wish to inflict on any man one loved. When Alex came in, looking haggard and depressed, she found that there was nothing to do but smile at him. His face lit up with relief. Bending over the back of her chair, he kissed her.

"Alex, you idiot! What a risk to take!" She glanced towards the window, at the snow lying thick and undisturbed on the garden lawn.

"It was the relief. I thought you were going to scold me."

He did not add "as well".

"I ought to."

"But you won't. You're much too nice." He stared at her with an odd, brooding expression, as though he were seeing some quality in her for the first time. "You're much too nice for me."

It was Naomi who had suggested in the afternoon that Miss Simpson might like to go for a walk with the children and Miss Glover. She would lend her some Wellington boots. After all, she could just as well type after tea, since Alex had said it was useless to post in the village now—the letters would get there far quicker if posted in London next day. Elizabeth had agreed to the suggestion with distinct relief. Each hour she spent in company with Alex in this house was an added strain. Besides, it would be pleasant to walk in country lanes under snow.

"Miss Glover, can't we have a slide too?" Sally demanded, jumping up and down. "Ask them, Miss Glover, *please*, Miss Glover! Ask the boys if they'll give us a slide!"

"Donald wants to slide—Donald wants to slide in the snow," her brother backed her up.

"They're big boys—grown-ups," Miss Glover chided. "They won't want to be bothered with you."

"We're not a bother, are we, Miss Simpson?" Sally demanded, changing her tactics. "*You* ask them, Miss Simpson."

Elizabeth was staring across the hedge at the tobogganists, her eyes screwed up against the glare of the snow. The dark one of the two, who had just reached the end of his run and was preparing to pull the sledge back up the slope, had a vaguely familiar look, he reminded her of someone. Absently, she shook her head at Sally's request. Miss Glover, annoyed at having her authority by-passed, repeated her refusal even more firmly; but harmony was restored by Elizabeth's suggestion, that they should make a giant snowball. They rolled it all the way home, and by the time it was piloted into the safety of the drive, it had achieved very satisfactory proportions.

"I thought for a moment those people were going to butt in," Owen gasped out when he got to the top of the slope.

"I know. I'd rather have liked to give the kids a run, but we don't want a couple of females tagging around. I wonder who they are? No one I know in the village. I say, if there isn't a thaw, we ought to get Ann Parsons up here tomorrow."

Owen mumbled agreement. He was suddenly aware of being cold and damp and muscularly weary. He didn't want Ann Parsons, and he had also guessed the probable identity of the strangers who had watched them from the lane.

"Would you mind if we packed up after you've had another run?" he asked abruptly.

"Had enough? All right. We'll go home and shoot a line about our terrific technique. We won't mention the crash-landings."

Owen hoped that this was the last he would see or hear of Elizabeth Simpson over the period of Derek's leave (a funny time for her to take a holiday, wasn't it?), but there was to be a third and final incident. Early the following morning, which was cold but sunny, a man appeared at the door, asking for Mrs. Hammond. The family was gathered together in the drawing-room, occupying themselves in their several ways.

"Mr. Foster," the parlour-maid announced.

He hesitated, smiling, in the doorway—a youngish man with fair hair growing thin and pleasant grey eyes.

"I hope I haven't chosen a moment when you're all very busy," he said.

"Why, Mr. Foster!" Aunt Susan shook hands with him warmly. "You know my daughters—this is my son, home on ten days' leave, and my nephew, who is staying with us. I've been meaning to come and see your wife. You haven't been well, I hear?"

"Just a chill and a touch of bronchitis. This is the first time I've been out since Christmas, actually. It's so sunny, I thought it would be a good day to begin, in spite of the snow."

"You must sit down and rest a little."

He accepted the chair that Derek pushed towards him and went on: "I've come to borrow, I'm afraid. My wife said that last year, when it snowed, you very kindly lent her some chains for the car."

"But of course! Our car, unfortunately, is laid up for the duration, but the chains are quite handy, only in the garage."

"I've had my secretary down for a couple of days," Alex explained. "It's so difficult to transact business over the 'phone. But she's going back to town today and my wife wants to drive her to the station."

"The boys will bring the chains down for you, they're much too heavy for you to carry, only just out of bed. Derek—Owen—go and look them out for Mr. Foster."

Going back to town today, Owen's heart sang. Two days left with no fear of running into her. But he had no intention of helping to carry the chains to Downside.

In the garage, he said as casually as he could:

"Derek, I don't want to join this party. I don't feel sociable. Get me out of it."

"O.K. I'll say you took a pill last night and daren't leave the house. No, seriously, I'll invent something for you."

Most admirable, beloved and trustworthy Derek—the one person in the world who would never let you down. Owen resolved, humble in his gratitude to fate in general and his cousin in particular, that he would clamp down the lid on all black thoughts for the rest of Derek's leave. He would not even be jealous of Ann Parsons. He would be the Owen Cathcart that Derek thought he was.

CHAPTER IX

LONELY WITHOUT OWEN, Daisy tried to talk to her husband in the evenings. She read the paper and made rather obvious comments on the news items.

"Really, these Black Markets are a disgrace! And they don't seem to give the men nearly heavy enough sentences. It says here, they can easily afford the fines and it's never the ones at the top that get sent to prison."

"If people are willing to take the stuff, you can't blame the men with brains and guts enough to provide it for them," Lionel said in the rather aggressive tone he used at home. "They're all equally to blame, if you're going to be Sunday School about it—"

"Oh, Lionel, I don't think that's quite the case! Surely it's more wicked to tempt people than to yield to temptation?"

"There's only one wicked thing about this war, and that's the fact that it was ever started. We're too damned interfering—that's our trouble as a nation. You can take it from me, our generation is never going to know what it is to see prosperity again. No, nor Owen's generation either. Whichever way it ends."

"Lionel, you don't mean you think that Germany might *win*? Why—why—I'd kill myself if I thought that that would happen."

"Then you'd be a fool," Lionel said grimly. "Ordinary people get along all right whatever happens, if they keep quiet and don't stick their necks out. But you needn't run round Saffron Park saying I said so. Before I knew where I was, I'd be reported to the police for signalling with my torch in the blackout, or some such nonsense."

Indeed, nothing short of torture would have persuaded Daisy to repeat her husband's words. They confirmed all the niggling little fears she had persistently suppressed for months past. Lionel was dreadfully defeatist and critical of everything, even of Mr. Churchill. He didn't talk like that outside the house (at least, not in her hearing), but he always seemed to take any opportunity that occurred for saying nasty, hinting things about the government and the public's reaction to air-raids and how much worse our shipping losses were than we were told. He always said it in such a genial, confidential way that people didn't appear to get annoyed, though she had seen Mr. Simpson look at him once or twice with a queer expression when he had come over the other evening to discuss this new fire-guard business. Of course, she told herself, it wasn't that Lionel was *unpatriotic*. His firm was really working for the government now and he was always quite generous about subscribing to war charities. But he did take a very cynical view of everything, and you couldn't help realising, when you'd lived with him for over twenty years, that his own affairs came first. Anything that was bad for business always annoyed him very much. He was never so angry about what Hitler had done to the Poles or the Jews, or about the suffering of the poor brave people in the East End.

"Owen will be home tomorrow," she said, changing the subject.

"About time he got back to work," Lionel grunted. "I dare say the break has done him no harm, but it mustn't be repeated."

"He says that they've had quite heavy falls of snow in the West," Daisy persevered.

"I know they have. A damned nuisance it's been, too. I lost a van-load of stuff for twenty-four hours."

"What sort of stuff?" she enquired, not because she cared but because she wanted to encourage her husband to talk to her.

"Just furniture," he said shortly.

His business was furniture-making. Wartime shortage of timber would have brought it almost to a standstill, but he was saved by his government contracts for army equipment and shelter-bunks. A number of his vans and lorries had been commandeered, but he still ran a small fleet and had always more petrol for his own car than could be accounted for by the most generous allowances. Daisy knew this, and it was one of the things that made her uneasy. Of course, she realised that ever so many people wangled extra petrol and thought nothing of it—even boasted about it—but it made her feel very uncomfortable when there were bits in the papers about oil-tankers being torpedoed and merchant seamen blown up. She never read aloud those particular items to Lionel. She was a coward and she knew it. She even prayed about it.

Dropping the evening paper on the floor, an untidy habit which always made Lionel frown, she returned to knitting socks for Owen. Then, with needles poised, she stopped.

"That's a German 'plane."

"Nobody else seems to think so. There's no siren and no gunfire."

"All the same, it is. I don't care what they say on the wireless, I always know the difference. There! The guns have started."

"Still no Alert. I suppose they haven't been officially informed yet—aren't allowed to accept the evidence of their own ears." He had hardly finished speaking when a distant siren broke into its contagious wail, to be echoed by another and another until the nearest shrieked in imminent anguish. As it de-crescendoed, others could be heard beyond, sinking into a final moan of protest.

"It's like the Zoo," Daisy said. "First one animal starts and then all the others join in. . . . That was a bomb, quite near." She spoke with great calmness, unassumed. Owen was in the country. Whoever had been killed or maimed by that bomb, it was not Owen. Whoever would be killed or maimed by the next bomb, it would not be Owen. She did not actually formulate this thought, which would have shocked her by its selfishness, but it was the reason that her heart did not miss a single beat.

"I'm not fire-watching tonight," Lionel said, dissociating himself from the raid. "By the way, I put Owen down to do from black-out till 1 a.m. on Sundays."

"Oh." It couldn't be helped, of course, but she didn't like the idea. How silly you are, she told herself; he'll be in the Air Force soon and then what are you going to do? "You'll be on with him, I suppose?"

"No, I thought it was better not to have two from the same house on duty together. I'm doing from 1 a.m. onwards on Fridays."

Why was it better not to have two from the same house? Sometimes she almost thought that Lionel didn't *like* Owen. But that kind of thought led to a number of other unpleasing speculations. She hurriedly shut the door on them.

"If you don't mind being left," Lionel said perfunctorily, "I'll go round to the 'Crown and Anchor'. I half promised to meet a man there tonight and discuss some business."

"I don't mind. But do be careful. Take your tin hat."

As he stood up to go, the door-bell rang. It was Henry Simpson.

"I'm on my way to the Post," he explained. "I thought I'd drop in as I passed and give you a copy of the fire-watch rota as it was finally worked out."

"I'll walk with you as far as the 'Crown and Anchor'," Lionel said in the jovial voice he kept for visitors.

Henry smiled at Daisy. "So you're going to be alone too, Mrs. Cathcart. My wife is not at all pleased with me for leaving her this evening. Elizabeth has had to stay late at the office. The man she works for is away ill and she has a lot to do."

"Well, now, I wonder if Mrs. Simpson would like me to go and spend a little while with her?" Daisy suggested. "It's not very nice to be alone when there's a raid on. Not that I mind myself," she said quickly, out of loyalty to Lionel, who was only going to the 'Crown and Anchor'.

Mr. Simpson looked pleased, almost relieved, she thought.

"Are you sure you don't mind? I won't press you. I'm superstitious about inviting people to leave their own houses these days."

"Of course I don't mind. And I'm not at all superstitious. Just let me put a coat on . . ."

Since Mrs. Cathcart's arrival on her doorstep coincided with a particularly thunderous crash of gunfire, Alice Simpson was very genuinely pleased to see her. She had been rather desperately trying to talk to Peter. But Peter could wait. Tonight in bed she would summon him again. He would sit on the edge and hold her hand. "Good old Mother," he would say, "never turn a hair, do you? Those German women ought to see you—they all cower in cellars and shriek when we go over and bomb them to blazes." For Peter was now in the Bomber Command. She had installed him there since the night that Bob Craven had spent with them. Presently, when Owen Cathcart joined the R.A.F., he would get to know him and report that he was completely dumb and decidedly windy. Nothing of all this, however, was discernible in her greeting to Daisy.

"It *is* kind of you to come and keep me company," she said quite warmly. "I don't know when Elizabeth will be back. She's been terribly busy ever since Christmas. The man she works for was taken ill when he went home to spend it with his family, and Elizabeth had to go down to Lampton herself for two nights this week."

"Not Lampton near Oxford? What an extraordinary coincidence! That's where my sister-in-law lives—where Owen is staying now. How funny if they had run into each other!"

The amusement of this discovery lasted for some time. It gave Daisy an opportunity to talk about the Hammonds, whom she loved, and Alice Simpson also took the chance to boast of Elizabeth's efficiency and value at the office.

"Mr. Foster is an exporter," she said rather vaguely. "The business is all with America, so he and his partner are reserved. It's something to do with dollars—Elizabeth explained it to me but I've forgotten the details. They're always getting cables telling them to buy things, and then they have to arrange about the shipping. It's much more difficult in wartime, of course. And so many forms to fill up! My daughter says they just dread the sight of new forms. I tell her I think she must be very clever to know what to do with them. But then, I never had a business training. Girls in our day never did, did they? But all they seem to think about now is a career."

"I sometimes wish that Owen were my daughter and not my son," Daisy said surprisingly, busy with her knitting. "Especially since the war. One can keep a daughter at home longer. And when they marry, one stays in touch more."

Alice thought this a very odd idea. She thought that Mrs. Cathcart must be a very stupid woman. She and Peter would laugh at her tonight. It was extraordinary how real a person Peter seemed. She even knew exactly how he looked. He was not at all like Henry.

"What news of that pleasant Mr. Craven who came and thanked me so nicely for the tins I lent you?" Daisy asked, prompted by a rather obvious train of thought.

"He writes very regularly but Elizabeth never tells me much of what he says." This was a grievance and her voice showed it. "He wants to go overseas but he's afraid they'll keep most of our troops here in case of an invasion in the spring. What does your husband think the chances are of an invasion?"

Daisy did not want to be made to dwell on her husband's views on the war.

"Oh, I don't think he's worrying about it much," she said vaguely.

"Henry worries terribly. It's his temperament to worry. He doesn't say much, but I always know when there's something on his mind. He gets so silent. He's working too hard, too—all this warden duty on top of being short-staffed at the office. Both his clerks are called up now. The girls are very good, he says, but they have to be taught everything from the beginning."

"I used to think I'd like Owen to be a solicitor," Daisy said. "Perhaps after the war . . ."

Her words were drowned in the roar of a gun apparently stationed on the doorstep. Alice jumped and covered her ears with her hands.

"That must be one of those mobile guns," Daisy continued placidly. "They say that they're driven about on lorries. I'd like to see one, but Owen won't ever let me go out to look—he's frightened I shall be hit by shrapnel."

It occurred to her that this was an excellent opportunity to play truant; the lorry must be quite near; but the expression on Mrs. Simpson's face kept her silent. Poor woman—she had turned quite pale. It must be terrible for her to have her daughter out in a raid and not know where she was. She began to talk, raising her voice above the recurrent clamour, about summer holidays abroad before the war. She was still talking about them, with some success, when Elizabeth returned.

The click of her latchkey in the front door was the last move in a game Elizabeth often played on raid nights. It started at the office. If she stopped to wash her hands before she left, it might make all the difference to whether she were killed or not. If she walked to the Underground by way of Cambridge Circus and Charing Cross Road or by way of Greek Street and Shaftesbury Avenue, it might make all the difference. If she waited for the escalator to carry her or walked down it to the bottom, thus possibly catching an earlier train, it might make all the difference. This game pleased her very much. It added a perceptible spice to the general mixed flavour of life. It also nourished her inherent fatalism.

She was surprised to find Mrs. Cathcart with her mother and to be greeted by her with the relief which Daisy felt vicariously for Mrs. Simpson. While Alice fetched the soup she had been keeping hot for her, to eat on a tray in front of the fire, Daisy told her about the strange coincidence.

"Wouldn't it have been funny if you'd run into each other?" Dimly Elizabeth recalled a likeness which had momentarily puzzled her . . . of course, the dark young man tobogganing in the snow. She spoke of the incident.

"That must have been Owen!" Daisy cried, as pleased as if she had suddenly caught sight of him herself. "With Derek, his cousin. Such a handsome boy! Did you notice him?"

But Elizabeth had not noticed Derek. She was rather surprised that she had recognised Owen. She had only seen him occasionally, had spoken to him perhaps once. She remembered him vaguely as a moody-looking boy, self-conscious and a bit "wet".

"Well, you'll have something to talk about when you fire-watch together," Alice said, setting down the tray. "I see from the rota that you're both on the first half of Sunday nights."

Heavens, what a bore! Elizabeth thought. However, it might have been still worse, she supposed.

"Are we supposed to patrol all the time?" she asked.

"You needn't leave the house, unless there's a raid on, your father says. But you must be up and dressed. If there is a raid, you have to patrol in couples at short intervals. There's some talk of fitting up the empty garage at No. 17 as a headquarters. You could keep the ladder there and have chairs and an oil-stove."

And darts and a lending library, Elizabeth thought crossly. She tried to imagine herself playing darts in a garage with the shadowy Cathcart boy, and failed. This war became daily more fantastic.

"Well, it seems quite quiet now, so I'll go home," Daisy said.

Alice accompanied her to the door and was very amiable. Her gratitude was sincere. She might be glad of Mrs. Cathcart's company another night.

Alone together, Elizabeth and her mother found nothing to say to each other. They had gone over Elizabeth's account of her stay at Lampton the evening before. She tried to think of any incident in the day which might sound interesting or amusing, but none occurred to her. Because of the necessity for secrecy about herself and Alex, she had never encouraged her parents to come to the office ("Mr. Foster wouldn't mind, but Mr. Rowland is very strict about things like that") and never brought any of the staff home, though Joan Walsh had angled for an invitation once or twice. There were too many alibis which might be shattered by a casual word from the inhabitants of either of her worlds. So now there was nothing to discuss but the January sales. Should she buy a couple of dress lengths? Her mother said yes. The quality of material was bound to deteriorate. In the last war . . .

Lionel came back from the 'Crown and Anchor' in a very good humour which lasted for the rest of the evening. Yes, he had met his friend. They had settled their business. He got out a note-book and made calculations, looking well pleased, even whistling in a sibilant, tuneless way. Daisy felt much encouraged.

"Is he a government official, your friend?" she asked.

"No. Why do you say that?"

"Oh, only because you told me that most of your business nowadays was to do with government contracts."

"So it is. But not all of it. You don't talk about my business, do you?" he asked abruptly.

"Of course not, Lionel. Except just that it's furniture-making and that since the war you do it for the government." And that's all I know, anyhow, she reflected.

Apparently satisfied, he went back to his figures. She was surprised to hear him say, a moment later:

"Pity the war came when it did. I should like to have sent Owen to Oxford."

"But could you have afforded it, Lionel?"

He didn't reply directly.

"I'd like him to have had all the chances I missed," he said instead.

A wave of mingled relief and shame drowned Daisy in confusion. Surely no man could say that about a boy he didn't believe to be his own son? She thought, Oh, poor Lionel, and felt tears prick her eyes. But whether because she had deceived him or because he had had to make his way in the world without benefit of higher education, she did not know.

CHAPTER X

At breakfast Sunday morning, Henry Simpson said to his daughter:

"Would you like to come to Kew with me this afternoon?"

"Love to. But aren't you very tired?"

"I can get some sleep before lunch. It would do me good to have a little air and exercise. You too. There won't be anything in bloom in the Gardens, but we can walk about to keep ourselves warm. It's a little milder today."

"What about Mother?"

"I've asked her. She doesn't want to come."

Elizabeth was pleased to be spending an afternoon alone with her father. It was a long time since she had done so. Before the war, when she had lived in rooms in Chelsea, she had often come out to Saffron Park at week-ends and gone walking with him. Once or twice, on such occasions, she had almost given in to the impulse to confide in him about Alex. But that was not the kind of thing you told parents. It was one of the paradoxes of life that you rarely chose to confide in the people to whom your well-being was all-important. She knew what advice her father would give her and she knew that she would not take his advice. So why add to his worries unnecessarily? But sometimes she was almost sure that he guessed a great deal more about her than he could possibly know, and that she was a cause of concern to him already.

Immediately after lunch they set off by 'bus.

"We'll go in by the main gate and walk through to the river," Henry said. "Then we might follow the towpath into Richmond and have tea there. You've brought some bread for the birds? Good. Though I suppose that's an offence under Food Ministry regulations now."

"Probably, but I don't care. I've put it in my gas-mask case. I have an idea there's something faintly symbolical in that—an anti-Hitler gesture of some kind."

Inside the big iron gates of the Gardens, a notice warned visitors that they walked there at their own risk, no shelters were provided and in the event of an air-raid they were advised to keep away from the glass-houses.

"If the court of George III haunts the Gardens, how puzzled the ghosts must be to read that," Henry said.

"Is there any reason why they should?"

"George and Charlotte used to stay at Kew Palace. He had one of his attacks of madness here. Fannie Burney, who was lady-in-waiting to the Queen, encountered him once in the grounds. He escaped from his keepers and ran after her. She was not unnaturally terrified. But when he caught up with her, he talked very rationally and kindly."

"Darling, what a lot you know. Let's see what's out . . . winter aconite on the mound and something called Chinese witch-hazel near King William's Temple. Not exactly a riot of bloom. Do you know, before the war one of the firm's American customers, a man we export a lot of stuff to, came over on a business-cum-pleasure trip and went to Kew. He was terribly disappointed—compared it most unfavourably with Yellowstone Park. I felt rather indignant. I wouldn't like it at all if we kept bears in the Bluebell Wood. That was the man who offered me a job in New York. Imagine if I'd accepted!"

"You'd have missed the raids."

"I know. Horrible. I should have felt an outcast from my generation for the rest of my life—"

They circled the Blue Garden, which at the moment contained nothing blue at all, and walked past the water-lily pond to the Rockery. The little stream that ran through it was covered with ice. Elizabeth threw out some of her bread here for the birds. The robins were so tame that they fed out of her hands. What extra convolution in their minute brains gave them their superior confidence? Henry said he didn't know. Undoubtedly birds had distinctive temperaments. Take coots, for instance. (For they had arrived at the pond behind the Palm House.)

"Coots are very ill-mannered and egotistic birds. Look at the way the ducks and moor-hens give them a wide berth."

"All the same, they're very attractive to look at. Black and white is very *chic*!"

They watched a pair of them picking their way from one floating patch of paper-thin ice to the next. The ice gave out a tinkling, bell-like sound and the coots snapped their beaks with a harsh, derisive click, impossible to imitate.

"I'll throw them a piece of bread, even if they are bad-tempered," Elizabeth said. "Maybe they've had their dispositions soured by the rude way people always talk about their bald patches."

She felt care-free and childish with her father, as sometimes, on very good days, she still felt with Alex. Alex would be back at the office tomorrow. . . . Oh my darling, I was horrible to you. You wanted to see me and I should have been touched and happy, but I could find nothing better to do than gibe at you and moan about my silly pride. Tomorrow night I'll make it all up.

Suddenly the ritual of feeding the ducks seemed futile and boring, and she gave the rest of her bread to a pleased and surprised little girl. One noticed children a great deal these days; they had become almost a rarity. It was delightful to see a child, but worrying too. One looked rather truculently at their parents and their parents had a guilty air. All the same, the raids didn't seem to be doing the average child much harm mentally. Elizabeth remembered a story she had heard about a little boy of four, placidly lying in his bed in a reinforced, ground-floor room, calling out to his mother in a dreamy voice: "Mummy, there are fire-bombs on the roof. But don't worry, I'm putting them out." She told the story to her father and was pleased to hear him laugh. There was not much about the war that amused him.

Walking down the wide expanse of Sion Vista towards the river, he disconcerted her by demanding abruptly:

"Do you regret having left Chelsea?"

"Good Lord, no. I'd much rather be at home with you and Mother in the raids." And that would be true, she justified herself, if it weren't for Alex.

"I hope you're not lying to me, out of courtesy," he went on still more dismayingly. "I feel that we put a certain amount of constraint on your movements, simply by worrying about you." (He used the plural, but both of them knew that it was only he who really worried.) "You mustn't give in to that. It's very often only cowardly to be unselfish."

"I'm not that kind of coward," she said in a low voice. "I'm frightened of quite different things."

"What sort of things?" he asked gently.

"Just ordinary things . . . loneliness, for one. Finding myself middle-aged and tired out, holding the handle of a shopping-basket with a hole in the bottom, looking down at a horrible mess of smashed eggs on the pavement." She laughed rather defensively. "It's easier to express in proverbs—"

"You don't think it would be a good idea to give away some of the eggs in advance, so as to be sure of always having a number of invitations to share a nice omelette?" he asked lightly.

"Oh, a very good idea!" She laughed again, more naturally. "But who wants my eggs?"

"My dear, there is always a demand for eggs—far more than the available supply. And yours are very good eggs."

"I doubt very much if they are." She abandoned the metaphor, since it had served its purpose. "You're such a different sort of person from me—kinder and gentler. I'm hard and egotistical—I very rarely think for long of anything except myself and my own affairs."

"Who does?"

"Well, you do. Or I think you do. Don't disillusion me."

"My dear, absurd daughter! You seem determined to be miserable either way. What is it really?"

She shook her head, alarmed to find herself on the verge of tears which would spill over at a word. Henry glanced sharply at her and then away. They walked on for a little while in silence. Then he said, as if at random:

"Do you like your work?"

"Of course." There was surprise in her tone, but a guarded surprise.

"I've wondered lately. When you first went to the firm you were always talking about it. Nowadays, you never seem to mention it. I've wondered."

"One outgrows one's first enthusiasm, naturally. One gets used to things and then they don't seem quite so interesting. That's all."

Suddenly he stopped walking.

"Let's rest on that seat for a few minutes. I'm getting tired."

There was nothing for Elizabeth to do but sit down beside him. She would have liked to change the subject, but she could not think of anything which would not sound suspiciously irrelevant. They stared ahead of them at the Long Water but neither of them was seeing it. Henry played with the handle of his stick, revolving it absently between his thin, large-knuckled fingers which bore two rings, a broad, old-fashioned wedding ring and a signet ring with an incised crest. His hands looked older than the rest of him, Elizabeth noticed with a pang of tenderness.

"Then, if it isn't your work . . ." he began tentatively. He broke off and tried again. "No one can be very happy nowadays. But you've been unhappy for a longer period than the war. I know it's easier to talk to your contemporaries, but you can't be as important to them as you are to me. What is it, Elizabeth?"

He turned his head and looked at her directly and gravely. But she could not bring herself to look at him.

"If I told you," she said unsteadily, "what would be the use? You couldn't do anything. You've got worries enough of your own. It's nothing very bad or serious. Only just an ordinary kind of mess."

"I dare say. But it matters very much to you and so it matters to me too. A love affair, of course."

"Of course. Rather a sordid one, actually. With Alex Foster."

"He's married, isn't he?"

"Yes. Two children. And he means to stay married. So you see there's no end to it. But I've no excuse for moaning. I went into it with my eyes open."

"My darling child, what do you suppose you mean by saying that you went into it with your eyes open?" he asked gently.

"We none of us have our eyes open. We grope our way the whole time."

"But I knew what I was doing," she said stubbornly. "I weighed things up and I thought it would be worth it. I still do, really. I mean, I think it's better than the alternative of having nothing. But it isn't very . . . satisfactory."

"Is Foster satisfied?"

"He seems to be. Oh, not for me, of course. He says he feels a cad—I ought to marry someone else and be happy. I don't believe he'd try to stop me if there were anyone else. But there isn't."

"What about Bob Craven? Your mother thinks you're going to marry him."

"I've never told him so," she said defensively. "It's not my fault if he won't take no for an answer." But she was conscious of her father's eyes regarding her appraisingly and she felt ashamed. "He's useful," she said defiantly. "He's an alibi. I suppose that shocks you."

"If you mean that I don't like it—no, I don't. You were never meant to be a bitter, calculating person, Elizabeth."

"Poor darling." She took his hand and raised it to her cheek in a brief caress. "It's disappointing to see your swan hatch out into an ugly duckling, isn't it? But lots of people are as good as gold until things start to go a little wrong with them. I'm the kind that doesn't improve with adversity, that's all."

"I've never quite believed that anybody did. Not with emotional adversity, at any rate. But I don't think you'll spoil so easily. You'll have to find your own solution, and you will."

"Then you aren't going to tell me that I ought to break with Alex?"

"Would it be any use?" he asked in his turn. "You know I think that. But I can't force the issue. The most important thing for me is to make sure you understand that I am always here and that I love you more than anyone or anything else in the world. It's a passive role. I've never been much good at active ones."

His smile was wry.

"I think you're perfect as you are." She squeezed his hand, on the verge of tears again. "Don't alter. You're much the nicest kind of father. I wish that I were more deserving of you. I'd so much rather be an average, satisfactory daughter, and present you with an average, satisfactory son-in-law and grandchildren to match. Perhaps I will, one day."

"I'm sure you will."

"Are you really sure?" she asked wistfully.

"Quite sure," he lied.

She laughed nervously.

"Isn't it silly—I feel quite a pang of disloyalty when I say that. I'm hopelessly illogical. I want to be out of the mess I'm in and yet I want to keep Alex too. I do love him, you know. He's very sweet. I couldn't bear it if you thought of him as just an ordinary seducer. He really is unhappy with his wife. It isn't the routine story of the misunderstood husband casting round for any available female sympathy. We quarrel sometimes, but I know he loves me too. It isn't just a passing thing. It's lasted three years already."

"Three years! That's a long time to keep a secret."

"Yes. It gets you down. It makes you very shut in on yourself. I've never found it easy to confide and now it's practically impossible. I think when people fall in love they're meant to shout about it to the whole world, and when you can't it shrivels something up inside you. Perhaps you're right about adversity not doing anybody any good. It's had a definitely bad effect on me."

Henry noticed with relief that she was talking much more fluently now. He felt cold, but he was afraid that he would make her self-conscious again if he stood up and began walking.

"Doesn't it often occur to you," he said, "that everybody has at least one secret they're ashamed or reluctant to discuss? I've never known anyone intimately without discovering that, sooner or later. I think you make a mistake in feeling yourself cut off and alien. One has a curious idea of the norm, as a being full of conventional virtue, free from temptation, rather stupid but nevertheless someone whose judgment of one's own sins and weaknesses one fears or resents. Yet there is probably more sympathy and understanding abroad than one will ever risk discovering."

"I don't want to be pitied," Elizabeth muttered.

"Why not? We are all to be pitied, in one degree or another. The dangerous thing is to pity oneself."

"Yes, I suppose so. I try not to, but I don't succeed very well." She smiled rather waveringly. "It's nice to talk to you. I feel better now—"

"Do you think that you'll be able to talk to me at other times, when things aren't going well with you?"

"I can't promise. A part of me will want to, but it's hard to break a habit of secrecy, even when you've found out that it's a bad habit."

"I don't want you to promise. I only want you to remember that, this time, you did feel better afterwards." Dramatically, he sneezed. "There! I've been struggling to suppress that for several minutes."

"You're cold! I am a selfish pig. Let's walk along the tow-path into Richmond and find a tea-shop where you can get warm again."

But the river gate was closed and they had to turn back. Outside the Gardens, while they were still searching for somewhere to have tea, a side street brought them unexpectedly into the area of an "incident"—a double row of small houses, some of them no more than piles of bricks and others without tiles or windows. In the Sabbath quiet, nothing stirred. The little street was lifeless and deserted, as if the Plague had struck down its inhabitants, killing some and putting the rest to light.

"It's lonely," Elizabeth said, unconsciously lowering her voice. "Horribly lonely. I wonder where everyone has gone? They can't all be dead." This devastation of a whole area seemed to her more frightening and pathetic than the ragged gaps which disfigured the West End. "I suppose this is what the East End must be like. It's one of the odd things about this war that most people only know the damage in their own immediate neighbourhood. They don't bother to go and look at a smash-up even a couple of streets away. Because they're afraid of being made to feel afraid, perhaps."

"Yet after a little while you cease to notice the ruins you see every day. They might be the result of ordinary demolition. That's something I don't think the German High Command has reckoned with."

"I know. You can't even remember what the shops sold when they've gone."

Mixed with the rubble of one little house, a number of household objects had remained intact: a saucepan, a knife-box, a coloured supplement in a frame with its glass miraculously unbroken, and a bound volume of "The Family Herald". Here, too, were the remains of cheap, worn furniture; an armchair covered in green plush, its original colour almost completely obscured by dust; fragments of coarse white china and a single felt slipper. The whole built up a picture of elderly, old-fashioned people, living decently on very small means. Once again that afternoon Elizabeth felt her eyes fill with tears, but this time she was not ashamed of them.

"It gives you a queer feeling," she said almost in a whisper. "I mean—when they bought that knife-box they couldn't possibly have thought that it would be one of the few things left intact, when everything else they possessed had gone. Even their lives, perhaps. Do you think people will come and take these things and use them in an ordinary way? Forget, even, where they came from? I wouldn't use them. I'd be afraid they'd bring their own ghosts with them."

"I don't think the average looter is troubled with so much imagination," Henry said rather grimly.

Elizabeth shivered. "Let's get away from here. It's a sad place."

"But salutary, don't you think?" her father suggested mildly. "It sets things in their right proportions."

"Yes," she agreed soberly. "Yes, it does." Then she laughed. "For the moment, anyhow," she mocked herself.

Henry laughed too, and slipped his arm through hers. They felt very close to one another. The feeling persisted for the rest of the afternoon, although they did not speak again of personal things. Tea, when they eventually found a shop to serve them with it, was quite a gay affair. But on the 'bus going home, Elizabeth yawned.

"Bother! It's my first fire-watch tonight. I'm on duty with the Cathcart boy."

CHAPTER XI

THAT FIRST SUNDAY evening the Alert sounded early, but nothing happened. It was obvious that London was not the main or even a subsidiary target. At seven o'clock the telephone rang in the Cathcarts' house and Owen answered it. He felt his mouth go dry as the voice over the 'phone said:

"Is that Owen Cathcart? This is Elizabeth Simpson. Unless anything more exciting occurs than at present, shall we just take turns to patrol once an hour? I'll do nine and eleven and one, if you'll do eight and ten and midnight."

"That's all right as far as I'm concerned," he announced in a tone that he knew sounded ungracious.

"Very well. I'll come over and rattle your letter-box if things brisk up later in the evening."

But the evening continued quiet and the All Clear sounded before eleven. It was the first of a succession of nights only occasionally punctuated by brief alerts and sporadic gunfire. No bombs fell within hearing of Wordsworth Road and it was not until towards the end of February that Owen and Elizabeth found themselves at last committed to an evening spent together in the garage of No. 17, by now the accepted rendezvous of fire-watchers in the road.

Besides the equipment of ladders, stirrup-pumps and buckets, various people had provided two deck-chairs and a card-table, an oil-stove and a reading-lamp connected with the ceiling fitment. Owen was already there, lighting the oil-stove, when Elizabeth arrived. He had brought two rugs with him, one of which he offered to Elizabeth in an off-hand way.

"My mother thought you might be cold."

"How nice of her! I think your mother must be the kindest person in the road."

He did not reply, except with a stiff smile, and Elizabeth, who had spoken quite sincerely, was made to feel that she had sounded gushing. He was really rather a tiresome boy, she thought, even if it were only shyness that made him *gauche*. She decided not to bother to try to talk to him, was glad that she had brought a book and relieved to see that he had done the same.

Owen, who had been thinking very similarly, opened his own book hurriedly. But he found it difficult to concentrate on what he was reading. This was the first time he had ever been alone with his enemy. Now, if he put out his hand, he could touch her. But she looked different tonight, because she had on no make-up and was wearing slacks and an old Burberry and a scarf twisted round her head. He was accustomed to seeing her rather well dressed and well made-up, on her way to or from her work. Like this she seemed a less hostile figure, because more vulnerable herself.

It was bad luck that out of all the people living in the road, they two should have been chosen to go on duty as a pair. He wondered how she felt about it. He imagined, inevitably, her comment on the news. "What? That pansy Cathcart boy!" A wave of heat burned upwards through his skin and he ducked his head behind the pages of his book. Blushing! He must be crazy. It was just what she would expect of him.

When his skin felt cool again he dared to glance up quickly to satisfy himself that she was paying no attention to him. He saw that her book lay unregarded on her knee, that she was staring straight ahead of her with the blank, indrawn gaze of those whose thoughts have carried them a long distance. Absurdly, his relief was succeeded by a feeling almost of chagrin. She had forgotten him. He was such a nonentity to her that in his presence she could afford to contract those invisible, delicate tendrils which grow on the surface of social consciousness, alert to grasp or to repel. There was something very wounding in that unawareness.

Determinedly, he went back to his book. Why should he care what she thought about him, whether she thought about him at all? She had no personal interest for him. She was just a type, a symbol of a point of view. It was only as a symbol that he feared and hated her. Feared and hated. They were very big words. You put yourself in the power of anyone you feared and hated. I don't really feel as strongly as that about her, he reassured himself. It's just that I don't like her and I know that she doesn't like me. And after tonight I shan't have to see her for another week at least. He turned a page he had not really read.

The barrage was heavy tonight and quite a lot of 'planes seemed to be going over. It would be funny if a bomb fell on this garage and he and Elizabeth Simpson went floating up together. A moment would come, no doubt, when they must separate—before or after the Interrogation? Would it count in their favour that they had been engaged on work of national and civic importance? "A couple of fire-watchers, Lord." But they might not go up at all, of course. It might already be a stock joke in Hell about fire-watchers. "Fire-watchers, eh? You'll find plenty to watch here!" And a sycophantic cackle from all the demons standing round. That was quite a funny idea. If Elizabeth Simpson had been a different sort of person—like Cynthia, for instance—he would have told her about it and they would have laughed.

Cynthia. It was pleasant to think about Cynthia. Next to Derek and his mother, she was the person he loved best. She was fond of him, too. She called him Tudor, as Derek did. He ought to write to her, congratulate her on her engagement. "Dear Cynthia, I hear you are engaged to marry a Flight Lieutenant. I hope quite soon to be in a position to salute him as a superior officer. Meanwhile, I salute him for having the excellent judgment . . ." It sounded stilted and pedantic. Cynthia would laugh. "Just listen to this from funny old Tudor!" But he didn't mind when Cynthia laughed at him. He wasn't—couldn't ever be—a pansy boy to Cynthia.

A gun went off with a noise like the bursting of a giant paper-bag. There was Jerry, bumbling overhead. Why bumbling?

Because it was a sound rather like a bumble-bee, perhaps. An angry, insect noise. You could write a verse about that.

> "Death in the sky,
> The monstrous bumble-bee . . ."

Nice easy rhymes, anyhow. At school he had been rather in demand for writing verses—comic ones, of course. They had won him the only personal popularity he had achieved there. Every term he had one accepted for the school magazine. Derek had been very proud of them.

Jerry had gone over. Soon he would drop his bombs and someone would be killed. All over London people knew that, but it didn't stop them chewing away at their own thoughts and preoccupations, worrying about money and love affairs and far less important things besides. That might go into the poem too. He wondered if it were worth slipping home to fetch some writing paper and decided against it. *She* might ask him questions about it. He would be made to feel silly. He would dislike her more than ever.

"Do you think we ought to go out and have a look round?" Elizabeth asked suddenly. "Now that those 'planes have gone? We shouldn't necessarily have heard a few incendiaries come down."

"Good idea," Owen agreed politely.

They stepped out of their enveloping rugs and were aware of being cold and cramped. Owen handed Elizabeth one of the tin-hats which were part of their equipment and put on one himself. Action, even such limited action, was a relief. Outside, the night was overcast and very dark. The moon was in its last quarter and only the searchlights, patiently running their fingers through the thick mesh of the sky, gave them a brief and fitful illumination. Although there were no fires visible, they groped their way down one side of the road and up the other. From behind blacked-out windows came muffled items of the nine o'clock news bulletin. There were nearly four more hours to go. Elizabeth sighed.

"Do you play cards?" she asked.

"Some games."

"Cribbage? Piquet?"

"I've played both those."

"When we get to No. 26 I'll go in and collect some cards. It would help us to pass the time."

How does one "pass" time? Owen wondered idly, waiting for her on the doorstep. Is time, then, something to be slipped from hand to hand, or a competitor in a race whom one must overtake?

When Elizabeth came out again she was carrying a thermos and biscuit tin.

"We'll have a picnic," she announced.

The garage, when they returned to it, had already an air of friendliness because it had acquired the impression of their personalities—the books they had been reading, the angle at which they had set their chairs. Eating and drinking together, they felt themselves to be a unit apart from the rest of the lazy world who stayed in warm rooms, listening to the radio, secure from all anxiety about incendiary bombs. And since they were together and apart, far away and deep down something stirred in both of them—the genesis of comradeship.

"Shall we play Piquet?" Elizabeth suggested when they had wound up with some chocolate which Owen had provided.

"I've forgotten it a bit—You'll have to teach me."

"It'll soon come back to you."

This was a good idea, she thought. Already he seemed less painfully shy and self-conscious. He was intelligent, too, and played well, though the cards went against him. A good loser. She liked that. Intent on the game they neither of them noticed that for a long time the guns had been quite silent, and it was a surprise to them both when, soon after ten o'clock, the All Clear sounded.

"I wonder if they've really packed up for the night?" Elizabeth said.

"Probably not. But we might as well go home till they come back, don't you think?"

"I think so. It won't be so cold."

They folded their rugs, closed their books, extinguished the stove and the light and locked the door behind them. Well, it hadn't been such a bad evening after all. They wished each ether good night. It was going to be hard to keep awake till one o'clock.

Elizabeth found her parents preparing to go to bed. She stoked up the fire, made herself a cup of tea and lit a cigarette.

"I've run in the bath," her mother said, "but I've left you to cut off the gas. You'll want to fill your hot-water bottle before you go to bed."

It seemed doubtful whether these precautions were of much use, but Henry, as a warden, was firm in enforcing them.

Elizabeth decided to write to Bob. She had not answered either of his last letters and the second had been plaintive in tone. Oddly enough, it was Alex who had reminded her about Bob, one evening they had spent together recently.

"Heard from Craven lately?" he had asked.

"Yes. I owe him two letters."

"Is he still as browned off with life in the Army?"

"Rather more so, I think."

"You ought to write to the poor chap."

They had been dining out, on one of those wet, wild February nights which had become so popular with Londoners since the blitz. She had put down her coffee-cup and looked at him quizzically.

"What does this signify? Impressive demonstration of non-jealousy?"

"Don't be silly. You know that I've never been jealous of Craven."

"Nor have you. Rather impolite of you, I think. Or is it just that you're impenetrably vain?"

"Jealousy is a vice, you may remember."

"But quite an endearing one sometimes."

He had stubbed his cigarette with an angry, nervous gesture, frowning.

"Are you trying to pick a quarrel?"

"Good gracious no, darling. Only teasing you. Of course I'm going to write to Bob, and it shows a very nice spirit in you to suggest it."

But he had not allowed himself to be immediately appeased and now she remembered the conversation with a feeling of slight disquiet. It seemed to her that when they were not actually in bed together or working at the office, they hovered too often on the edge of acrimony. She was almost sure that it was Alex' fault. No doubt he was suffering from a certain amount of nerve strain as the result of the raids. It hadn't been apparent in the months before Christmas, but that sort of thing was usually delayed in its effect. She told herself that she must be gentle with him. He had a lot to worry him. She was not exactly free from anxiety herself, but it was the feminine role from time immemorial to comfort the uneasy and temperamental male.

With a smile and a sigh, she picked up her fountain pen. "Dear Bob . . ." she began.

Just before eleven o'clock, the siren sounded again. Elizabeth swore. The worst of fire-watching was that one had to take the raids so seriously. One couldn't just turn over in bed or sleep through the damned noise. She pulled on her coat and let herself quietly out of the house. A gleam of light from across the road signalled the appearance of her fellow-watcher and a distant nimble of gunfire greeted them both.

"Hello." She smiled at him, although in the darkness he could not distinguish her face. "Back again. I thought it was too good to last."

They unlocked the garage. Inside it seemed colder even than before. Owen lit the stove, but they neither of them sat down. Disconsolately they stamped their feet and swung their arms.

"I remembered to bring some cigarettes this time," Elizabeth said. "Have one?"

"No thanks. I don't smoke."

"Getting into training for the R.A.F., I suppose."

"Partly that. I never smoked, anyhow."

"You'll be called up quite soon, won't you?"

"Well, I register in April. I'm hoping they'll call me up soon after."

She remembered suddenly that ages ago she had pigeon-holed a subject for conversation with him.

"Your mother told me that you knew Lampton. I stayed there a couple of nights last month."

"Yes, I know it very well. Some relations of ours live there."

"I should imagine that it's rather lovely in the spring and summer."

"Yes, it is. I've spent most of my holidays there."

There seemed nothing more to say about it. She wished he would occasionally make an opening for talk himself, instead of merely answering her questions in a polite, flat voice. It was like interrogating a prisoner.

"I'm sorry for the poor devils who'll take over from us at one o'clock," she began again.

"Yes, I'd rather do the first half of the night."

"We ought to make three shifts of it, really."

"Apparently they can't get enough people to volunteer."

She went to the door and looked out.

"Nothing seems to be happening. I believe it's a false alarm."

"Shall we have another game of Piquet?" he suggested unexpectedly.

"Good idea." She was pleased, though she suspected that he was chiefly anxious to avoid the strain of further conversation.

They had only played four hands when the All Clear sounded, half an hour after the Alert.

"What shall we do now?" Elizabeth asked.

"I think I'll stay here till one o'clock. The other couple have to come here to take over officially, even if they go home afterwards."

"Well, I'll stay if you do."

"It's not a bit necessary for both of us. You'd far better go back and keep warm." He sounded quite firm and determined.

"All right," Elizabeth agreed meekly. "We'll finish the game next week. Thank you for staying. Good night."

"Good night." For the first time he smiled at her in a quite friendly, spontaneous way. "Don't bother to come back if there's another warning in the next forty minutes," he called after her.

Alone in the garage he gave a sigh of relief. He felt pleased with himself. He had been masterful and she had submitted. That was how he meant things to be if they ever had bombs on the road. He would give the orders and she would obey them without argument, instinctively realising that here was someone with a keen, clear grasp of the situation. Afterwards she would tell everyone she met: "Owen Cathcart was wonderful. He didn't lose his head at all. Things might have been really serious if he hadn't acted so promptly." Of course, if there were high explosives he might even have the chance to win the George Medal . . .

At this point in his reverie, Owen broke off and grinned to himself. How Derek would laugh if he could overhear his thoughts! He employed the rest of his time composing a self-derisive limerick about young Tudor, fire-watching one night, who was feeling remarkably bright until the bombs fell, when he let out a yell and nearly passed out with the fright. Cheered by this success, he greeted amiably the yawning pair who came to relieve him and took himself home to bed.

CHAPTER XII

In March the raids became heavier again and Alice Simpson's powers of resistance, already perilously stretched, snapped suddenly. One Monday morning, after two successive nights of little sleep, she decided to go to the West End for a day's shopping. This was her ostensible purpose. Actually, the expedition was cover for one purchase only.

It was the first time she had visited the London shopping centre since the beginning of the raids and the damage and destruction suffered by familiar landmarks frightened her. Everyone had told her about John Lewis's—Elizabeth had seen it still in flames—but it was quite different personally to behold its wilderness of blackened girders. All those lovely materials gone! At that moment she would willingly have signed a peace treaty with Hitler on any terms.

She met Elizabeth for lunch in one of the Soho restaurants.

"I nearly suggested one in Dean Street," Elizabeth said grimly, "but it was just as well I didn't because it was bombed over the week-end. Wardour Street got a hit, too. And the Café de Paris, of course. You've heard about that?"

"They were talking about it in the train coming up."

"Everyone's talking about it. It seems to have captured the public imagination."

Elizabeth was distrait and in some indefinable way different against her workaday background. She looked tired, too. Her fire-watching duty the night before had been to the almost continuous accompaniment of a particularly heavy barrage and a procession of German 'planes overhead. The Cathcart boy had been good, she reported. They had patrolled most of the time and once or twice had had to take shelter in doorways from the shrapnel. Henry had been on duty too, at the wardens' post, but Alice's sympathy was all for herself. They had both had companionship; she had been alone. And to be alone in a heavy air raid, she thought with some justification, increased its terrors tenfold.

"What are you going to do this afternoon?" Elizabeth asked her.

"Oh, just buy a few things. I want to try and match some wool . . . And your father asked me to get him some special sort of tobacco he can't buy locally."

"Well, don't be frightened if you hear some bangs. A lot of time-bombs have been going off."

Alice bought the wool and the tobacco and was then free to make the only purchase which really interested her. With a certain amount of self-consciousness she went into a wine-merchant's shop in Oxford Street.

"I wonder if you can help me," she began hesitantly. "My son is coming home on leave." She paused for so long that the assistant, though obviously uninterested, made a sound of encouragement. "He's in the Navy," she added finally. "So I thought . . . I'd like to buy him a bottle of rum." The last words came out in a little rush of embarrassment.

"Certainly, madam. Jamaica rum, of course."

"Of course." She gave the man a wavering smile. "They call it Nelson's blood. In the Navy, I mean."

"Really, madam?" He was very bored.

Outside in the street again, carefully cradling the bottle in her arms, she told herself that it had not been at all difficult. She wouldn't mind another time. Not, of course, that there was likely to be another time. She would probably never open the bottle. But it would be a comfort to know that it was there, to steady her nerves on bad nights. She was sure that Bob would approve. After all, it was he who had prescribed it for her. But she didn't think she would mention it to him, all the same. It might reach Henry's and Elizabeth's ears that way and they would both be very surprised and almost certainly disapproving. Just because they had no nerves themselves, they didn't understand how more sensitive people felt.

When she got home she hid the bottle very carefully on a shelf at the top of the built-in cupboard in her bedroom. She was almost disappointed when that evening there was only a very brief and quite uneventful Alert.

The following week-end Elizabeth agreed to go away with Alex to Brighton. Brighton! The perfectly conventional choice for an illicit holiday, exactly the place where you would expect a man to take his secretary. Alex didn't, or wouldn't, see it like that. Someone had told him that the weather on the South Coast was almost spring-like, and in another week's time the Coastal ban on visitors would come into force. Why should they run into anyone they knew? They never had. He was obstinate about it and a little irritable. He had still not quite recovered from his illness at Christmas and looked pale and fine-drawn. Elizabeth gave in. She told her parents that she would be staying with Joan Walsh. It wasn't worth while leaving an address. She would ring up if there were a raid on London either night.

They left the office separately, as usual, and met again at Victoria. Alex had booked a room at a small hotel on the seafront. In the train Elizabeth put on the wedding ring which Alex had bought her three years ago. It slipped on in an accustomed way. Long since she had outlived the embarrassment of signing hotel registers as Elizabeth Foster. It was necessary now to fill in one's registration number too, but no one had ever asked to look at her identity card.

The first evening passed without incident. They arrived late for dinner and by the end of the meal were alone in the dining-room. The occupants of the lounge had a residential air; middle-aged people, evading the problem of rationing, gathered in little groups to do their cross-words or to knit. Alex and Elizabeth went out, warned by the hall-porter to be back by half-past ten when the curfew came into operation. It was a mild night and the moon was up. An Alert had sounded at eight o'clock but no 'planes were going over on their way to bomb London or the Midlands. There were no guns in the town, apparently, which was restful though a little disconcerting to people accustomed to hitting back at their attackers. The sea lapped quietly at beaches strewn with driftwood and protected by barbed wire, and the Palace Pier, blown up half-way along its length, had a desolate and lonely air, stripped of its slot-machines and deck-chairs. Elizabeth had a feeling of nostalgia for her childhood, a period, it seemed to her, of unbroken peace, since she was too young to remember the 1914-1918 war. There was a time when sixpence to spend on the Palace Pier at Brighton had been the utmost limit of desire.

"Used you to come to Brighton for your summer holidays when you were a child?" she asked Alex.

"We spent a couple here."

"Do you suppose we were ever here at the same time?"

"We might have been. But I shouldn't have had any use for you. You were a little girl when I was a big boy."

"Maybe I admired you from afar. You were probably a lordly being who patronised the rifle range, while I was only turning a handle to race a blue bicyclist against a red one with some condescending grown-up who always let me win."

"It would be rather fun to do that now." He looked regretfully at the barbed wire.

"Would you let me win?"

"Not on your life, my sweet. But you might beat me, all the same."

They walked back arm in arm to the hotel, in perfect amity and accord. Now we shall go to bed and sleep together all night long, Elizabeth thought. If I wake up in the dark and hear the pulsing of a German bomber, I shall not have to lie and wonder if it carries death for you, or if you are already dead or trapped in fear and agony. You will be there beside me, tangible and living. And when the daylight comes I shall not have to greet you with "Good morning, Mr. Foster". It made it all worth while—the subterfuge, shifts and lying, the apprehension and humiliation.

"Do you ever have any regrets that you met me?" he asked her abruptly that night.

"Sometimes," she said honestly. "But not for long. And even then it isn't you I regret, only the circumstances."

"You'd be married by now," he said gloomily.

"Not necessarily. I'm not very susceptible, nor am I everybody's cup of tea."

"You're Bob Craven's cup of tea, apparently."

"Good lord, don't start on Bob again! Besides, I'm not. He only thinks I am. He'd find me a very sour-tasting brew in practice."

"You haven't given him any practice, then?"

She sat up on her elbow, switched on the light beside the bed and stared down at him in astonishment. Blinking, he evaded meeting her eyes.

"What on earth are you driving at?" she demanded.

"I wish you'd turn that light off and lie down again," he said peevishly. "Don't take me so seriously. I'm not accusing you of anything."

"Then I don't know what you're talking about."

"I only meant . . . Well, I suppose you must give him a certain amount of encouragement or he'd have packed up long ago."

She lay down beside him again, but she did not switch off the light.

"Yes, I give him a certain amount of encouragement," she said in a low, flat voice. "I treat him rather badly, if you want to know. I make use of him, as a cover for . . . this. Last time he was home on leave I let him kiss me, but I'm not particularly ashamed of that. That was more generous than my usual treatment of him, even though I was a little drunk at the time. Up till now, I've simply kept him dangling on a string with no reward at all, simply for our joint convenience. Is there anything else?"

To her horror and astonishment, he laughed.

"Don't be such a tragedy queen about it, darling." He stretched his arm across her and switched off the light himself. "I'm not jealous. Merely curious, if you like." He drew her to him, but she remained taut and unresponsive. "Don't let's waste any more time discussing the poor mutt."

Hours later, she was still awake though Alex slept beside her tranquilly. Puzzled and profoundly uneasy, she listened to the echo of their voices in her mind. A curious and extremely disagreeable impression remained with her. Alex had *wanted* her to say that Bob made love to her. But that was crazy. Why on earth should he? There was only one possible reason and that she rejected fiercely. If he were getting tired of her, were preparing to break off their relationship, he might want to quiet his conscience that way. But that simply wasn't true! She *knew* that he was still in love with her. It was always he who made the opportunities, who was aggrieved when she could not fall in with his plans, who had, only a short time ago, fretted at their separation and risked disclosure for the sake of seeing her. Bewildered and unhappy, she lay beside him in the darkness and listened to his even breathing. A few hours ago this was where she had longed to be. But now she wished that she were far away and quite alone.

In the morning their conversation of the night before seemed slightly unreal and diminished in significance. The sun shone, and the war, though undeniably existent, had shifted its focus. Brighton might be shabby, underpopulated and pathetic—a once prosperous town now showing symptoms of acute economic stress—but even the empty shops had glass in their windows, and bomb damage, though large in the eyes of its inhabitants, appeared trivial to the Londoner. To go down streets which presented an unbroken line of buildings standing trimly shoulder to shoulder; to look at houses with their faces all decently composed, not one of them brutally forced to reveal the private lives of former inmates to the curious passer-by; never to meet a road-diversion sign or cross a wooden bridge thrown over a gaping pit in the surface of the thoroughfare: that was a holiday far outstripping the effects of the sun, the sea air and the clean wind off the Sussex Downs.

"I hadn't realised before how sick I was of seeing bomb damage," Elizabeth said. "Isn't this heaven? All the anti-invasion devices have a sort of comic opera air, by comparison. Even the soldiers don't look quite like the real thing. I can't help imagining they're all on leave."

"Don't let them hear you say that," Alex warned. "What are we going to do this afternoon?"

"Take a 'bus on to the downs and walk. Up to the Dyke, maybe. That's in the tradition of Brighton trippers. I feel a tripper this week-end." She thought, too, but did not say, that they were less likely to run into people they knew on the downs than strolling up and down the sea-front.

In the woods below Poynings they found primroses. Alex filled his hat with them, picking seriously and deliberately, the wind ruffling his fair, thin hair. He looked absurdly like his son. Elizabeth loved him very much. Bending over the same cluster their heads met and they kissed, fleetingly but tenderly.

"You've very nice," she said.

"I'm nicest when I'm with you. You're very nice too, of course," he added.

She laughed rather ruefully.

"Sometimes I think I'm nastiest with you. But it doesn't mean anything."

Against her will she saw them both objectively, a man and a woman, obviously townsfolk, stooping among the pale grey saplings. Before the war there would have been a large, expensive car drawn up on the road alongside. He looked what he was, successful, sedentary, a married man and father of a family. She looked, no doubt, the kind of woman he would choose as wife—sophisticated, self-possessed, a little hard. Out of place among the primroses, both of them. No one, seeing them, would guess on what a knife-edge their relationship balanced, how threatened it was from within and without. But I know that he loves me, she told herself fiercely. Whatever's wrong, it isn't that.

"I think we've picked enough," he said. "It's getting cold. Do we have to walk back up that hill?"

"No. We can get on to the London-Brighton road from here and catch a 'bus."

But actually they did not return by 'bus, for the driver of a car, passing where they waited by the roadside, slowed down and offered them a lift.

"Very kind of you," Alex said in thanking him on their arrival in the town again. "My wife was tired."

"My wife!" It tripped off his tongue so glibly. But naturally he was used to calling Naomi that.

They had dinner early and went to a cinema in the evening. The second night was unmarred by any argument.

On Sunday morning Alex went down to breakfast earlier than Elizabeth. She found him waiting for her at the foot of the stairs, talking to a Canadian officer they had noticed dining alone the night before. He was a pleasant, garrulous man—on leave, he told them—and it soon became obvious that he intended to spend the rest of the day with them. Someone had given him an itinerary of places to visit in Brighton and its neighbourhood. Rottingdean was not on any account to be missed, he said—they must give him the pleasure of lunching with him there. Before they quite knew what was happening, he had despatched them upstairs to put on their coats while he consulted the porter about 'bus times.

"Alex, you fool!" Elizabeth protested. "Now look what a mess we're in."

"I'm terribly sorry. He just fastened on me. He's desperately bored and lonely, poor chap. But I never imagined it would lead to all this."

"We can't possibly snub him now. Canadians always say the English are so stand-offish. But it isn't at all the way I'd planned to spend the day."

Subdued but acquiescent they let themselves be taken on the 'bus to Rottingdean, inspected (from a distance) the coastal defences, admired the village green and ate lunch at the pleasant Canadian's expense. It was obvious that he was "a man's man". He found little to say to Elizabeth, but to Alex he talked practically without ceasing. Alex seemed interested. They discussed America, politically, commercially and from the propaganda point of view. It might have been an interview with a salesman anxious to increase his export trade. Elizabeth felt she should have had her shorthand notebook on her knee.

"I'm stationed quite near London," the Canadian said enthusiastically, over the liqueurs which Alex had insisted on contributing to the meal. "You folk must have dinner with me one evening, if you don't mind being out in the raids."

"That would be lovely," Elizabeth murmured.

She tried to catch Alex' eyes. This was exactly what she had feared. In another moment he would ask for their address.

"I think I'll go and tidy up before we start back," she said hurriedly, and escaped to the sanctuary of the ladies' cloakroom.

She knew, when she returned, that Alex had told him. The atmosphere had very slightly altered. The Canadian was a simple soul and he was embarrassed for her. He made a marked effort to draw her into the conversation, was rather too self-conscious attentive. Stupidly, it made her want to cry. She knew that she ought to play up to him, talk, laugh, be aggressively natural; but the effort was too great. Going back on the 'bus she was almost completely silent, listening without interest to the conversation of the two men. In Castle Square the Canadian left them—to keep a date, he said; they murmured that they had a train to catch. Nothing was said about a further meeting.

Alex and Elizabeth walked back along the front to their hotel without speaking.

In the bedroom, he stood and watched her pack, looking a little helpless. Then suddenly he took her in his arms and kissed her fiercely.

"Sorry, darling, about today. But you have enjoyed the week-end, haven't you?"

"Of course I have. It's been heavenly."

"We'll have dinner in town. You must go home tonight, I suppose?"

"I'm afraid so. I'm on fire-watch duty, anyhow, from black-out. But I warned the boy I'm on with that I might be late."

"I'll call a taxi, if you're ready."

When he had left the room, she closed the suit-cases and took the primroses out of the wash-basin. There was quite a big bunch of them and she tied them together carefully, with darning-silk. Their faint, virginal scent made her want to cry again, though she didn't know exactly why. It *had* been a lovely week-end. They were very lucky to have had it. There was no reason at all to feel so hopelessly, irreparably sad.

CHAPTER XIII

WHEN THE TAXI drew up at the end of Wordsworth Road, Owen was standing in his old look-out, the doorway of the shop facing the Common. The Alert had sounded but he had not yet bothered to unlock the garage. In the moonlight he recognised Elizabeth as she got out and he watched her turn to speak to someone who was still inside the taxi. There seemed to be some kind of discussion going on—the taxi driver was taking part too. Then the door opened again and a man emerged and joined Elizabeth on the pavement. The argument continued until it appeared to reach an amicable conclusion, when the driver nodded and slid back into his seat and the man climbed into the taxi again. Elizabeth gave a quick glance round and leant forward over the lowered window. Her head and the head of the man merged for an instant in one dark blur. Then the taxi moved on. She picked up her suit-case and walked past the shop and out of sight.

This incident, which had occupied perhaps three minutes, left Owen in a state of considerable mental confusion. For he had not only recognised Elizabeth; he had also recognised the man whom she had kissed good-bye. Clearly, in his mind, he saw him standing in the doorway of the drawing-room at Lampton, heard him say:

"I've had my secretary down for a couple of days . . . she's going back to town today and my wife wants to drive her to the station."

Owen's astonishment was naïve and complete.

Ten minutes later, Elizabeth joined him in the garage. She apologised for being late.

"I've just come back from Brighton. I went there for the week-end. The weather's lovely there."

"I've never been to Brighton." He tried to sound as casual as she did.

"Haven't you? I thought everybody had. It's not a bad place."

It was the fourth Sunday they had spent together and they were almost friendly now. The noisy night the week before had gone a long way towards abolishing Owen's constraint and Elizabeth's slightly patronising reaction to it. They had arrived now at a point where they could be silent together without embarrassment and this evening they were both glad to take advantage of the fact. Elizabeth wanted to think about Alex, and Owen wanted to think about Elizabeth.

He did not himself realise what an enormous advance this was. In the past he had been forced, against his will, to think about her; he had been obsessed by her, and always in relation to himself—what she thought, said or guessed about him. Now, for the first time, he was interested in her as an individual, with a separate, surprising and rather mysterious life of her own.

So everyone, then, had a secret; that was the conclusion to be drawn. Turn up any stone and out would crawl some naked, shameful maggot of the mind. Well, perhaps not every stone but most, at least. Here was Elizabeth Simpson, so fluent in her scorn of other people, engaged in an intrigue with her employer (a married man with children), going away with him for an illicit week-end, coming back and picking up her mask again with a steady hand. There was satisfaction mixed with Owen's curiosity. He had acquired a certain power over her, although she did not know it. He need never feel guilty or embarrassed in her presence any more. Surreptitiously, he looked to see if even her outward appearance had been changed to him. Yes, she had changed—or perhaps only his own focus had shifted. He saw for the first time that she was very unhappy. It was a disconcerting revelation.

When people were unhappy, you were forced to pity them. He did not want to pity Elizabeth Simpson. It was he who was to be pitied—though only by himself. He conceded that it was rather bad luck for her to be in love (he supposed she was in love) with a man she couldn't marry, but it was a very ordinary situation; it happened all the time. She could know nothing approaching his own intense loneliness of spirit. He felt indignant with her for competing, as it were.

All the same, she did look sad. She wasn't even pretending to read the newspaper on her lap. She looked tired, too, and rather plain. He tried to recall the strong emotions—fear and hate and resentment—which he had felt that evening outside the Post Office at Lampton, when it had seemed that a powerful and ubiquitous enemy had tracked him down on purpose to torment him. That girl had nothing to do with the one sitting with him in the garage now. In the light of this reality she dwindled to the dimensions of a booby-trap to frighten children—a candle in a scooped-out turnip. People who were unhappy themselves, who had something to conceal themselves, had no time or thought to spare for other people's secret lives. He realised, soberly and conclusively, that he had built up an entirely imaginary persecution and indictment. It made no fundamental difference to the truth about himself as it was known to him; but it did lift a weight of shame and apprehension from his mind. Henceforward he would see her as she really was—an ordinary human being with ordinary human problems. No longer feared, she was no longer fabulous. But she was much more likable.

"I brought home some primroses," Elizabeth said suddenly. "We picked them in a wood."

"Nice wood?" Owen questioned, trying to sound encouraging. It seemed to him that she wanted to talk, to distract her mind.

"A very young wood, all new trees."

"There's one like that at Lampton." He said it without thinking and then flushed at his tactlessness.

"Tell me about Lampton, and about your relations there. Talk to me." The pleading in her voice was unmistakable.

Owen began very haltingly, but after a moment or two he found a surprising fluency. It was really quite easy, he discovered, to talk about a place you loved and people whom you loved. It was almost like thinking aloud. He could not bring himself to speak of Derek, except very casually and briefly, but he told her all about the things they had done together—"my cousins and I"—bird-watching by day and moth-hunting by night, camping out in summer and skating on the pond in winter, about a holiday when they had had a craze for geology and collected all sorts of useless specimens which wore holes in their pockets, and a glider they had built which ignominiously crashed the first time it was air-borne. It was like turning over the pages of an album of old snapshots. It made him very happy in a nostalgic way.

"Then you're not really an only child," Elizabeth said when he paused at last, suddenly rather self-conscious again. "Your cousins must be just the same as brothers and sisters to you. I envy you that."

"It's almost the same, but not quite. I think I'd . . . take them more for granted if they were."

"They'd be less romantic, you mean?"

"Yes, I suppose that's what I mean, really." He looked at her with respect for her intuition.

"Well, that's better still. More fun."

"Yes. Yes, it is."

They had forgotten all about the air raid, but now a sudden burst of gunfire in the near neighbourhood reminded them of their responsibilities.

"How we gas!" Elizabeth exclaimed. "Let's go out and have a look round. The whole road may be one blazing inferno for all we know."

She's nice, Owen thought, still surprised at his discovery; I like her.

When they reached his own front door he glanced at his watch and saw that it was time to go and collect the coffee and sandwiches his mother had prepared for him. Daisy was just about to bring the basket along to the garage herself. She insisted on accompanying them back.

"It's terribly cheerless," she lamented. "I don't wonder all you fire-watchers catch cold."

"Your rugs make a lot of difference," Elizabeth said. "I'm immensely grateful to you for lending me one."

Daisy smiled rather absently. Her thoughts had gone ahead.

"Owen, such a queer thing happened after you went out tonight. A man called to see your father—my husband is away on business for a few days," she explained to Elizabeth in parenthesis—"and asked me all sorts of curious questions—where he'd gone, how long he'd be away and if I could remember if he were at home the second week in February. He was very polite but I thought it rather impertinent of him. I didn't tell him anything. I'm sure your father will be very angry when he hears about it."

"Perhaps he was a plain-clothes copper and Father's knocked someone down with the car," Owen suggested with a grin.

"Owen, what a dreadful thing to say, even in fun! You know what a careful driver he is."

"Well, it's a very easy thing to do in the black-out. You might just feel a bump and think it was a bit of bad road surface." But he saw that she was looking really worried and changed his tone. "It's all right, I'm only kidding. He was probably just a business acquaintance of Father's. Forget about it."

"Yes, of course." But she sounded rather doubtful of her ability to comply. "I'd better go back now, in case anyone should ring up. One isn't supposed to ring up during an air raid, I know, but I'm afraid people do, all the same—"

The spell had been broken. Alone together again, Elizabeth and Owen ate and drank companionably enough but talked only of general things. For the rest of the period of Alert they played cards, yawned and shivered.

In the morning Joan Walsh did not turn up at the office. By ten o'clock Elizabeth was frightened. It hadn't seemed a bad raid the night before, but bombs had certainly been dropped somewhere. At half-past ten she had just decided to go down to Earl's Court and look for her (as usual, the exchange was out of commission) when Joan rang through from a public call-box. Her voice sounded unnaturally composed.

"Elizabeth? I can't come in today. I've got to go home."

"You haven't been bombed out?"

"No." She paused for seconds that seemed like minutes. "Tim's been killed."

"Oh, Joan!"

But she had rung off. Elizabeth swallowed a lump in her throat. She had never met Tim, who was Joan's brother in the Navy, but she had always imagined him as her male counterpart, cheerful, disrespectful and dependable. He had served in a destroyer, which probably meant that a good many other Tims had been killed too. There was nothing about it in the papers yet. She would have to tell Rowland when he came in.

Alex was in already. He was very genuinely upset at Elizabeth's news.

"Poor kid. What rotten luck. Where do her people live?"

"Somewhere in Suffolk. Her father's a doctor."

"Better write and tell her to take the week off. No, Rowland must do that, but I'll suggest it to him."

Any discussion of the week-end at Brighton seemed unfeeling and distasteful after that. So neither of them spoke of it.

On Wednesday Elizabeth had a letter from Joan which thanked her for her painfully and inadequately worded condolences and asked her to go to her rooms and send on one or two things she needed. Elizabeth left the office early and arrived at the house in Earl's Court with a certain amount of curiosity in her mind. Joan's account of her fellow-boarders was always very highly coloured. She wondered what they were really like.

The landlady, Mrs. Henley, opened the door to her. She looked hopefully enquiring until Elizabeth explained her errand and then her face, which was foolish, pale and slightly puffy, assumed an expression of dolour and disappointment. Perhaps she thought I'd come to rent a room, Elizabeth speculated. Joan had said that the house was almost empty.

"Ah, poor Miss Walsh—yes. She wrote me that you would be coming. I'll take you to her room."

She lingered while Elizabeth looked out the things Joan had asked for and put them in the case she had brought with her. On the mantelpiece stood a photograph of a young man in naval uniform whom it was easy to identify by the likeness to Joan. Mrs. Henley saw her glance at it.

"I'm going to put a nice vase of flowers beside it the day Miss Walsh comes back," she said with gloomy satisfaction.

Elizabeth thought this an appalling idea and one which Joan would detest, but cowardice made her murmur something that sounded approving.

"Very sad, isn't it?" Mrs. Henley went on. "Not only him, poor young fellow. It's a terrible war. You can't see an end to it, can you?"

Irrationally, Elizabeth had at once an inclination to deny that Tim Walsh's death was sad and that the war was terrible and to forecast total victory in time for August Bank Holiday.

"I see you've had your share of bombs round here," she remarked instead.

"Ah!" Mrs. Henley's face lit up. All the way down the stairs, across the hall and out to the pavement she enlarged on the peculiar dangers she had had to undergo. "And I can't do the sensible thing and go down to my sister in the country," she explained. "I've got the house on a long lease, you see; it's my livelihood, as you might say. Though goodness knows it's not much of a one now."

A short, spare man with a grizzled moustache and a very straight back turned in at the gate and raised his hat to them.

"Good evening, Major," Mrs. Henley said.

Yes, the Major was exactly as Joan had described him. Elizabeth wished that she could see the redoubtable Miss Dalrymple, but this was not to be.

"He thinks the world of Miss Walsh," Mrs. Henley sighed. "Always so bright—she keeps us all cheered up. But we mustn't expect her to be bright now."

"I'm sure she won't want her . . . bereavement to depress everyone else," Elizabeth said hurriedly. "I must really go now or I shan't get home before the black-out. Good-bye, and thank you very much."

Though what I have to thank her for I don't know, she reflected as she walked away quickly. God, what an awful woman! How on earth can Joan stick living in that house? I shall tell Alex he must give her a rise, so that she can afford to move somewhere else.

But that thought was succeeded by another: would Joan want to stay with Foster and Rowland's any more? Her brother's death might finally decide her to go into the Wrens. It was selfish to feel so dismayed at the idea and out of proportion to the circumstances, but nevertheless Elizabeth's heart sank. Carter would be leaving to join the Navy quite soon now. Everything threatened change, at a time when one's instinct was to cling desperately to the accustomed and the routine. The world rocked, buildings and lives collapsed, yet as long as one could add up figures in the same ledger, measure out material on the same counter, wash the same kitchen floor, one could endure. At the back of her mind, she knew, was the latent fear that change would bring about eventually the finish of the firm and separation between Alex and herself. But it was stupid to anticipate. She excused herself with the recollection that it had been pretty hellish last night. She had scarcely slept at all and she was tired.

She hoped very much there would not be another heavy raid that night, a hope which was not to be fulfilled.

CHAPTER XIV

THE SIRENS SOUNDED soon after eight o'clock and it became evident almost immediately that this was going to be a memorable night. "It was that terrible Wednesday," people would say. For it was a curious trait in the national character that the ordinary citizen thought in terms of week-days rather than dates. Days of the week meant early closings, Home Guard drills, spells of duty at First Aid Posts or leisure to wash one's hair; happenings on which to hang, as on a hook in the wall, one's recollections of abnormal things like fires and land-mines. Dates of the month meant only birthdays and What the Stars had Foretold for the year to come in the morning papers.

At the Wardens' Post they said that Jerry was having quite a party. None of them was enjoying the almost incessant drone of enemy 'planes, the thud of falling bombs and a barrage which was heavier than anyone had heard before, but they kept up their spirits with the usual rather silly jokes, tags quoted from radio comedians or personal jibes in which there was no malice and no humour except that of repetition. Although their gaiety was a little strained, each man and woman, Henry thought, was principally afraid of one thing which was not lethal at all; they were afraid of their own possible incapacity to rise to the occasion, keep cool heads, act correctly in the split second which might make all the difference between lives saved or thrown away. That was his fear too. He was conscious of being middle-aged, inwardly irresolute and very weary. At the same time, he was upheld by a false elation and excitement which he recognised from the last war.

"If we don't get an incident in our area tonight," Thorne said, "it will be very surprising."

And very disappointing too, he might have added. Thorne's mentality was constructed to deal with emergencies; he had invention but no imagination and a quiet, unboastful self-confidence. By an accident of residence he was responsible for a number of suburban roads containing only secondary targets for the enemy, but by temperament he was fitted for the hot spots, the East End, the City and the river boroughs. He felt ashamed that in six months of blitz he had been given nothing better to do than put out stray incendiaries, calm apprehensive householders and uphold the sanctity of the black-out.

"It looks to me as though they were funking the inner London barrage and jettisoning their bombs more or less at random on the outskirts," Henry said. "A good thing too."

"Yes, it's our night to howl," Thorne misquoted pensively. He broke off as the scream of a bomb ended with the unmistakable crash of falling masonry. "That was pretty close! Come with me, Simpson, and we'll find out where it landed. O'Neal and Mrs. Brown, you stay here."

Outside in the street they bumped into Buckley, gasping as he ran.

"It's at the angle of Longden Avenue and The Chase," he panted. "Direct hit. The dust's so thick you can't see much." He spoke as though the black-out did not exist, and indeed the night was so lit up by fires, gun-flashes, searchlights and the serenely neutral stars that visibility was relatively good.

They were all three running now and Henry felt his heart labour with the effort. As they rounded the last corner, Thorne pulled up with a grunt. A thick fog seemed to have rolled up out of the ground like a protective smoke-screen, a fog which filled their eyes with a smarting pain and caught at their throats, choking them. Gas! Henry thought with a moment's panic memory of 1915. But it was only dust, of course. All houses were solidified dust. Mankind was dust and to dust would return. Behind the fog a large house standing in its own grounds gaped at them with outrage. One corner still remained, like the open covers of a book stood on end. Rubble from the rest had been thrown across the road, blocking their approach. Disconcertingly, Thorne laughed.

"The Nursing Home. It's empty. That's one on Hitler."

They were filled with an enormous relief. Henry knew it as the measure of his terrified anticipation.

Somewhere a woman was screaming, but she sounded frightened rather than hurt. The house opposite had a skeleton look, its bones were showing, the ribs of its roof. Up and down the road light shone from houses that had lost their curtains with their window-panes.

"Tell those fools to douse their lights," Thorne commanded, beginning to pick his way unsteadily through the debris. "No, Buckley and I'll do that. You go back to the Post, Simpson, and report."

Henry began to run again. He felt ashamed of his muscles, already tired, and of his bursting lungs. A solicitor, he thought; too sedentary a life. I ought to take up golf, he thought ridiculously. He arrived so out of breath that O'Neal had to relay his message over the telephone.

"Have a cup of tea before you go back," Mrs. Brown insisted, always kindly and maternal. "It'll clear away some of that dust in your throat."

"What's the betting there's a crop of time bombs?" O'Neal commented with grim relish. "Well, we'll all have to take our chance of that. There's hours to go yet before we can start looking for 'em."

Hours to go yet, Henry's mind echoed him. The German 'planes still chugged overhead but they pretended not to hear. He wondered whether anything had dropped on Wordsworth Road. But it was no good thinking about that now. He gulped down the tea without tasting it and walked back as fast as he could to the scene of the incident. The police had arrived and two people suffering from cuts were being put into a car, drawn up a little way along the road. The dust was beginning to settle already, but mixed with its gritty smell was the pungent smell of burning. Henry saw that there were flames coming from a tall building near the railway line. Thorne's words kept running through his head in an irritating repetition—"It's our night to howl . . . it's our night to howl . . ."

Thorne himself seemed very much at home and in command. The incident officer had not arrived; he was dealing with a worse mess somewhere else, it seemed; and Thorne's carefully cultivated good relations with the police were obviously bearing fruit. He was talking to one of them now, while a little man in shirt-sleeves hovered at their elbows. Henry could see quite distinctly the gleam of his spectacles as he turned his head from one to the other of the tall men in uniform. Then the policeman nodded and moved away, the little man ran with a stumbling, ducking motion into the house opposite which had lost all its windows and tiles, and Thorne turned to Henry.

"That chap's afraid his son may be somewhere under this lot. It seems that the young fool went out to look at the fires and he hasn't come back. He may have been inside the grounds of the Home when the bomb fell. But the police say they can't do anything till daylight. The rescue parties are all out working at other places and we can't waste their time to look for a boy who may be safe and sound somewhere else."

Henry agreed, but he felt very sorry for the little man in shirt-sleeves. It would seem a long night to him if his son did not return. He wondered whether, presently, he could ask Thorne to let him slip home for a minute, to make sure they were all right there.

Elizabeth had slept the first part of the night. A few months ago she would not have believed it possible to do so, but nowadays, if she were sufficiently tired, fear was not enough to keep her wakeful. She did not deny the existence of fear in herself. At the whistle of a bomb or its shattering explosion, an invisible hand closed on her heart and squeezed it gently. That was all. Always the same reaction. It was what people meant, she supposed, when they said: "My heart stopped beating." There was also the fact that she invariably felt extremely hungry in a bad air raid.

But tonight neither of these symptoms had been able to compete with a fatigue that was like a drug spreading lassitude throughout her body, a lassitude which had in it a perverse element of pleasure in pain. The ear-splitting thunder of the guns did not even make her twitch in her sleep. Her subconscious mind consoled her with a reassuring whisper: "This noise is harmless and no concern of yours." What woke her finally was by comparison a slight sound—the crash and tinkle of breaking glass.

In an instant she was out of bed and pulling on shoes, trousers, and a coat, placed ready beside her. The sound seemed to her to have come from the back of the house. She ran into her father's room and wrenched apart the heavy curtains. A high wall skirted the gardens that side of the road and behind it stretched a row of small shops. One of these, directly in a line with No. 26, was the show-room of a garage, with a yard adjoining which was used for storing caravans and lorries. A bright blaze of fire was already visible there and she could hear the abominable, cheerful crackle of the flames. With one ricocheting movement of her mind she thought: "Petrol—explosives—Mother." In the next instant she was in her mother's room.

She was asleep. Having made sure that the curtains were drawn, Elizabeth switched on the bedside lamp. Alice lay on her back, breathing very heavily. Her face was flushed. A curious smell pervaded the room—familiar but for the moment unidentifiable. Elizabeth shook her arm.

"Mother! Wake up! There's a fire in the garage at the back."

She roused very slowly. Her eyes when she opened them looked dull and vacant. But she did not seem afraid when she realised at last what Elizabeth was saying. In a fumbling, unhurried way she began to put on some clothes.

With a pang of guilt Elizabeth remembered that she was a fire-watcher. It was obvious that no stirrup-pump could cope with the blaze at the garage. Smiling to herself, she dialled 999 on the telephone and made her report. She had always wanted to do that. A present from Hitler. A moment later she was outside the front door. About a dozen incendiaries were burning brilliantly, two of them on the roofs of houses. Whoever was on fire-watch duty that night had failed to rouse the whole road, but she saw that all three of the Cathcarts were on the job and a man and his wife whom she knew by sight were struggling to put the ladder into position against one of the houses. Elizabeth turned back for a bucket of sand. Cautiously approaching the nearest bomb she tried to empty out the sand in one neat cast, but it was damp and would not scatter. Feeling inefficient and extravagant, she crowned the bomb with the whole bucket and left it to burn itself out. Sand-bags would have been better, she thought. We ought to have had sand-bags.

In the few seconds that had elapsed, the road seemed to have filled with people. The incendiaries were now definitely out-numbered. Well, I put out one, anyhow, she consoled herself. It was time to return to her mother.

She had not made much progress with her dressing. Elizabeth could not understand it.

"Mother, I don't want to frighten you but you really ought to hurry. That place is full of petrol. It may explode any minute and it's only ten or fifteen yards away from us. I think we ought to collect a few things and get out of the house."

"Don't fuss me," Alice said pettishly. "I'm coming as fast as I can. But I don't believe a word you say. We're perfectly safe in this house. It's probably the safest house in London."

"Mother, what *are* you talking about? You're still half asleep. Here! Have a look!"

She switched off the light, pulled back the curtains and led Alice over to the window. The flames were now rather dramatically lurid. If the fire brigade had arrived, it had not yet been able to make much impression on them. For the first time it occurred to Elizabeth, with a shock of unpleasant surprise, that they formed an excellent target for high explosives.

"Fire!" Alice muttered, as though it were the first time the word had been spoken that night. "Fire! We must get away! Where are we to go?"

"The nearest shelter, I suppose. I've got the case I always keep packed and you have yours. I can carry Father's for him. Is there anything else you want to take?"

"Nothing. Nothing." She seemed at last in a frenzy to be out of the house.

"Hand-bag? Jewellery? All right—let's go."

At that moment there was a loud knocking on the front door. Elizabeth ran to open it. A policeman stood outside.

"Everybody this side of the road is advised to move out, Miss. The firemen are afraid the petrol will explode."

"Thanks very much. We'd thought of that already. Where do you suggest we go?"

"I'd go into one of the houses opposite, if you've got friends there. It's only a precaution, like." He was already knocking at the house next door.

Elizabeth turned to find her mother just behind her. She seemed to have lost her head entirely. She had dropped everything she had been carrying and was swaying as she stood.

"What is it?" she demanded in a voice that rose almost to a shout. "What was that man saying to you?"

"It's all right, Mother—it's perfectly all right." Half irritated, half concerned, Elizabeth took her arm to steady her. "We're going to the Cathcarts. They'll let us stay there for the rest of the night."

She had almost to drag her across the roadway. Owen was standing on his doorstep and he peered at them with a surprised expression as they approached him.

"We're refugees," Elizabeth explained. "Turned out by the police. May we come in, please?"

"Of course." He opened the door behind him and called to Daisy.

"I've some bags to fetch. Take care of my mother, will you?"

Almost at once he joined her and took two of the cases from her.

"Rather exciting, isn't it?" he said with satisfaction in his voice.

"Yes. I shall begin to enjoy it in a minute. I've been rather worried about Mother. She doesn't seem well."

"We've got her lying down on the couch. We're all going to have some tea."

"What time is it?" She was surprised at herself for not having wondered that before.

"One o'clock, just about."

"How awful! Hours to go yet."

Only Daisy was with Alice. Lionel, she explained, was still in one of the houses which had caught fire. The bomb had burnt through the roof, but he and the owner had succeeded in putting it out. The owner's principal fear had been lest the fire-brigade should get wind of it and turn on a hose. The water, he said, would do far more damage to his furniture than the incendiary.

"Your mother is feeling rather shocked, dear," Daisy said compassionately. "I've tucked her up in blankets on the couch and I'm going to give her a cup of hot, sweet tea. That's the treatment for shock, you know. Stay with her, dear, while I see if the kettle has boiled."

Alice appeared to have gone to sleep again. Elizabeth leant over her, puzzled and alarmed. She looked so flushed—perhaps she was sickening for something, had a temperature? Again she was aware of that odd, familiar, unnameable smell. It was almost like . . . But of course it couldn't be that. What nonsense!

"Wake up, Mother!" She shook her gently. "Mrs. Cathcart's bringing you a cup of tea."

Alice opened her eyes. In the bright light of the Cathcarts' sitting-room, Elizabeth saw that she was squinting horribly.

"Let me alone," she articulated very slowly and thickly. "I'm tired. I don't care if there's a raid or if there isn't." She made a gesture that was meant to be emphatic and sweeping, but she seemed to have no control over her arm and it fell limply at her side. "I want to go to sleep." Her eyes closed.

Elizabeth realised that her mother was drunk. It was one of the most unpleasant moments of her life.

Daisy bustled in with Owen behind her, carrying the tea-tray. "There! I think we all deserve this. How does your mother . . ."

"I think it would really be kinder to let her sleep," Elizabeth interrupted quickly. "She seems absolutely . . . exhausted."

"Well, it's a dreadful thing to be roused up in the middle of the night and turned out of the house like that," Daisy said sympathetically. "I'm sure I should feel the same." This was not true, and they both knew it, but Elizabeth was grateful for the lie.

"I think I ought to write a note for my father and stick it on the front door," she said, sipping her tea. "He might come back to make sure we were safe and find us disappeared."

"I'll take it across for you," Owen volunteered.

She smiled at him. "No, you won't, thank you. I don't want you blown up and on my conscience. I'll go myself in a minute."

I ought to get her back and into bed before Father sees her, she thought unhappily. He mustn't ever know. But supposing it happens again? She wondered then, for the first time, whether it had happened before. Oh, poor Mother! She must have been so much more frightened than they realised.

"Cigarette?" Owen asked her.

"I'm pining for one. Thank you. Bad luck we weren't on duty tonight!"

"Yes." He grinned. "I've always wanted to beat the lid of a dustbin and wake everybody up—"

"Who was on?"

"Mr. and Mrs. George." His tone was scornful. "They forgot all about rousing people. All they did was fool about with the ladder, trying to get on the roof of No. 12, and by the time they got up there the bomb had burned its way through. That's where Father is now."

"You three were all on the spot pretty quickly."

"I hadn't been to bed. I woke the others up."

"I wasn't asleep, I'm afraid," Daisy apologised. "Such a noisy night! There are several other fires quite near, you know."

"I wish Father would come back." Elizabeth felt suddenly restless. "I'm going to write that note now."

"Owen, give Miss Simpson a piece of paper."

"Oh, please call me Elizabeth. After tonight—we do know each other fairly well, don't we?"

"Of course, dear, I should like to."

That was the pleasant side of the war, Daisy reflected happily. Everyone was so neighbourly and friendly. Poor Mrs. Simpson! Her daughter was quite right—she seemed absolutely exhausted.

"I want to see what's happening at the garage," Owen said. "I'm going to have a look."

"Must you?" Daisy pleaded.

"Don't be silly, darling. The firemen won't let me go near enough for it to be dangerous."

"But the raid's still on. And people always say they're attracted to fires." She spoke as though the German 'planes were a rather obscene kind of moth.

"I'll only just dash there and back."

"Don't go, Owen," Elizabeth broke in suddenly. "Someone's sure to let us know when the fire's under control. I think it would be taking rather a silly, unnecessary risk."

He was surprised at her concern and absurdly gratified. When his mother seconded her eagerly, he allowed himself to be persuaded.

"I've heard nineteen bombs tonight," he said proudly. "That's not counting our own bread-basket. I suppose that wouldn't be much of a score for the East End, but it's a devil of a lot for Saffron Park."

"Sixty-eight incidents in one night is the record for the borough up to date," Elizabeth contributed. "That was back in October."

"The night our bedroom windows went," Daisy remembered.

"We were lucky. We only lost one pane, in the bathroom. Blast is a queer thing."

They talked about blast and its vagaries for some while. It was oddly soothing to make an academic subject of a danger which threatened them so nearly. Presently Lionel returned. He was pleased with himself and in an excellent humour. About Alice he showed genuine concern; Alice admired him and he knew it; but it seemed to Elizabeth, taut with apprehension, that he looked at her mother with a puzzled and surprised expression. She slept on very heavily. They were no longer even bothering to keep their voices lowered.

In his father's presence Owen stopped talking. Presently he slipped out of the room and when he returned a few minutes later he made a surreptitious thumbs-up sign to Elizabeth. She interpreted that to mean that the fire was now under control. The note she had written for her father had disappeared. Owen must have taken it when he went out. While she was still wondering whether it would be worse to rouse her mother to come home or for Henry to find her as she was, the All Clear sounded. It was only an hour since they had left the house.

She stood up.

"I must wake my mother now. You'll want to get some sleep yourselves."

"But the petrol—the explosion!" Daisy protested.

Elizabeth glanced at Owen.

"That's all right now, Mother," he put in. "The fire's practically out."

"What a relief! But don't you think you ought to let your mother sleep on, dear? She seems quite comfortable here."

"I think I ought to take her home, thank you all the same. My father may come back at any moment."

Tactfully and courteously, the Cathcarts all became very busy in other parts of the house, leaving her alone to rouse her mother. It took quite a long time and longer still to make her understand that they were in the Cathcarts' house and now must leave it; But finally Elizabeth got her to her feet and to the door. There they were joined by Lionel. He took Alice's other arm and helped her very solicitously across the road and into her own room. Elizabeth tried to thank him but he would not let her finish.

"It may be the other way round tomorrow night. We've very likely got a time bomb in the garden at this moment. Yes, yes—I'll give my wife your message."

Elizabeth had only just succeeded in putting Alice back to bed when Henry returned. They exchanged brief outlines of the night's events.

"I shouldn't go in to see Mother now," Elizabeth finished. "She's quite tired out and half asleep already."

Even if she had to tell him the truth eventually, she thought, it would be needlessly cruel to do so now.

Getting into bed beside his wife, Lionel remarked:

"That woman was drunk."

"What woman? I don't know what you're talking about."

"Mrs. Simpson. Drunk as a lord. I felt sorry for the girl."

"Lionel! You can't mean what you're saying!"

He laughed. "It was plain as a pikestaff, my dear. She reeked of rum. You can't mistake that smell. Curious tipple for a secret drinker."

"Oh, Lionel, how terrible! Poor woman! And that poor daughter! You won't breathe a word of this to Owen, will you?" she asked anxiously.

"Of course not. It's no business of his. No business of ours, if it comes to that. But it's funny."

Tired though she was, Daisy lay awake for quite a long while, compassionately mourning for the Simpsons.

CHAPTER XV

IN THE MORNING Alice did not get up for breakfast. She had a hangover, although she did not recognise it by that name. Elizabeth brought her a cup of tea and lingered, wondering how to make sure that her mother remembered enough about the night's events not to make a fool of herself. Alice remembered very little. She said tentatively: "It was a terrible night," hoping that Elizabeth would enlarge on the subject.

Elizabeth sat at the dressing-table, making up her face. She could see her mother's reflection in the mirror and she watched it surreptitiously.

"Mrs. Cathcart was very kind," she said. "You ought to thank her—send her some flowers or something. She kept you resting on her sofa for a long while."

"I felt so faint," Alice murmured defensively.

"She said she thought you were suffering from shock," Elizabeth coached her. "They put out the garage fire quite quickly—it never reached the petrol. I took across our emergency suitcases with me, but I forgot to bring them back with me last night when the All Clear went. I expect Owen Cathcart will turn up with them some time this morning."

That was about as much as her mother could take in at the moment, she thought. She left her and joined her father at the breakfast table. They were both going to be late arriving at their work.

Over breakfast they discussed the raid. Henry told her about the missing boy.

"He never turned up. I spent about an hour with his father and his aunt. They were both pretty shocked, poor things. The house is badly blasted, too. I got Mrs. Brown to come along and put the aunt to bed. Not in her own bed, the ceiling was down in that room. I doubt very much if the boy is under the debris of the nursing home, but it looks as though he has met with some calamity."

"Perhaps he was scared and took shelter somewhere."

"I waited for several minutes after the All Clear had sounded."

"I'm sure you were very kind, darling." She patted his hand.

"That appears to be my only useful function as an Air Raid Warden," he said dryly. But he looked pleased.

Inevitably, the Underground line had been hit, but Elizabeth reached Soho Square eventually. Alex was there before her. Because he had been afraid for her he was rather short-tempered. Why hadn't she 'phoned the flat?

"I tried to. I couldn't get a connection. I was just as much worried about you."

"It was a hell of a night," he muttered. "They hit the block of flats next to ours. Lot of people trapped in a basement shelter. I've always sworn I'd never sleep in one."

"Alex, do you think these raids will ever end? I don't see any chance unless our defences become so strong that we can bring down a really big proportion every night. The winter's over now. Weather conditions are improving all the time."

"I don't see an end of any kind, just between ourselves. Not to the raids or the war. Though I suppose America will come in eventually."

"Oh—America! The Greeks are the only people with any guts, it seems to me. My father found a lovely quotation from Boswell's 'Life of Johnson'. He wrote it down for me. Listen: 'Rome, sir, had the panoply of power, but 'twas the Goths that did their fighting for them. When it came to saving their own precious hides, the Latins could move with the best of them; ask the Greeks; they had a word for it.'"

They both laughed and felt more cheerful. Elizabeth wished that she could confide in him about her mother—ask his advice; she felt helpless and at a loss how to deal with the situation; but it would be too disloyal. She wondered where her mother had hidden the rum and how often she had consoled herself with it before. It was easy to deduce why she had chosen that particular drink; Bob was the innocent cause of that. Bob was coming on leave again in a few weeks' time—he had written to say so. She pushed the thought away. There were other things nearer at hand to worry about.

One person, had she only known it, would at least have given Elizabeth sympathy about her mother—Daisy Cathcart. All that morning as Daisy went about the town, condoling with weary-eyed shop assistants, dropping in at the W.V.S. headquarters to undertake fresh service for the newly bombed-out, she thought about the Simpsons and wondered if she could do anything to help them. Perhaps if she could persuade Mrs. Simpson to join her in her work for the poor harmless people who were always so bewildered and (at first) so tractable, it might give her a fresh interest in life? This very day there was a great deal to be done. The empty houses requisitioned by the town council and furnished with a minimum of necessities had not provided accommodation enough for a whole street of families evacuated because of time bombs. New houses had been hastily opened up and must be provided with a temporary black-out before dusk. Owen had promised to help. But it was not likely, Daisy thought considerately, that Mrs. Simpson would be feeling well enough to join in any such activity today. Should she call to make enquiries how she was? It would have seemed the obvious thing to do, if Lionel had not opened her eyes to the real explanation of the poor thing's odd behaviour. Now she was afraid she would say something clumsy out of sheer embarrassment. But if she failed to call, would Mrs. Simpson guess the reason?

At noon this seemed to her a real problem. By one o'clock she had forgotten all about it.

For Lionel had come home. She had never before known him to leave the office at midday in all the years they had been married. He had looked so strange that at first she thought he must be ill, but he denied the suggestion almost angrily. No, he hadn't had any lunch; no, he didn't want any. He had gone into the little dressing-room which led off their bedroom, in which he kept a desk and easy chair, and shut the door behind him. She suspected that he had even locked it.

An hour later she summoned up courage to knock.

"Lionel, I'm going out now. I don't expect I shall be home before black-out. Is there anything you want?"

"Nothing," he called back impatiently.

"Shall I tell Norah to bring you some tea at four o'clock?"

"If I want anything I'll ask for it." He sounded preoccupied and uncompromising.

There was nothing more she could do. She set out on her task of charity with a heavy heart. Owen, who went with her, had not made any comment on his father's unexpected appearance. He was unusually tactful and sensitive for a boy of his age, she thought. She felt happier about him than she had done for some while. She was sure that he was happier. How useful and considerate he had been last night! It was obvious that he had been enjoying himself, too. Young men were very odd, even one's own sons.

At dinner that night Lionel appeared as usual. He was very silent, but there was nothing out of the way in that. Daisy talked too much, from nervousness, telling stories of the bombed-out families to which Lionel paid no attention and which Owen, although he did his best to help her out, had heard already. One of the time bombs had killed a woman outright, piercing the house and burying itself under the stairs where she had taken shelter. Her daughter beside her had suffered no more than a fractured arm. Her husband, in the kitchen, was entirely unhurt. Daisy had been painfully impressed by this man's quiet, almost apologetic demeanour. He seemed principally concerned to give no trouble—a tidy, self-respecting, thin man. There was something very pathetic in his faintly bewildered dignity. All his life he had been independent. Now strangers, kind, well-meaning, irritating strangers, surrounded him with clumsy sympathy and lent him soap, a pocket handkerchief, another man's pyjamas.

When the Alert sounded that evening, Daisy sighed.

"Not three bad raids in succession! I shall go to bed when I've heard the news at nine o'clock. I really feel I'd sleep through anything tonight."

Lionel did not look up from his paper. The gloom surrounding him was almost palpable. But when Daisy kept her word and rose to go up to her room soon after nine, she ventured to address him directly.

"You won't be late either, will you, Lionel? We had so little sleep last night and you're on fire-watch tomorrow."

For a moment she was afraid that he was going to ignore her completely. Owen was watching him with a very queer expression. But he said at last, almost inaudibly and without looking at her:

"I'll be up soon!"

Tired as she was, she lay awake waiting for him, staring into the darkness, oppressed by a forewarning of disaster. It was very quiet outside. At ten o'clock she heard him come upstairs and go into his dressing-room. A few minutes later he opened the communicating door. Without turning on the light he groped his way across the room and climbed into bed beside her.

"Lionel," she whispered.

"Aren't you asleep yet?"

"No. I can't sleep. I'm worried about you. What's the matter?"

He stirred and she thought she heard him sigh. But his voice in the darkness was unexpectedly vigorous and dry.

"Plenty," he said.

"Is it business?"

"You might call it that."

"You've lost a lot of money? Tell me, Lionel, *please*. I'm not a silly woman about that sort of thing. I shan't make a fuss."

"You're not going to like this. But I suppose you'll have to know eventually. I've been charged with a technical offence against one of these damned wartime restrictions. I've got to appear before a magistrate. I'll probably be fined several hundred pounds."

"Oh, Lionel! And can't you pay?"

"I can pay all right. It isn't that. It's what will happen afterwards."

"What will happen?"

"Oh Lord, it's difficult to explain it simply enough for you to understand. I tell you, it's just a technicality. The only way I can get any timber now is by government licence and I'm supposed to use the largest percentage of that for contracted stuff, like bunks. Well, I didn't use the full amount, that's all. I sold some of it. Damn it, I'd paid for the bloody stuff."

"It doesn't sound so terribly serious," Daisy said timidly and hopefully.

"That's not the whole of it. It means I shall have my licence taken away. I shan't be able to get any more timber while the war lasts. It's the end of the firm. We're smashed."

"Smashed! Do you mean we shan't have any money at all?"

He laughed, and something in the sound made Daisy realise for the first time that what he had done was calculated and unscrupulous, a part of his whole attitude to the war, his creed of primary self-interest. He had cheated and lied and on this occasion he had been found out. But it was only a temporary set-back. He was far too clever to suffer as foolish, honest men might suffer.

"I've not let every opportunity slip, my dear. There are more kinds of business than one. We're not yet quite on the rocks. But this case isn't going to be a help. It's a lucky thing people don't read their papers very carefully."

"The papers!" Daisy gasped. "You don't mean it will be in the papers?"

"Bound to be. I can see the headlines now—'Black Market in Timber'." He laughed again, ironically. "That's the pretty name they give everything now, though they all know damn' well that nobody can stay in business who doesn't buy and sell at the back door."

Daisy did not answer and her silence seemed to irk him.

"There's no need for you to be so upset about it. It's I who've got to stand the racket."

"But if it's in the papers," she whispered, "all that about . . . the Black Market, Owen will see it. All our friends will see it. What will they think?"

"Let them think what they bloody well like," he said aggressively. But she knew from his voice that he would mind a great deal. "As for Owen—I don't want any criticism from him. He's been glad enough to spend the money I earn—he's never taken any interest before in where it came from. I'm not ashamed of what I've done—so get that clear in your mind! It's no worse than hundreds—thousands—of other men are doing every day, and getting away with it. What sticks in my gullet is that it's come out. And not through my own books, but just because some snivelling, long-nosed busybody had to talk."

Everything he said made it worse. She listened to him with increasing horror. If he had been unhappy, conscience-stricken, apprehensive, she would have closed the door on all her personal scruples and standards of conduct in order to comfort and reassure him. But how could she console him for the ignominy of being found out? They stood on opposite sides of a frontier. They did not even speak the same language.

"Well, that's enough about it now." He had lost his earlier gloom in irritation. "I don't want to discuss it again. I shall have plenty to think about and worry about in the next few days without having a nightly inquest into the bargain."

"I only want to ask you one more question: when does the case come up?"

"Monday week. I shall plead guilty. That's my solicitor's advice. You'd better tell Owen before he reads about it in the papers, but warn him not to talk to me about it. No son of mine is going to tell me what I ought to do."

He turned over in bed and lay with his back to her, presenting, as it were, his most obstinate angle—broad, thickened shoulders and bull neck. Daisy did not answer him, but inwardly she cried out:

"He's not your son! Thank God, he's not your son!"

CHAPTER XVI

IN SPITE OF the fact that things in general were going better for them, Elizabeth and Alex had begun to quarrel. The surprising thing was, perhaps, that they had quarrelled so seldom hitherto. Now there was less excuse. London was, for the moment, no longer the chief target for the Luftwaffe. Londoners caught up with their sleep, their nerves relaxed, they even ceased to imagine they heard the siren every time a car changed gear. Elizabeth and Alex could spend almost every evening together. Yet they quarrelled.

Always under the surface of their relationship there had existed a latent hostility; now, every day, it pushed itself a little further upwards. They loved each other, but they loved themselves more. Elizabeth never quite forgot that she had sacrificed certain things she deeply craved—security, children, all that could be summed up in the word legitimacy; Alex never quite forgave her for the sacrifice. In the past this had not mattered enough to outweigh all the rest, but now it seemed to matter a great deal. Elizabeth thought that it was Alex's fault. He was so restless, on edge and quick to take offence—particularly after he had gone home for the week-end. She decided privately that Naomi must be proving more than usually tiresome. But she wouldn't be sympathetic with him about Naomi.

He went down to Lampton the last week-end in March. He came back midday on Monday. Elizabeth found him in his office when she returned after lunching with Joan. It was apparent at a glance that he was in a bad mood and she did not feel prepared to deal with it. She was depressed herself because Joan had just told her that she was leaving almost at once. She had already volunteered to join the Wrens and her parents wanted her to live at home until her call-up. They were suddenly terrified of losing their remaining child in an air raid.

"But I won't go until you've found someone to take over from me," Joan had said. "I can't let old Roly-Poly down, in spite of his silly little ways. He'd better leave me to choose my own successor. I shall know who'll suit him far better than he will."

"She must suit me too," Elizabeth had sighed.

"That won't be so easy to find. You're much more discriminating."

It had been evident from the day of her return that Joan did not intend to embarrass or sadden her colleagues by a display of grief over her loss. Nevertheless, she had subtly but unmistakably changed since her brother's death. She had grown up. Watching her, Elizabeth knew a pain that was half maternal. She had often found her irritating, but she had come to love her too. Compassion for Joan, regret at parting with her, made her feel annoyed at the sight of Alex scowling at the correspondence on his desk. He should have a better sense of proportion.

"You ought to have wired or 'phoned me about this cable," he said immediately, without greeting her.

"It hadn't arrived when I left the office on Saturday."

"Oh. Well, I suppose you couldn't then," he admitted grudgingly. "Take a cable now. Please," he added as an afterthought.

That he was business-like seemed to her entirely correct, but she did not see any reason why he should be brusque. Throughout the afternoon they were cool with each other. An onlooker might have placed them as an employer dissatisfied with his employee, an employee only waiting for an opportunity to change her job. Childishly, they were both of them more than usually cordial to everyone else in the office. They were neither of them feeling at all happy.

As usual, at the end of the day everyone left earlier than they. With the exchange of the last "Good night", a different constraint fell on them. They were alone, and the atmosphere surrounding them must now be formally recognised. Tension must relax into emotion—anger or regret.

Elizabeth lingered for unnecessary minutes in her room, covering up her typewriter, tidying first her own and then Joan's desk of a litter of pencils, rubbers and paper-clips. Carefully and deliberately she made up her face, from force of habit more than any conscious wish to improve her looks. Only when there was nothing else at all that could detain her did she cross the passage into Alex's room.

He was still sitting at his desk where she had left him. He sat with his elbows resting on it, pressing his finger-tips against his eyelids, as if his eyes were tired and over-strained. It was difficult to feel aggrieved with anyone who seemed so weary and dispirited. She took a cigarette from the box before her, lit it with her own lighter and sat down in the arm-chair.

After a moment he sighed, leant back and lit a cigarette himself. But he did not look at her.

"Well?" she said at last.

"Well what?"

"Are you feeling any better now?"

"I suppose you mean better-tempered. I feel as if I'd like to cut my throat, to be explicit."

"But why? What's different about today?"

"I've felt it before, if you want to know. It's slightly accentuated today, that's all."

"Plenty of people feel suicidal at the moment," she said shortly. "Fortunately we're not Hungarians or Japanese."

"No, I've certainly no intention of actually cutting my throat. But I shouldn't cold-shoulder a nice little H.E."

"Alex! Don't be so . . . theatrical," she said almost roughly. "What's the matter with you? Not only today—for weeks past? You've been different ever since Christmas."

He looked at her with an expression she could not define and slowly stubbed out his cigarette. Then he walked across the room and stood in front of her.

"Stand up."

Astonished, almost frightened, she obeyed. He sat down in her place.

"Now sit down again."

"I won't. You're being childish."

"Please sit down again."

She visualised herself perched primly and protestingly on his knee, and against her will the picture made her smile. Having smiled, it was easy to sit down, to allow herself to be drawn into the depth of the chair, with her head resting on his shoulder. "Better?" he asked.

"You've got it wrong. In all right-minded films the hero says 'Happy?' and the heroine just purrs ecstatically. I'm not so docile. I won't be fobbed off with an arm-chair for two."

"But you'll admit it's more comfortable?"

"I'll admit nothing." She twisted her head until she could see his face. "You're a slippery customer, aren't you? I love you, but I think you're slippery."

"Don't you love me for my faults?"

"No. I know I ought to, according to the text-books, but I don't. I love you for your virtues and your graces. If you develop a lot of new faults, I'll love you less."

"You're hard," he said. He was not joking.

"I've always told you so. People are like sweets—hard, with soft centres, or soft, with hard centres. I'm the latter kind."

"You're not even soft outside. You're rather a horrid girl, as a matter of fact."

"You're not much of a man yourself. This is a silly conversation, isn't it?"

"It's better than the one we were having before."

"It's the same one, in different words. Tell me what's the matter. Tell me."

"Nothing's the matter."

"You're lying."

"Like this, nothing is the matter."

"'Like this!' That's the trouble with us now. We're only on completely easy terms when we're in bed together, or the equivalent. But I know you too well. Do you suppose I don't realise that there's something gnawing away at the back of your mind all the time?"

"There's nothing gnawing. Only time itself. Let's live by the day."

"Women aren't much good at that. Days become weeks, months years . . ."

He tightened hold on her and stopped her speaking. "Did you mean what you said—about only loving my virtues and graces?"

"Yes, I meant it, I think it's true, though it may not be. I love you in spite of your faults, not because of them. I prefer you to love me that way too."

"You wouldn't love me whatever I did—however I fell short of your estimation of me?"

"I don't think so." She spoke slowly and reflectively. "I don't think I'm big enough for that. I should hurt myself as much as you'd hurt me, but I wouldn't feel the same about you any more. I don't think I would. . . . But why are we talking about such a stupid thing? Are you working up to a confession? . . . trying to tell me that you want a change of secretary?"

"No, I don't want another secretary."

"Or another mistress?" She kept her tone light and even.

"Don't call yourself that!" he said violently. "I won't stand for it."

She laughed gently and dropped her head back on his shoulder. "Then that's the only thing that matters. If I come first and last in that capacity, the rest doesn't matter. Nothing matters. Not even the nameless crimes you may be going to commit. I'll forgive them all in advance."

She felt his lips on her forehead.

"Oh Lord," he murmured. "Oh Lord, oh Lord, oh Lord."

"Now what is it?" she whispered,

"Nothing. Nothing and everything. Let's go."

"I can't go back with you this evening. My mother's alone and I don't think it's good for her to be alone these days."

"You're talking nonsense," he said firmly. "You can't excite my animal passions and then walk out on me like that. Of course you're coming back."

There was a little further argument, but she gave in in the end.

As usual, they went to the Sherry Bar for a drink before dinner. Alex bought an. evening paper on the way and Elizabeth took it from him.

"Do you think there'll be a raid tonight?" she asked.

"I haven't any special hunch. Why should there be, any more than any other night?"

"I thought they might be cross with us for bombing those battleships at Brest."

"Yes, that was a good show. Here, give me one sheet! I want to see the news too."

"Wait a minute. I've found something most extraordinary. Read that paragraph."

"'Black Market in Timber . . . Lionel Cathcart, described as a company director, was today charged . . . resale of timber restricted to government use . . . fined five hundred pounds . . .' I don't see anything extraordinary about that. There are dozens of similar cases up before the courts every day."

"Yes, but it's my Cathcarts. Our neighbours at Saffron Park. Lionel Cathcart—it's not a very ordinary name and I know his business is to do with furniture. Oh, poor Mrs. Cathcart! And poor Owen."

"Who's Owen?"

"The son. I fire-watch with him. They're such nice people. They were so kind when we got turned out of our house the night the garage caught fire."

"Well, I'm afraid the magistrate didn't think that Lionel was particularly nice. I'm sick of these Black Market men. We ought to make an example of one or two particularly flagrant cases—stick 'em up against a wall and shoot 'em. They're worse than the looters—"

She was not listening to him.

"What does one do in a situation like this? Pretend one doesn't know anything about it, I suppose. How awkward, though! I hope there isn't an Alert next Sunday. It would be so difficult to talk to Owen all the evening and never mention anything to do with the law or profiteering or parents or the newspapers."

"You seem to cover a wide range of subjects as a rule. I want to know some more about this young man. You've kept very quiet about him."

"Oh, you needn't be jealous. He's only a boy—eighteen. Painfully shy and self-conscious until you get to know him, but really very pleasant and intelligent. I feel rather sorry for him, though I don't know exactly why. He's terribly shut in on himself—a complete introvert."

"Sounds most attractive. Here, finish your drink and I'll get you another."

When he came back to their table from the bar he asked, as though continuing a train of thought:

"How's Craven these days?"

"Quite well. He's coming on leave this week."

"Are you heavily dated up?"

"It depends on what you call heavily."

"Every lunch-hour? Every evening?"

"Not, not every one."

"Better be careful or he'll find another girl. There are plenty about, only too anxious to entertain lonely officers on leave; kinder, more accommodating girls."

"Are you advising me to be kinder and more accommodating?"

"Apparently you don't need to be. He likes to be treated rough."

"Don't sneer at him. You know it rubs me up the wrong way."

"I wasn't sneering at him. I rather admire him. He's dogged, at least."

"I've told you before—he's a much nicer person than either of us."

"I know—I know. Don't be so earnest, darling. Go ahead and brighten up his leave. I'm not objecting."

She found herself back, in her mind, in the hotel bedroom at Brighton. But that was something she didn't want to think about. Why must Alex harp on Bob? It filled her with a peculiar disquiet, just when she had been feeling happier than for weeks past. Once more she was aware of an irrational conviction that Alex *wanted* her to go out with Bob, that he took a perverse pleasure in subtly encouraging her to do so. It would be understandable if he had a bad conscience himself and sought a twisted means to ease it. But that implied another woman, and tonight she was surer than ever that none existed.

"Let's go and eat," she said abruptly. "I don't want to be home late."

Nevertheless, she was not home very early.

Lionel Cathcart, also, did not return to Wordsworth Road until long after his accustomed time. Late as he was, Daisy had sat up to speak to him. This was an act of courage which offset many smaller acts of cowardice. She was very much afraid of what he might say, a little afraid even of what he might do, but she could not bring herself to feign sleep and be the first of many who would cover up embarrassment by avoiding him. She did not think this consciously, but it was the motive behind her resolution.

Lionel did not look at all pleased to see her. He had been drinking, though he was not drunk. He was in a morose and truculent mood, aggrieved and resentful. A number of people had been sympathising with him on his bad luck, and the fact that they were people for whom he normally had a deep contempt (though not on moral grounds) had not prevented him from enjoying their sycophancy. But the part of his mind which was cold and shrewd, the very much larger proportion, was aware all the time that a crisis had come in his affairs, that he was faced with a difficult and even dangerous situation and that ahead of him lay months of anxious scheming and extremely hard work. The last thing he wanted now was a "scene" with Daisy.

"No need for you to have waited up," he grunted.

"I thought there might be something you wanted," she said timidly.

"Only to get to bed. I'm tired." He felt sorry for himself at the sound of the last two words and the whisky he had drunk nearly brought tears to his eyes.

"Was it . . . very terrible?" she asked, hardly above a whisper.

"Terrible? That's a damned silly word. I didn't enjoy it—who would? A smug, phara. . . pharasaical magistrate yapping away about things that had nothing to do with the case. I bet he does a bit on the side himself, if it comes to that. Did you see the papers?" he finished abruptly.

"Yes. Five hundred pounds. It's a lot of money, isn't it?"

"What's Owen got to say about it?"

It was the question she had been dreading and inevitably she hesitated. An expression of anger, almost of fury, came over Lionel's face.

"Thinks I'm not good enough for him now, does he?" he shouted. "That's just what I expected. That's the thanks I get for working all. these years to give him a good education and safeguard his future. A nice sissy you've brought him up to be! He's nothing better than a damned young prig."

"Lionel, hush!" she entreated in an agony of apprehension. (Supposing Owen heard him and came in?) "You're imagining things. He didn't say anything like that. Naturally he's upset . . . but he didn't say anything that . . . that you could have objected to. You can't expect either of us to feel happy about it."

The sadness in her voice penetrated his anger to the uneasiness that lay behind it. He was a sociable man, away from his own family. He had enjoyed his popularity among his fellows, the welcome that greeted him at week-ends on the golf course, the prestige he enjoyed in local circles as a good chap and a sound business man. All that was threatened, perhaps irretrievably. It was of less concern than the ruin of his business, but of far more concern than the comments of the magistrate.

"I'm going to bed," he said gruffly. "You ought to have gone there yourself, hours ago. I never wanted to drag it all up tonight. I'm sick and tired of the whole thing. Well, why don't you go?"

"I'm just going," she said hastily.

She tried to think of something conciliatory to finish with, but nothing occurred to her. For the first and last time in her life she wished that there were an air raid in progress. A heavy barrage or a stick of bombs would somehow have relieved the awkwardness of the occasion. But the sky was as empty and as quiet as it had been fifty years before. It provided no diversion. So Daisy went upstairs to bed, and surprisingly fell asleep before her husband joined her there.

CHAPTER XVII

DAISY HAD NOT summoned up courage to tell Owen about the charge against Lionel until the day the case was heard. She had persuaded herself that it would lessen the tension of the intervening days if Owen knew nothing of what lay ahead, and she had found that Lionel agreed with her. Owen realised well enough that something was "up", that his father was in a worse mood than usual and that his mother was expectant and on edge, but he guessed nowhere near the truth. He was no more interested in Lionel than Lionel was in him. There was no open antagonism between them but a complete absence of sympathy. Although he did not know it and would never know it, Owen was badly in need of the understanding and affection of the man who had begotten him, whom he very greatly resembled temperamentally. Only Daisy was aware of that, and she accepted the knowledge as part of her merited punishment. More was to come.

That Monday morning breakfast was apparently as usual. Lionel ate in silence and left for the office, Owen went to his tutor, Daisy shopped. Mother and son met again for lunch, and now, with a dry mouth, Daisy took the plunge.

"What are you doing this afternoon, dear?"

"Nothing particular. I thought I'd probably go to the flicks. Do you want me to do something for you?"

"No . . . well, yes . . . I mean, I want to talk to you. About something important—"

Something important, at eighteen, is something to do with oneself. Importance implies intimacy and intimacy implies the secret places of the heart, all one would conceal, the untellable. A number of wild and alarming ideas scurried through Owen's mind in the space of the next few seconds.

"What is it?" he asked, his mouth as dry as Daisy's.

"It's about your father."

"Oh." He was enormously relieved.

"He's been very worried lately."

"Yes, I thought he had."

"It's about business."

Immediately Owen decided, as his mother had done before him, that they were penniless, and his first thought, of which subsequently he felt ashamed, was that his own education was safely completed and that you didn't need any money to get into the R.A.F. After that, sheepishly, he thought of the effect upon her.

"Are we broke?"

"Not exactly. It doesn't seem so much the money . . . Oh dear, it's so difficult to explain. It's just a technicality, really. You see, your father's done something that's against the law and he has to go before a magistrate today and be charged."

"I told you that man was a plain-clothes policeman!"

"What man?" She stared at him in bewilderment.

"That man who came one night and asked you questions. Did you tell Father about that?"

"Well, no, dear, I didn't. I'm afraid I forgot all about it." This was a lie and they both knew it. "You don't think it made any difference, do you?"

"I shouldn't think so. What is the charge exactly?"

"It's something to do with timber. Your father bought some timber and then he sold some of it again, and apparently he ought not to have sold it, because the government meant him to use it on work for them. That's as nearly as I can understand it."

Owen whistled.

"That sounds pretty serious. They're awfully down on things like that. It's nothing more or less than a racket. Doesn't Father get his timber now by government licence?"

"Yes. That's just the trouble. He says they won't allow him to have any more. It's the end of the business."

"No wonder he's been jumpy lately."

He was taking it quite differently from how she had imagined, in an impersonal, emotionless way which revealed more clearly than any quarrels or disagreements could have done the extent of the chasm which divided him from Lionel. He seemed neither shocked nor surprised but as if he had anticipated something of the kind. It frightened her to realise that she understood her son as little as her husband.

"Owen, don't you *mind*?" she asked timidly.

"I mind for you," he said slowly, "and I mind the disgrace of it. It is a disgrace, you know—it will be in all the papers, too. But I can't feel really . . . involved. I mean, we've never really been a trio, have we? You and I—we're a pair—but Father's always been almost a stranger living with us. It sounds mean to say that now, when he's in a jam, but it's true, isn't it? And I don't think it's been our fault."

For one crazy, hysterical moment she had an impulse to confess everything—bring down her house about her ears, clear Owen of the stigma of relationship to a man he could neither love nor respect, proclaim defiantly the happiness she had enjoyed so briefly and repented of so long. What kept her silent was not fear for herself in Owen's judgment or dread of the effect of such revelation on his own self-respect; she kept silence out of loyalty to Lionel. The hand of society was against him, whether justly or unjustly was beside the point. At such a time, she could not follow up her first betrayal with a second.

"Perhaps every . . . estrangement from someone else is partly one's own fault," she murmured. And she knew that now she would never tell Owen the truth about his parentage.

"I dare say." But he was not interested. "What will happen now? What's Father going to do?"

"I don't know. He said to me, 'There are more kinds of business than one'. I don't know what he meant. I think—something he said gave me the impression—he's made a lot of money lately. He didn't seem to mind at all about the fine he'll have to pay."

Owen looked serious. He was beginning to feel worried. It occurred to him that his father must be pretty deeply involved in more than one illicit transaction. He had probably gone in for a bit of income-tax evasion, too. Where did all this sort of thing end up eventually? It was not pleasant to imagine his mother tagging along in the wake of a man whose every enterprise henceforward would be under the observation of the police. On how many more occasions would an officer in plain clothes call to make discreet enquiries? Already, in his mind, he saw her seeking refuge, with Aunt Susan and himself supporting her (well, partially) out of his R.A.F. pay. This business wouldn't help him when it came to trying for a commission, either. They always asked you what your father was.

Thinking of Aunt Susan made him think of all the Hammonds. They would see it in the papers, too. They wouldn't know what to say about it. Oh, hell! His mother would hate that and he wouldn't like it himself. Why couldn't Father be ordinary, like Mr. Simpson, for instance—a respectable solicitor and part-time air raid warden? Or did Mr. Simpson systematically defraud his clients? He didn't think so. He would be very much surprised to hear it, and he had not been surprised at all about his father. That was rather terrible, when you came to consider it. Most sons, nowadays, were friendly with their fathers. Why was it that they two had never travelled further than acquaintanceship?

Daisy was watching him. He looked stern, she thought, and very grown up—a young man, not a schoolboy any longer. For the first time, she was conscious of a feeling of feminine dependence on him; he seemed to understand it all much better than she did, to be anticipating and planning. The sensation was rather enjoyable to her.

"What are you thinking about?" she asked.

He roused himself. "Oh, lots of things. But nothing you need worry about. Did Father mention me, in all this?"

"He said he didn't want you to refer to it. You must be very careful, Owen. He'll resent it terribly if you seem at all critical."

"Oh, I shan't say anything to upset him. We've never had a straight talk about anything in our lives. We should neither of us know where to begin. It's funny, though—he knows I'm going into the R.A.F. and I'm his only child. You'd think, wouldn't you, that he'd want to do everything in his power to get the war won as quickly as possible, to increase my chances of coming through?"

To his horror, she covered her face with her hands and began to cry.

"Oh, don't say that! I hoped you wouldn't think of that. It's the thing I can't forgive him."

"Mother, darling! Don't take it so seriously!" He put his arms round her. "I wish to God I'd never said it. He's probably never seen it like that. I expect he quite honestly believes that the war will go all the better if private interests are allowed to carry on. He may even be right, for all I know."

But she was not to be so easily consoled. She knew better than Owen what Lionel thought about the war.

"Don't pay any attention to me, dear. I'm just overstrained. I've known about this for ten days now and I've been working myself up." She smiled at him and dabbed at her eyes with the handkerchief he gave her. "I don't know what time your father will be back this evening, but I expect he'll be late. I'd rather you didn't see him until the morning."

"All right, darling. I'll take my books to my room and do some work there after dinner." He hesitated. "Are you going to write and tell Aunt Susan?"

"I shall have to eventually. But not till I know how things stand. Presently, I want you to slip out and buy the late editions of the evening papers. I've been reading them very carefully lately. They always seem to put in bits about the cases that have come up in court during the day."

They read the account together at the same time that Elizabeth was reading it aloud to Alex. Alice Simpson also read it. She was enjoyably shocked and astonished. Who would have supposed that harmless, ordinary people like the Cathcarts could be mixed up in such a scandal? The mildly sentimental feeling she had had for Lionel Cathcart died immediately. She burned with curiosity to know if Daisy had been aware of her husband's nefarious doings. It seemed unlikely, on the whole. But that sly-looking boy must certainly have had a hand in it. She said as much to Henry, who disagreed very testily. He seemed quite upset about it, which was absurd. He had never liked Lionel Cathcart. Naturally one was sorry for Mrs. Cathcart, but that was no reason for Henry to lose his temper. Thank goodness she would have a rest from his gloomy moods and Elizabeth's secretiveness and independence in a few days' time.

For Alice was at last going away to visit her Aunt Lucy in the country. Now that the worst of the raids was apparently over, Elizabeth had woken up to a realisation of all her mother had gone through and had persuaded Henry that she mustn't be allowed to stay in London any longer. Alice had put up a show of demur, but she had not risked protesting too much. She was greatly looking forward to telling all Aunt Lucy's friends about the horrors of the raids and what she had endured. If she could have been quite certain that these quiet nights would continue for another week or so, she would have liked to have waited to see Bob on his next leave, but that would be tempting Providence. As it was, she was leaving in two days' time. Elizabeth ought to have come home early, to help her with all there was to do—especially as Henry went on duty at eight o'clock. But Elizabeth, as so often, had rung up to say she would be late.

Nevertheless, Alice decided to go ahead with her packing alone. She could at least put some things in the bottom of her trunk which there would be no need to disturb again. She used the plural, but there was only one thing which she did not mean to be observed by other people. She went to the shelf above her built-in cupboard to get it out. But the bottle of rum was gone.

She did not believe it at first. With unsteady hands she searched every corner, recklessly tumbling on to the floor the accumulated odds and ends of years. In the end she had cleared the cupboard completely. But she had not found the bottle.

What did it mean? Had someone—Henry or Elizabeth—found it and suspected, or had the search and the discovery come after the suspicion? She remembered the night of the garage lire. She had felt very queer that night. In the morning she had realised that she must have taken a little too much of her consoling tonic. Elizabeth had been with her—Henry had not seen her till the following evening. It must have been Elizabeth who had secretly ransacked her room and stolen her private possession. She saw in the looking-glass her face grow red with anger. How dared Elizabeth! She would make her feel sorry for that.

Or would she? It wasn't going to be a very easy thing to say outright. In fact, she could imagine no form of words which would not cause them both acute embarrassment. No, she could say nothing. Elizabeth had won without a fight. But she would never forgive her for it.

Coming home on the Underground, Elizabeth, too, was thinking of the theft she had committed. But her tired, uneasy reflections were constantly interrupted. She sat facing the sliding doors of the train and at every station, until the line moved out into the open, a peculiar section of other people's lives presented itself to her. Three-tiered sleeping bunks with wire mattresses which stretched between steel uprights had been erected along the length of the platforms and by now some of the ticket-holding occupiers had retired to bed. From modesty, or to shut out the glare of the lights overhead, a few of them had hung makeshift curtains round their bunks. Others lay with their backs turned to curious eyes, their heads almost covered by nondescript bedding, with curl-papers or a hair-net adding an occasional touch of oddly intimate domesticity. There was something rather touchingly dependent in these sleeping ones, for they were mostly young and had, Elizabeth imagined, hard work behind them and an early rising ahead. But the middle-aged and the old, women who had gossiped, arms akimbo, on their doorsteps, walrus-moustached men who had collected at street corners for companionship, these sat or stood in groups of two and three, eating, drinking and talking, unaggressively but consciously a community of their own. The passengers stared out at them, but the shelterers ignored their curiosity. It was the passengers who were intruders.

Up and down the platform, women in a gay uniform of green overall and scarlet bandeau walked with steaming enamel jugs of tea and trays of buns and chocolate. But the passengers could not buy, however thirsty or hungry they might be. From an hour determined by the black-out, the passengers were incidental, must stand waiting for their trains at the extreme edge of the platform, lonely and self-conscious figures on the fringe of other people's home lives. The white-faced children still awake whimpered or strained their eyes to read or darted with shrill cries from one group to the other. Their tired mothers slapped them, without effect. An argument broke out and someone quelled it. A Red Cross nurse was greeted with appreciative smiles. The doors slid open and slid to, and the train moved on.

Like many Londoners who habitually and defiantly slept in their own beds throughout the air raids, Elizabeth had a slight contempt for the Tube shelterers and needed to remind herself that many of them were homeless or had suffered damage to their nerves in proportion to the damage to their backgrounds. On behalf of stout hearts who clung to certain decencies and privacies at the risk of death in fourth-floor rooms or damp basements, she resented the colourful compassion of visiting journalists towards those less stout-hearted who had burrowed underground and left the warfare of the night to be conducted by the tougher souls who stayed at street level. Nor could she feel much sympathy for parents who preferred their children to exist in such conditions rather than evacuate them to the country. But even now, after seven months of intermittent bombing, the Londoners below or above ground remained commendably cheerful. That, after all, was the chief thing to be noted. The English had invincible good humour, a virtue not to be despised in time of war.

When the train moved out into the open, the carriage lights were dimmed to a faint, mysterious blue and the station platforms appeared deserted. Elizabeth could no longer find distraction from her thoughts about her mother.

She wondered if she had found out yet that the rum was gone. There had been no raids worth mentioning since the bad night of the 19th, so perhaps she had not had recourse to it. Her manner had been as usual—rather more affectionate, if anything, since Elizabeth had urged, her to take a holiday away from London. Elizabeth felt guilty, remembering that. She and her father, so immersed in their inward, private lives, had shown themselves peculiarly callous to the person who had shared their outward lives most closely. Physical courage had become very important in the last few months; or perhaps, more accurately, it was its assumption which was important. But to have an ugly weakness was no worse than to have an ugly face. Both she and Henry, at the back of their minds, had known that Alice was afraid. The idea had offended something in them and they had deliberately pushed it away. Bob, in his mistaken kindness, had been wiser than they.

Elizabeth had sought and removed the bottle of rum on impulse, a rather cowardly impulse. There had been three alternatives: to do nothing, to confront her mother or to enlist her father's aid. The first had seemed to her too negligent, the second too painful, the third too damaging to all their lives. She had taken the easiest course. She was not at all sure that it had been the best one.

When she reached home that night her mother had gone to her room, but there was a light showing under her door. Elizabeth knocked and, although she received no answer, went in. Alice was lying in bed, but she was not reading. Her trunk stood open in the middle of the floor, surrounded by a miscellany of objects. She looked at her daughter unsmilingly and without returning her greeting.

"I'm sorry I'm so late," Elizabeth apologised. "I went home with Joan and we got talking."

"It didn't matter," Alice said dryly.

"I see you've begun your packing."

"Yes."

There was no need to say any more. Both of them understood perfectly. A feeling of chill, almost of fear, invaded Elizabeth's heart. The open trunk was like the coffin of something which had died and would not come to life again however desperately one worked its limbs. Reluctantly, compelling herself, she crossed to the bed, bent down and touched her mother's cheek with her own.

"Well, good night. You must be tired."

"Good night."

The door closed between them. Saddest of all, they neither of them wept.

CHAPTER XVIII

ON THE NIGHT of April 16th Elizabeth felt glad that her mother had gone away. When her father had left for the Post, she decided to use the excuse of being alone in the house to visit the Cathcarts. She had been waiting for the past fortnight for the opportunity to make some such gesture of friendliness.

Owen opened the door to her. He looked surprised to see her but pleased. Preceding him into the sitting-room, Elizabeth received the impression that they had all three been sitting in silence, Owen reading (his book lay face down on the arm of his chair), Mr. Cathcart working on some papers, Mrs. Cathcart darning socks. Lionel greeted her with his usual heartiness; he did not seem at all embarrassed. Daisy was obviously touched by her visit and called her "Elizabeth", squeezing her hand.

There was a jigsaw puzzle, half pieced together, spread out on a table and Elizabeth accepted an invitation to continue with it. She was glad to occupy herself while she talked and it made a helpful and innocuous subject with which to fill in awkward pauses in the conversation. Domestic animals served the same purpose. She sometimes wondered if that were not one of the principal reasons why people kept them.

"You heard those bombs earlier, of course," Daisy said.

"Yes. Some way off, I thought."

"It's going to be a bad night, I'm afraid. Such a lot of 'planes ... they sound as if they were going over in a procession. Listen!"

"The most horrible noise in the world," Elizabeth said with conviction. "Except the bombs themselves, of course. Owen, have you got a picture of this puzzle?"

"I have, but you ought not to look at it," he grinned.

"I always cheat. Hand it over. I want to see where all these red bits go."

He came and stood beside her, helping her to sort the pieces. "The sky part is boring," he said. "I leave that to the end."

"There's that gun that sounds like tearing calico," Daisy went on. "Owen calls it Smee, after the pirate in 'Peter Pan'. And there's another one that sounds just like a door slamming in the sky. I always imagine it's St. Peter shutting the gates of Heaven in case any of the German bombers try to raid up there."

Owen and Elizabeth both laughed, and Owen murmured:

"You never told me that before, Mother. It's a nice idea."

Elizabeth remembered an evening in October when she and Alex had ridden in a taxi, making up silly rhymes about the anti-aircraft guns. They had been happy that night, in spite of the war. But some quality had gone from their relationship since then. She realised it more clearly than ever by comparison.

"What was the news at nine o'clock?" she asked. "I didn't listen."

Lionel joined in the conversation for the first time since he had greeted her.

"Not very cheerful. Things look bad in Libya and worse still in Greece. We've made a big mistake, throwing troops away in Greece. We'll only have to stage another of our celebrated evacuations."

"Oh, but we couldn't just abandon the Greeks!" Elizabeth protested. "We should never have been able to hold up our heads again."

"You can't win a war by making gestures," Lionel said dryly. "The trouble with this government is that it has no clear coordinated plan. Everything we do is just a makeshift, an improvisation."

"I don't see how we can do anything else at the moment. If you're caught as unprepared as we were, you have just to stave off the enemy where and how you can and play for time."

"You seem quite sure that time is on our side, Miss Simpson," Lionel smiled.

"Well, I am," Elizabeth said stoutly. "Plus other things too, of course. Something's got to be on our side."

Even if it's only poor old God, she added inwardly; though He doesn't seem to be having much success lately.

"Ah, that's the feminine point of view. You're like my wife. I'm afraid I'm more realistic. I don't see any hope for us except in a negotiated peace with Germany. Otherwise, the best that can happen is a long war of attrition ending with the complete economic collapse of both sides."

"A negotiated peace! For how long? No, thanks. I'd rather have this every night." She jerked her head towards the ceiling.

"That's just what I say," Daisy supported her eagerly, "Let's get it over, once and for all, whatever the cost."

Lionel laughed and began gathering up his papers.

"Well, I'm afraid nothing we decide in this room will make a ha'p'orth of difference to the result either way."

"I don't agree with you. I think that what people like us decide in suburban sitting-rooms with Jerry chug-chugging overhead is going to make all the difference in the world."

"Perhaps you're right."

He sounded genial enough, but it was the rather patronising geniality of an adult towards a child and Elizabeth found it irritating. Her father was frequently critical of the conduct of the war, but his criticism was based on anxiety, fear for the survival of the ideals by which he lived and a wincing pain at the thought of one hour's unnecessary prolongation of the world's suffering. Lionel Cathcart was too glib in his omniscience. She thought it ill became a man who, in his fashion, had done his best to sabotage his own side, and she was glad when he added:

"You'll excuse me, won't you? I have a lot of work to do and I must take it upstairs to my study."

"I'm afraid I've driven you away from your fireside," she apologised insincerely.

"Not at all. I usually work up there—my wife will tell you. Good night—if I don't see you again."

"Good night."

Though Elizabeth's relief at his going was secretly shared by Daisy and Owen, the immediate effect was to throw a constraint on them. Each of them was thinking of the same thing and they each knew it. Infected by their embarrassment, humiliated by their humiliation, Elizabeth bent over the jigsaw puzzle.

"I believe there's a piece missing," she said. "It *must* be a certain shade of blue and there isn't any more of it left."

Owen strolled over again and stood beside her.

"There you are!" he announced after a moment, holding out the piece to her.

"Clever." She put out her hand to take it and then paused, arrested. "Listen!"

A high whistling noise passed overhead, a sound of extreme urgency.

"Shell," Owen said.

"No. Bomb."

The thud and tremor were confirmation. It was as if, Owen thought, somewhere in the bowels of the earth a giant had swung an enormous sledge-hammer upwards against the floor of the world above him; as if the forces of darkness were joining in, synchronising their blows with the crash of each descending bomb, widening each man-made flaw in the earth's surface. People said lightly: "It was one of those nights when all hell was let loose." But supposing, Owen wondered, hell should really get loose—the demons of hell streaming up through the cracks which mankind had blasted for them, released by the power of evil which directed bombing raids? The fancy pleased him, but he did not put it into words.

"I'll have that piece now," Elizabeth said composedly.

Daisy laughed. "Oh, dear. I think I'll make some tea."

All over London that night women sighed and said: "I think I'll make some tea." Other people lit cigarettes, a fresh cigarette from the butt of the last one. Blacked-out rooms grew hazy with the smoke of cigarettes. For there was no doubt that it was unpleasant to sit waiting for the bomber overhead to release his load, and most unpleasant of all for those who had already experienced a near miss. The closer one's experience of bombs, the less one liked them. Since neither Elizabeth nor the Cathcarts had actually suffered the terror of sudden darkness, crumbling walls and burial alive, their calm, though creditable, was not unduly so. Secretly, like the majority, they believed in their hearts (but would not dare to say) that bombs were things that fell on other people. At the sound of one approaching, their conviction wavered but quickly reasserted itself when the immediate danger passed. Combined with the feeling that it would be flattering to Hitler to appear over-concerned, it was easy to light yet one more cigarette with a steady hand, pick up the dropped stitch, count the tricks and find the missing piece in the jigsaw puzzle. In any case supposing, just supposing, that the next bomb was meant for you—well, it was meant. Then and not before. Why die before you must?

"I'll make the tea," Owen said. He went out of the room.

Immediately Daisy's manner changed. She glanced at Elizabeth with an oddly timid, enquiring look.

"It was kind of you to come," she said.

"It's kind of you to let me spend the evening," Elizabeth answered, deliberately misunderstanding her. "I don't like being alone in raids."

"Oh, you don't have to pretend that you came because of the raid. I appreciate it very much, dear. Some people have been very hurtful. Mrs. Bennett cut me, coming out of church. I don't blame her. Her son was killed, you know."

"Don't you think you're imagining things?" Elizabeth abandoned her subterfuge. "People are embarrassed by . . . anything like that. They don't know quite how to behave."

Daisy shook her head.

"It isn't only that. I'm not defending Lionel; he did wrong; but you should search your own heart before you judge others. It isn't fair to Owen. After all, he might be killed too." She spoke with great dignity. "But good comes out of evil. He went to church with me the Sunday after. Usually I can't persuade him. It was to give me countenance, I know."

"Owen's growing up," Elizabeth said. She felt touched and amused.

"You've noticed that too? He likes you so much, you know."

"Does he?" She was surprised. "I like him too. But I used to be rather afraid of him. He seemed such a stern, disapproving young man."

"Oh, no!" Daisy laughed. "I expect he was shy. But we mustn't let him catch us talking about him—he wouldn't care for that at all. Tell me about your mother, dear. Is she liking it in the country?"

She made only one more reference to the subject before Owen came back with the tea-tray. She said:

"Don't think because Lionel doesn't show it that he's not upset. He feels it very much."

But she was not sure herself if what he felt were regret at wrong-doing or at its publication only.

Elizabeth stayed with the Cathcarts till eleven o'clock. But though, once in bed, she went to sleep quickly and heard no more of it, the raid went on all night.

In the morning she caught a train to Oxford Circus. She had meant to do some shopping in one of the big stores before going into the office, but when she came up the steps into the open, one glance was enough to show her that the shop had been too badly blasted to do any business that day. An abnormal, rather terrifying quiet brooded over Oxford Street east of the Circus, a quiet broken only by the tinkle and crunch of shattered glass. Every few yards there was a gap in the façade of buildings either side, and of those which remained not one seemed to have escaped damage. The road blocks had been heaved up into undulating mounds, forcing her to pick her way gingerly and erratically, slowing down her impulse to hurry, hurry, and find out the worst. This time Soho Square could not possibly have escaped. She would look across it, beyond the shabby little garden in its centre, and where the office had stood there would be a blank.

Very few people were about as yet and those who were had a strained, stunned look. Perhaps that was how she looked herself. Already it was an effort to remember what some of the shops had been. Bombed, blasted, burnt out—they had all become anonymous in their misfortune. Only here and there a display of muddy, soaked dresses clung limply and incongruously to their stands, no longer protected, no longer needing protection from the passer-by. A menu still hung on the lintel of a door which framed only rubble. Heavy shutters had been wrenched off and curtains blown into the street. Outside the least damaged buildings, commissionaires and assistants armed with brooms and shovels were clearing the pavement of an indescribable litter of glass and window fittings. The acrid smell of dust and charred wood filled the air.

A little way further on, she came to a road barricade. Beyond it firemen were still at work, playing their hoses on smouldering buildings either side of the road. A small group of people stood at the barricade, forlornly staring at the wreckage of their livelihoods. One girl was crying, soundlessly, the tears slowly running down her face unchecked. Perhaps she was not even aware of them. Elizabeth realised that she could go no further that way. She turned down a side street, and now she began almost to run.

Suddenly she heard her name called: "Elizabeth!" She looked round and saw Joan waving as she ran to catch her up. They linked arms, breathless, laughing with relief and pleasure.

"What's the betting that the office is still there?" Joan demanded. "I refuse to believe that it could disappear two days before I leave it for good. Come on!"

They were round the corner and in the square. Dust lay thickly on the tassels of the plane-trees in the garden and broken glass was strewn along one pavement. Nothing else was changed at all.

"It's positively uncanny," Joan said almost reproachfully. "We've got two churches and a hospital and *still* we don't get hit."

When Carter arrived he had a list of casualties to report, whether authentic or rumoured remained to be seen—Piccadilly and Jermyn Street again, one corner of Leicester Square, a store in Holborn, the Shaftesbury Theatre. . . .

"We can check up on the Shaftesbury and Leicester Square at lunch-time," Joan said. "Oh Lord, I'm getting sick of horror and destruction. I'd better send a wire home. They'll worry."

"You'll probably arrive there on Saturday before the wire does."

Elizabeth reflected rather bitterly that her own mother would be very much surprised to receive a telegram assuring her of her daughter's well-being.

"Your boss is late," Joan remarked idly. "I hope he's only overslept. I'm beginning to get quite fond of him on the eve of my departure."

"I expect he's all right," Elizabeth said placidly.

She knew that he was, for she had telephoned him before leaving that morning.

It was the day that Bob was due to start his leave. He had arranged to collect her from the office for lunch, but he had not arrived by two o'clock. It looked as though there had been damage done to the railway line in the night. Elizabeth left a message with Miss Lewis in case he should turn up and went out to get something to eat quickly in a Milk Bar.

Yes, they had hit the Shaftesbury Theatre sure enough. But it had been empty a long while. Far worse, was the fact that they had also hit the large blocks of tenement flats behind it. An enormous pile of debris, many feet high, made a funeral pyre for untold numbers. Underneath it were the brick and concrete surface shelters where some of the inhabitants had probably sought refuge. Firemen were still playing their hoses on the smouldering dust-heap and rescue party men, with the apparent aimlessness which characterised their kind, were picking their way delicately over the rubble, working in what seemed a desultory and uninterested manner. There was surely very little hope that anyone beneath could still be living.

Elizabeth remembered a pale, sickly child who had sat forlornly, unattended, in a push-cart outside one of the tenement blocks each time she happened to go past. She found that she was crying for this child and she went back to the office without having eaten any lunch after all.

Bob turned up at four o'clock. She found him sitting in the waiting-room when she came away from taking Alex's dictation. He was talking to Miss Lewis at the switch-board, about the raid, of course, and the damage it had done. He jumped up when Elizabeth appeared and grinned with relief and pleasure at seeing her.

"Terribly sorry I couldn't make lunch. My train ran over three hours late."

"I guessed that was what had happened. What are you going to do with yourself now? I shan't get away from here for another two hours."

"Oh, I'll go to a news reel, perhaps, or just walk about and look at the mess. I'll come back here sharp at six o'clock."

"No, don't do that. I'll meet you somewhere. The Café Royal? Is that still there?"

"I haven't heard it isn't. All right. In the foyer." He saluted Miss Lewis, who had been listening to the conversation with sympathetic interest, and clattered down the stairs.

Elizabeth was glad that he and Alex had not met. She had an instinctive aversion to the idea. As a matter of fact, Alex had announced his intention of going to sleep till his letters were ready to be signed. He had been fire-watching on the roof of the flats the night before and was feeling very weary. As a spectacle it had been magnificent, he reported, but he did not want ever to spend such a night again. The intensity of the raid had driven from his mind the recollection that Bob's leave began to-day and Elizabeth had no intention of reminding him. She had made a resolve about Bob, and she did not mean to discuss it with Alex.

When she went in to say good night to him at six o'clock, he had fallen asleep again. It always touched her to see him sleeping. The weakness in his face softened to a more becoming look of childishness and dependence. She stood staring down at him for quite a long while, as if she were expecting some sign to be revealed to her, an answer to a question which she did not formulate. But there was no revelation and no answer. She closed the door behind her very gently and left him to wake and find himself alone.

Bob was awaiting her impatiently. He had already ordered cocktails of a peculiar potency, evidently having decided, she thought with a rather dreary amusement, that alcohol was his best means of approach. But she could not afford to get drunk this evening. It was important that she should find the right words in the right order.

That wasn't going to be easy. It was horrible to have to hurt Bob. She asked herself, as countless women had done before her, why she had not had the sense to fall in love with someone so obviously considerate, honourable and trustworthy; why she had put herself in bondage to a man who was not markedly any of these things? But it was a futile question. She knew perfectly well why she loved Alex rather than Bob: because they spoke the same language, saw the same jokes; because Alex reminded her of the little boy in dancing-class whom she had worshipped from afar and who, all unwittingly (where was he now?), had sentenced her for ever to admire a certain type of colouring and features; because chance had made her secretary to the one man and not the other; and finally because of some quite irrational element which it would be waste of time to try to analyse.

"You're looking tired," Bob said anxiously. "Did you have a terrible night?"

"No, thank you, Bob. Not terrible at all. But I suppose, sub-consciously, one feels the strain. I was probably more frightened than I realised."

"When I look at the results, I feel quite petrified. But I always hope my uniform would sustain me if I was actually in a bad raid."

"Yes, uniforms are very helpful," she agreed absently.

"Do you think there'll be another one tonight? I wanted you to come dancing with me. But I don't want to run you into any unnecessary risk. Not after the Café de Paris."

"Oh, I wouldn't mind. But I don't think you'll want . . . Bob, get me another drink. I've got to say something nasty to you."

"I'll have one too, then." His voice was suddenly grim. Neither of them spoke while he beckoned to the waiter and they waited for their drinks to come. But when they had exchanged a brief toast he prompted her:

"What is it?"

She spoke very slowly, looking at her glass and not at him. "Bob, I've made up my mind. You're wasting your time on me. It isn't fair. I've lied to you about a lot of things."

"What things?" He did not look at her either.

"I told you that there wasn't anybody else. It wasn't true. I've been in love with a man for years. I'm living with him as his mistress. And I shan't change."

There was a long pause. "Is that all?" he asked finally.

"That's all. I'm glad it's said. I ought to have told you long ago."

"Why didn't you?"

She answered with another question.

"Need I say that too?"

"Not if you don't want to. I don't suppose I'd understand in any case. I don't understand women."

"Don't blame other women on my account," she retorted quickly. "They're not all like me."

"Did you tell me this because you're going to marry him?"

"Oh no. He can't marry me. He has a wife and two children."

"But you went on writing," he said with sudden heat. "You went out with me on my leaves. You let me kiss you. I thought. . . . You always said you weren't in love with me, but I thought . . ."

He broke off and for one appalled moment she was afraid that he was going to burst into tears, but instead he emptied his glass in a gulp and lit a cigarette, forgetting to offer her one. "Well, I suppose I bought it," he added bitterly.

There was a certain amount of truth in that, but she could hardly assent to it. She felt helpless and inadequate, and more ashamed of herself than she had ever been in all the times she had deceived him. If this had been a draft leave, I should never have been able to tell him, she thought. She wanted to assure him that he would get over it and find a nicer girl with sense enough to love him; but it seemed too insulting a thing to say just now.

"I'm sorry, Bob." It was the best she could do.

"Yes, I expect you are. I expect you've tried to be decent and civilised about it. But I wish I'd never met you."

At his last words, unconsciously revengeful, Elizabeth felt a pique which filled her with self-contempt. For she was more honest with herself than she had been with him. He did well to wish that he had never met her; but she did not like to hear it said.

"I'm sorry," she repeated helplessly. "I'd better go now—"

She stood up and he got to his feet with automatic politeness but without trying to detain her. He looked so bewildered and at a loss that she welcomed the pain she felt for him because it seemed more just that she should suffer too.

"Bob, you won't cut quite adrift, will you?" she said impulsively. "I mean, you'll let me know if you go overseas or anything. I should hate not to hear."

"I don't know." He avoided meeting her eyes. "I haven't had time to think yet. I don't know."

She wondered how she was going to say good-bye—here, in the bar of the Café Royal, so publicly. She imagined him following her through the revolving doors, escorting her to the Tube station, watching her borne away on the escalator, mechanical and trivial parting. He had far better stay where he was.

"Don't come with me," she said. "I'd rather you didn't."

"All right." He looked at her directly for the first time and she saw a pleasant, nondescript young man with a small moustache and light brown eyes that were full of hurt surprise. "Good-bye."

"Good-bye, Bob. I didn't mean to be so beastly. No one ever means to be. One gets into a jam and takes it out on other people."

But it was too late now to explain all that. She turned away hurriedly and did not look back. Almost immediately she ceased to think of him purely as an individual. She was telling herself that Alex must never know about this. He would say something that might make her hate him. Whatever happened, Alex mustn't know.

CHAPTER XIX

THE TELEPHONE BELL rang very early in the Simpsons' house on Sunday morning. A woman's voice said:

"I want to speak to Miss Elizabeth Simpson."

"Speaking."

"This is Saffron Park Hospital. You are on our list of part-time nursing auxiliaries. Will you please report for duty immediately?" She rang off.

Elizabeth remembered the very loud explosion she had heard the evening before. It had sounded like something stupendous, perhaps a land-mine, a mile or two away. She roused her father, who for once had not been on duty, and he made her tea and toast while she hurriedly dressed. She ate and drank standing, struggling with a sick inclination to do neither. Henry 'phoned the Post.

"It was a land-mine," he said. "Casualties are very heavy. It hit a dance-hall and a crowded public-house. In God's name, why must people deliberately congregate at times like these?"

No 'bus was in sight, so Elizabeth set out to walk. She reached the hospital at half-past seven. Three other girls in the Civil Nursing Reserve arrived simultaneously. Slightly apprehensive but pleased to be made use of after months of dull, preliminary training, they waited for the matron to direct them to their posts.

The matron's pose was always to be self-possessed, calm and aloof, inspiring respect and awe. This morning, though she had been working all night and there was blood on her apron, she maintained her pose and its value became apparent. She dealt with Elizabeth first and sent her to report to the Women's Surgical Ward.

Near the door of the long ward, at the end where all the serious cases were always put, several beds had screens round them and an empty operation trolley was just being wheeled away; but the largest proportion of patients were of longer residence and it was these whom the Sister in charge told Elizabeth to attend to. Land-mines might fall and three hundred casualties require treatment of one kind or another, but the regular patients must have their breakfasts and the auxiliary nurses must see that they had them. The women all showed signs of strain, Elizabeth thought, but this did not prevent them from anxiously requesting that their eggs should be boiled the exact number of minutes they preferred, nor from eagerly identifying the particular pot of jam or marmalade which bore their name. They stared at Elizabeth with polite curiosity and asked her questions about the raid. She answered evasively but not too evasively, since obvious concealment seemed to her more frightening than the truth.

Presently, when breakfast had been served and cleared away, a nurse beckoned her over to one of the beds near the door, on which a woman had just been laid. She was an elderly woman with a blood-stained triangular bandage wound roughly round her head. Her eyes were closed and her face was extremely pale, but she groaned slightly and seemed semi-conscious.

"I want you to help me undress her," the nurse said.

The woman was wearing a nondescript skirt and too many woollen cardigans and jumpers. What colour there had been in these garments was now entirely lost under a thick coating of dust and grime. It dung to her blood-soaked collar and sleeve and matted her hair into a sinister paste—grey dust, black blood and the vivid stain of the bandage. The nurse was young and rather handsome in a slightly Malayan way, dark-eyed and olive-skinned, with flat cheek-bones. She seemed not so much ruffled by events as overcome by them and she worked gently but very slowly, trying to remove the layers of dirty clothing without disturbing the patient. It was Elizabeth who finally suggested that, since nothing she was wearing could ever be used again, it might be better to cut them off with scissors. After that, they both slashed away recklessly, Elizabeth with a certain guilty enjoyment. They cut, too, as much of the matted hair as showed beneath the bandage. Grit and rubble and fragments of glass fell out of her clothes into the clean white bed and her body beneath was stained with dust. But her feet were black with sheer uncleanliness—the nails uncut and curved grotesquely, the toes distorted with neglected corns and bunions. The nurse regarded them with distaste added to her air of faint helplessness, but she would not accept Elizabeth's offer to wash them for her.

Clean at last and in a flannel nightgown, the woman opened her eyes. She murmured something and Elizabeth bent down to hear.

"It was terrible, nurse. We were just sitting by the fire, my lodger and me. We were just talking about going up to bed. And then everything came down on our heads—the whole ceiling came down and buried us. I don't know what's happened to my lodger. And two beautiful cats I had—lovely cats, they were. I don't know what's happened to them."

There was more anxiety in her voice for the cats than for the lodger.

"You're all right now," Elizabeth said reassuringly. "Shut your eyes and go to sleep."

The nurse had disappeared and she looked round for someone else to give her orders. On the other side of the ward, beside a screened-off bed, another nurse with a determined little face and a brisk manner was shaving a patient's head. She caught Elizabeth's eye and Elizabeth went over to her.

"Want to look?" she said. "It's a fractured skull. I'm preparing her for operation."

Elizabeth saw the bone shattered like a tapped egg-shell. Something resembling a minute white flower bulb lay on the pillow.

"That's a bit of her brain," the little nurse said grimly.

She went on with her shaving, slowly, gingerly. The head on the pillow, plump and young and pretty in a buxom way, began to take on a grotesque likeness to a wax model in a shop window, waiting for the dresser to disguise its vacuity with a Spring hat.

"Not very nice, is it?" the nurse said.

She shot Elizabeth a glance of innocent malice, anticipating her revulsion. But Elizabeth did not give her the satisfaction of displaying any.

"Was she at the dance-hall?" she asked.

"Yes. Eighteen, she is. She won't live. At least, I hope not."

Sister Fuller came by and seized on Elizabeth with relief.

"Nurse, will you clean up the sluice? There are some draw-sheets to be washed and bowls to go in the steriliser."

Elizabeth scrubbed the draw-sheets, but the blood-stains still showed. She hung them out to dry on the verandah. The water in the steriliser wouldn't boil. A gas-main had been hit and the pressure was very low. A Probationer nurse, pleased to find someone to whom she was in a position of superiority, found a job to do to keep her company. The raid patients frightened her. One of them was dead already, she told Elizabeth, but they hadn't moved the body yet from behind the screens. There was a little girl in, too, with a shrapnel wound and internal haemorrhage. She had twice been a patient in the hospital before, suffering from pneumonia, and the surgeons wouldn't risk operating on her yet.

Somewhere about mid-morning (we shall be drinking coffee at this time tomorrow in the office, Elizabeth told herself incredulously), Humphreys, the nurse who had shaved the head of the girl with the fractured skull, commandeered her to help with the routine dressings. Elizabeth observed an odd distinction between the attitude of nurses to air-raid victims and to ordinary cases. It was as if the plight of the former had a more personal application. They themselves might be bombed, or their relations and friends, while there was an unspoken ruling among nurses to pretend that disease was something which afflicted only the curious race of people who came in as patients. They felt more kinship with the air-raid victims and showed less impatience. Though Humphreys was a good nurse and did her dressings competently and kindly. She was kind to Elizabeth too and answered her questions. This woman had had her breast removed and the tubes must be shortened; this old woman had to have a bladder wash-out; this girl was epileptic and had fallen on the fire—there was nothing to do for her but dab with yet more Gentian Violet the edges of the crinkled, blackish-purple crust that covered her from neck to thighs. Lying on her stomach under an electric cradle, she smiled in gratification at the interest she afforded. It was hard to believe that one day the loathsome film would peel away and leave her firm young body whole and unscarred beneath.

"You'd better start laying the lockers for dinner now, Nurse," Humphreys said at last.

But first Elizabeth stole a moment to put in hair-curlers for a pleasant, middle-aged woman recovering from an appendectomy, who confided cheerfully that she wanted to look nice for her husband and daughter when they came to visit her that afternoon. She had been terrified by the raid and wakeful most of the night because of the constant traffic in the ward, but it still seemed important to her that her back hair should not straggle. She seemed to Elizabeth to epitomise the healthy, egotistic *sang-froid* of the ordinary citizen.

Serving out dinners in the kitchen, Sister Fuller said amiably: "You can take forty-five minutes off for lunch, Nurse."

That meant the canteen. There wasn't time to go home. Eating beans on toast, she found that she was very tired and very hungry. She shared a table with two other emergency auxiliaries. They exchanged experiences, boasting of the horrors of their own particular ward. There were some bad cases on the Men's side, Elizabeth learned; most of those killed outright had been in the public-house. That was where the land-mine had actually fallen.

Back on the ward she found that the girl with the fractured skull had been returned from the theatre. Her poor shaved head was mercifully concealed now by snowy white bandages. She lay quite motionless and whatever was essential in her—soul, spirit, individuality—seemed very far away. Perhaps it would never come back.

Hers was the first bed by the door as one entered. In the third bed was the child with internal haemorrhage—conscious, not in any apparent pain, incredibly active. In the bed between lay something so terrible that one was frightened even to think about it.

It must be a woman, because this was a women's ward. A woman, then, a human being, like oneself; but she didn't look human. The eyes were covered; one of them, Elizabeth had been told, was gone. Bandages black with stale blood gave her head a mummified appearance. Her face was black too and made more ghastly by a coat of Gentian Violet. Her right arm also was heavily bandaged. She was nineteen years of age and had been to a dance.

No one had been behind those screens that morning but the Sister and the doctors. A young house surgeon who had been working all night had managed after an hour or more to insert the needle for a blood transfusion. He had had to cut down in three different places before succeeding, Nurse Humphreys told Elizabeth; the veins were so collapsed from shock. It was possible now that the girl might live. But would she thank them for saving her life, Elizabeth wondered?

Bed-pan round was done; it was the hour for visitors. The air-raid casualties had visitors as well.

A young man in khaki stood beside the second bed on the left. He stood and stared, making no comment. He was the brother, someone said. Presently he went away.

The little girl began to whimper when she saw her parents. She had not cried at all before. They were a young couple, quite unharmed themselves. They had evacuated her to the country but had not been able to resist the temptation to bring her home for just one week-end. She was the only child.

Sick at heart, Elizabeth sat on the edge of the bath and dropped her head in her hands. She was conscious of wanting nothing in the world as much as a cigarette. Normal life was more than a long way off; it no longer existed. This day had gone on for ever. Wearily she got to her feet again and began carbolising rubber sheets.

After the visitors left there was tea to serve. The Probationer nurse beckoned Elizabeth into the kitchen and gave her a cup out of the patients' pot and some bread and margarine. There was always a lot of surreptitious eating in the ward kitchens; nurses were invariably hungry, however adequately fed. When the time came for them to have their own tea, the tall, dark girl who had asked Elizabeth to help undress the woman with the head injury approached her again.

"Nurse, take my place for a little while. You've only got to make sure the blood is flowing properly and that she doesn't move that leg. And keep an eye on that child the other side of the screen—see she doesn't throw the bed-clothes off. She can have a sip of water every hour or so."

Elizabeth found herself behind the screens that flanked the second bed on the left. She felt extremely apprehensive and inadequate. It was frightening even to glance in passing at the poor, black featureless thing lying there. How could she take responsibility for such a tenuous thread of life? She looked at the blood in the glass container, slowly gathering to a drop, reluctantly falling, and then at the needle precariously thrust into the inert, scratched leg. It seemed a makeshift, oddly primitive arrangement—too obvious to be effective. Half hypnotised, she stared and stared, willing the blood to flow. It was as if it did not want to be the means of bringing life to anyone so far along the road which led away from life. But that was only stupid and fanciful. Remembering her duty, she laid her finger-tips on the unbandaged wrist. The pulse-beat was unexpectedly strong.

"Please, Nurse, can I have a drink of water?"

The little girl in the next bed was staring at her round the edge of the screen. Elizabeth turned and smiled, taking her ice-cold hand.

"Not just yet, darling."

"But, Nurse, I'm so thirsty."

"It isn't good for you. That's why you mustn't have it. What's your name?"

"Norah Jenkins."

"How old are you, Norah?"

"I'll be ten on September 4th. Please, Nurse, just a little sip!" She spoke very politely and reasonably, as though she had learned that those qualities took you further and that she must be careful not to antagonise the people who had her in their power.

"Presently, darling. What a dear little ring you're wearing! Was that a birthday present?"

"No, a Christmas present. From my mummy and daddy." She shifted fretfully, too weary for the strain of conversation, and Elizabeth pulled the blanket over her.

"Try not to move about too much, there's a good girl. You'll catch cold if you don't keep covered up."

"If I stay quiet, will you give me a drink?"

Desperately, Elizabeth looked at the ward clock.

"When it's half-past, you shall have just a sip. Lie still now."

She turned back to the quiet figure and the slowly dripping blood. Standing all these hours seemed unnecessarily exhausting, but pride would not let her ask to have a chair. If the professionals could stick it, so could she. She tried to keep her weight off her heels, from a vague recollection of hearing someone say that you were less likely to faint if you did. Suddenly her heart jumped. The figure on the bed was stirring—she shifted her legs and Elizabeth seized the ankle of the one in which the blood-transfusion needle was inserted. The black lips parted. An indistinct mumble came from between them. Elizabeth waited till she lay still again and then put her head round the end screen. She signalled to Sister Fuller, who was writing at her table.

"Sister, I think she's coming round."

Sister Fuller came over. She was a young woman, with a serene and pleasant face. From gossip in the canteen Elizabeth had learned that she was shortly leaving to be married. She said reassuringly:

"That's all right. You can give her a drink of water if she asks for it."

"Is it safe to lift her head?"

"Just slip your hand underneath and raise it as little as possible."

They stood together, looking down at what remained of a girl named Watson. The peculiar, sickening smell of bomb casualties, a mixture of charred flesh and stale blood, was heavy in the air. Elizabeth thought that it would linger in her nostrils for ever.

"The blood is dripping very slowly," she said. "She's only had about an eighth of a pint."

Sister Fuller watched the apparatus for a moment. Then she shrugged her shoulders and went back to her writing.

"Nurse, it's half-past now," Norah prompted.

Elizabeth took the feeding-cup and raised the child's head.

She felt the cup tilt urgently as Norah seized it with both hands. It needed force to take it away from her and she began to whimper.

"I'm so thirsty . . . It was so little . . . Please, Nurse, just another little sip!"

Elizabeth wondered why she had attended lectures and taken exams in order now to have to be an instrument of torture to a child. "The symptoms of internal haemorrhage," an impersonal voice recited in her brain, "are pallor, sighing respiration, a cold and clammy skin, pulse quick and feeble, temperature subnormal, restlessness and thirst. On no account must fluid be given by the mouth." She pulled the bed-clothes over Norah once again and stroked her damp forehead.

"Presently, darling," she said.

As she turned away, Miss Watson stirred again and mumbled more distinctly: "Drink . . . something to drink." Summoning all her courage, Elizabeth slid her left hand underneath the black, mummified head. The bandages were leaking—she felt a moist stickiness over her palm and fingers. The burnt lips parted, leaving a stain on the rim of the cup. She drank greedily, and Elizabeth saw Norah staring longingly round the edge of the screen. Absorbed in her own craving, she seemed to feel no shrinking at the sight of her neighbour. The thin, parched murmur came again:

"Please, Nurse, if I can't have another drink, will you put your finger in the cup and let me suck it? That's what the other nurses do."

Elizabeth thought, I'm not handling this child properly. She knows perfectly well that I find it hard to resist her pleading. It would be kinder to be more professional. She said in a brisk, slightly impatient voice:

"Now, Norah, you mustn't keep bothering. I'm not your nurse, you know—I'm here to look after this other patient. You only make yourself feel worse by talking all the time. Lie quietly and go to sleep."

Norah did not answer. Her small white face shut up with an expression of defensive resignation. Some hope went out of it. She lay and sucked the collar of her night-dress, which was damp where some of the water had trickled down from the feeding-cup.

Miss Watson was becoming increasingly conscious. She asked for tea. "With no sugar," she added unbelievably. So might Lazarus have spoken, astonishing his mourners. But Sister Fuller vetoed tea; a little glucose in the water, that was all.

Fatigue was making Elizabeth slightly hysterical. She became obsessed with the longing to wash the blood off her hand. It wasn't ordinary blood—it felt and smelt corrupt, impure, blood from a charnel-house. But the horror it inspired in her was separate, in some queer way, from her emotion for Miss Watson. Miss Watson was a person now, however little she resembled one. She liked her tea without sugar. She had regained humanity.

Even when all the nurses were back on the ward, no one came to relieve Elizabeth. She felt a certain pride in that, despite the long strain of standing. She was proud, too, when Humphreys gave her a thermometer and told her to take the temperatures and pulses of the patients she was specialling. "And the one in the first bed by the door. In the axilla, of course."

Norah submitted resignedly. She was used to hospital routine. For a long time Elizabeth held the thin little arm pressed tightly to the thin little chest. But the mercury stayed obstinately far below normal. When she had charted the figures she rewarded the child by moistening her lips. Their feverish tug on her finger reminded her of an occasion when she had helped to feed an orphaned lamb. She wiped the clammy forehead with a damp face-flannel and pulled up the tumbled bedclothes for what seemed the twentieth time. Then she went back to Miss Watson.

Miss Watson was easy to handle. Thick layers of sleep or of unconsciousness protected her. Again, Elizabeth was surprised at the strength of her pulse. She felt complete conviction that Miss Watson was going to live. Without an eye, with very little face, with other injuries unspecified, Miss Watson was going to live.

There only remained now the girl in the first bed. She looked very serene under her white coif and very alone. Elizabeth felt awed before that utter stillness and remoteness. Her pulse was almost impossible to find; Elizabeth could only guess its rate; but her temperature registered over 104 degrees. It was as if, deep down within her, a fire burned furiously in a final blaze before complete extinction.

Ten minutes after Elizabeth had gone back to her post, Sister Fuller went over to the first bed on the left. She emerged again almost at once and beckoned Humphreys, and another nurse. Humphreys caught Elizabeth's eye. "She's gone," she murmured as she went past. They stayed behind the screens for some while.

Norah was becoming increasingly restless. Her thin, cold fingers played incessantly with the edge of the screen, she had kicked off the bed-clothes again and she whimpered that it hurt her to lie flat . . . "Why can't I have a pillow, Nurse? Oh Nurse, I am so thirsty!"

Elizabeth bent over her and immediately the child's bony little arms slid round her neck and gripped her with surprising force. Using her hold on Elizabeth as a lever, she tried to raise her shoulders from the bed but fell back with an exclamation of pain. Her brown eyes looked enormous in her small white face.

"Nurse, can't you cry?" she whispered. "Cry, Nurse, and then I could drink your tears."

Elizabeth thought, this is so terrible that it cannot really be happening. She loosened the child's grip and straightened her back. She heard herself say in a rather too high-pitched voice:

"Now, darling, be a good girl and I'll give you just a sip of water."

The feeding-cup was half full. She had a crazy impulse to pour it down the child's throat in one gulp, to let her drink and drink until her thirst was sated and she died in peace. She could not cry for Norah now, but she felt that once outside this ward she would never be able to check her tears again.

Miss Watson was thirsty too. Her periods of unconsciousness were becoming shorter. In one of these, a Sister from another ward appeared, escorting two women. From their ages, Elizabeth guessed them to be Miss Watson's mother and sister. She tried to imagine how it would feel to see someone you loved look like the blackened mummy on the bed. They ought not to have come—oh, they ought not to have come!

But the Sister was speaking to Miss Watson, trying to make her understand that her mother and sister were there. Miss Watson was actually answering, almost collectedly, almost as if she understood. They were all three speaking to her, raising their voices as though the bandages were round her ears and not her eyes. Then, suddenly, it happened. Without warning, Miss Watson vomited. Her body jerked convulsively and Elizabeth darted forward to seize her leg. But it was too late. The needle had been pulled out. The blood that should be going into Miss Watson's veins was spilling all over the bed.

Somehow, order was restored. The visitors went away and the gentle little Sister reassured Miss Watson and went too. Sister Fuller came and disconnected the transfusion apparatus and bound up the wound in Miss Watson's leg. Nobody blamed Elizabeth except herself. It was a pity—the doctor would have to try and put it back; that was all. There was apparently no urgency about the matter.

But Elizabeth knew that she had failed. For two long hours she had watched life returning to Miss Watson in slow, reluctant drops and at the first threat, the first emergency, she had not acted quickly enough, she had lost her head, she had failed.

Miss Watson would recover but with no thanks to her. It seemed the crowning misery.

It was seven o'clock. She had been on the ward, and on her feet, for nearly twelve hours, with a break of forty-five minutes. Supper was being served, by other auxiliaries who had come on during the day, but Elizabeth had reached the limit of her endurance. She turned her back on Miss Watson and on Norah Jenkins and on the dead girl in the corner behind the screens and asked Sister Fuller for permission to go off duty.

"Certainly, Nurse. You've been a great help. Thank you very much."

She said it to all of them, of course, but it was comforting.

The journey home on the 'bus was like a dream. Nobody else in the world was real. No one who had not spent the day in the Women's Surgical Ward at Saffron Park Hospital had any conception of what life was really about.

Henry was waiting for her anxiously. He boiled her an egg and made her eat it lying on the sofa. Tomorrow she would have to talk about it, like a child who has acquired a piece of obscene information and can only find relief from its horror by communicating it in secret to another child. But tonight the weariness of finding words was too great. She lay back with her eyes half closed, smoking cigarettes in an unceasing chain.

At about ten o'clock the sirens began to wail. She heard them with more horror than in all the previous months. How must they sound to the victims of last night's raid? And then she remembered. It was Sunday.

"Oh, God, I'm supposed to be fire-watching!"

"Well, you're not going to fire-watch," Henry said decisively. "You're going to have a hot bath and get straight into bed. I'll take on your duty. I'm not due at the Post till midnight and we may have had an All Clear by then."

She did not protest. It was too much trouble. It was almost too much trouble to undress. Sliding her aching body down between the cool sheets, she longed for the comfort and tenderness of

Alex's body stretched beside her, whole, clean, unblemished. But until she slept she saw only images of horror in her mind's eye, and every breath she drew brought back the hateful smell of mutilated flesh.

CHAPTER XX

WHEN OWEN HAD unlocked the garage and lit the oil-stove, he waited with pleasurable anticipation for Elizabeth to join him. He was disappointed when Henry appeared instead and explained what had happened. He liked Henry, but he was almost a stranger, while Elizabeth now was a friend. He had been looking forward to telling her about Derek's accident, surprisingly confident of her interest and sympathy. Also, he suspected that Henry had never liked his father and now must like him less than ever, which was humiliating and embarrassing.

Henry had brought a book with him and after the preliminary exchange of civilities he seemed to want to settle down and read. But Owen felt too restless to imitate him. He was still excited and wrought up by Cynthia's visit and the news she had brought of Derek. For one sick, horrified moment, at the sight of her standing on the doorstep, unfamiliar in her Waaf uniform, he had thought that she had come to say that Derek had been killed. Even after she had begun to explain about the crash landing, Derek's concussion and unconsciousness, her own forty-eight hours' compassionate leave to see him in hospital—even then he had been half afraid that she was preparing him for something worse. But it was all right. The 'plane had been the chief casualty. X-ray photographs had shown no fractures and Derek would be out of hospital soon. He was going to have a week's sick leave, and Owen, said Cynthia, must come and spend it with him.

All this he had wanted to tell Elizabeth, since it was quite safe to talk to her about Derek. She took it for granted that everything that happened to any of his cousins was important and personal to him. Even though she had once called him a pansy boy, he knew that she didn't think him one now. That was the cream of the jest. Bitter cream of a sardonic jest. But there was no one with whom he could share it.

He stood in the doorway of the garage, looking out on the dark road but not seeing it. After a few minutes Henry joined him there. He had remembered that they had not met since Cathcart's prosecution and he did not want the boy to misinterpret his unsociability.

"All very quiet so far," he said, nodding at the sky. "No barrage, anyhow."

"Perhaps our night fighters are up, sir."

"Elizabeth tells me you're joining the R.A.F., as a pilot."

"If they'll accept me." The opening was irresistible. "My cousin's taking his training now. He's just had a bit of a smash-up. Bust the kite and gave himself concussion."

"Oh well. I expect it's like learning to ride. You're not really confident until you've fallen off the horse a couple of times. I'm glad it wasn't more serious."

"Derek's rather a lucky chap." Surreptitiously he crossed his fingers. "I dare say anybody else would have been killed." He meant to sound casual and unmoved, but there was a note in his voice, of pride and emotion and excitement, which made Henry smile to himself a little ruefully. The boy was very young still, not yet grown out of hero-worship. Henry, who felt tenderly towards the young, was oddly moved. He thought of his own adolescence, and sighed.

"You were brought up with your cousins?"

"More or less, sir. We went to school together and we've always done things together, though he's a year or so older than I am. You know how it is."

"Yes, I know how it is," Henry murmured. He added with a curious abruptness, "I had a friend like that when I was your age."

Knocking out his pipe on the lintel of the door, he moved into the interior of the garage again, rather aimlessly, as though his mind was elsewhere. Puzzled but polite, Owen followed him and sat down opposite him in the second deck-chair.

"Did you, sir?" he prompted.

"It's ancient history. I don't suppose that you'd be interested."

He spoke as though he already regretted what he had said and looked for a pretext to withdraw. But Owen said eagerly, with obvious sincerity:

"I'm sure I should be, sir."

"Oh well. He was a boy named Humphrey. His surname doesn't matter. We lived next door to each other, went to school together (a grammar school, as day boys), spent all our holidays together. I thought I knew everything about him. I thought we shared every interest and idea and experience. Then, one day, he committed suicide. Hanged himself, in the attic."

Owen stared at him with surprise and horror—surprise at the confidence and horror at its climax.

"Why did he do that?" he asked hardly above a whisper.

Henry did not reply immediately. He finished filling another pipe and struck two matches before it drew to his satisfaction.

"I don't know," he said finally. "I shall probably never know. He didn't leave a letter. His parents made up their minds that he must have been fooling about with the rope and hanged himself accidentally. But I knew better than that. He'd been rather quiet for a couple of days, but I hadn't thought anything of it. He was the quiet sort. I think what upset me almost more than his death was the knowledge that I must have failed him in some way, that he hadn't felt able to confide in me. It was the worst thing that had ever happened to me, and nothing that has happened to me since has been as bad."

He wondered why he was saying all this and why young Cathcart stared at him with an expression of such strained absorption. It was perhaps not fitting to display one's heart across the gulf of nearly forty years' difference in age. But then, regarding Humphrey he was still eighteen himself, could never grow any older. The friends he had made since, the women he had loved, had never replaced him. There was a quality attendant on one's first love, a purity and disinterestedness, which could not be recaptured. Only, if one were lucky, it merged with time and custom into something less ecstatic but more stable.

Owen said nervously, breaking the silence:

"Don't you think, sir, that nobody can ever really know what's going on in someone else's mind? I don't see that you need have blamed yourself. You might be awfully fond of someone and yet feel too ashamed to tell them everything about yourself. I mean, your friend . . . Perhaps people said things, without really meaning them very seriously. And then he got to worrying and didn't want to worry you too . . . And felt browned off and rather desperate and just sort of gave in to a sudden impulse. It wouldn't mean that he thought any the less of you or didn't trust you."

Henry, who had been thinking about himself, woke up suddenly and began thinking about Owen. It struck him that the boy had immediately applied the story in a personal way, casting himself in Humphrey's role. And what was behind that jumble of words about people who "said things"? He became a middle-aged man again, kindly and tolerant towards the distresses of youth.

"What sort of things do you suppose people might have said?" he asked.

Mentally, Owen shied violently and Henry was aware of the recoil.

"Oh, I don't know. Sometimes I think that people are sort of jealous. They try and spoil things if they can. They . . . hint things."

"I see." He saw quite a lot. "I wonder if you're right?" His tone was serious, as between adults. "You think that Humphrey might have got the idea that people were critical of his friendship for me, even suspicious of it?"

Owen nodded, not trusting himself to speak.

"It's possible. But that would be a kind of murder, wouldn't it? A totally needless and unprovoked murder. Because anyone who understands boys of that age realises that it's entirely natural for them to admire and love each other, especially if one is rather older and excels in things which the national tradition teaches are admirable and worthy of emulation. Take the Greeks, for instance. Socrates has underlined the virtues and the dangers of that national tradition. You've read the 'Symposium', of course?"

Yes, Owen had read the "Symposium", and everything else he could find which had a bearing on his problem. Again, he nodded without speaking.

"It always amuses me to hear people talk about Platonic Love as though it were a heterosexual relationship. Socrates was right, of course; he tried to combat what was decadent in his generation and class, a tendency which might have led to racial suicide. But he knew too much about human nature to condemn, *en bloc*, emotions which are fundamental and of value to the race. The only real danger lies in deliberate corruption by those already corrupted themselves. Hero-worship, and the tenderness which it evokes in those who receive it, is mostly a singularly pure and unselfish feeling between two people. To sow self-consciousness and self-distrust in their minds is a crime of the first order. We all learn soon enough to love possessively and greedily."

He broke off, waiting for a reaction, and Owen said breathlessly:

"What about jealousy, then? That's being possessive, isn't it? I mean, that's not very . . . pure."

"Oh, jealousy. That's only another name for insecurity, isn't it? You might call it the seamy side of humility. It's a quality you see sometimes, in very young children, an inherent characteristic, not an acquired vice. Certain people will be jealous in every relationship throughout their lives."

"I'm one of those, I'm afraid," Owen confessed.

"Are you?" Deliberately he made his voice uninterested. "Humphrey was a bit like that, too. It was the only thing we ever quarrelled about. He needn't have been, but we were at the age when we both felt rather shy of putting things into words and unfortunately I didn't know how to tell him so. The Anglo-Saxon is always at a disadvantage in such matters. I wish I could tell him so now. Does that sound sentimental to you?"

"I suppose it is rather sentimental," Owen said candidly. "But I'd feel just the same if I were you."

"Then we're both sentimentalists. Good." Henry's tone lightened and he smiled. "I don't know why I've told you all this. It's years since I've mentioned it to anyone. I'd rather you kept it to yourself. It's not of general interest, anyhow."

"Of course, sir. I'm glad you told me. I appreciate it very much."

They were silent, but it was a companionable silence. Owen felt extraordinarily happy—relaxed, tranquil, curiously cleansed. Sprawled in the deck-chair, he stared unseeingly at a stirrup-pump in the corner. Henry pulled at his pipe. They might have been a trusted master and his favourite pupil. Or a father and his son.

Suddenly the door was pushed wide. Daisy came in and regarded them with extreme surprise.

"Owen! Oh, good evening, Mr. Simpson. I didn't know that you were here. Are you going to stay till one o'clock?"

"No, Mother. Only till the All Clear."

"But it went ages ago! Didn't you hear it?"

Henry and Owen looked at each other and laughed.

"We were talking too hard," Henry said. "I'm sorry, Mrs. Cathcart. You can have your son. We'll lock up now."

"I've just made a pot of tea," she said rather hesitantly. "Would you like to come back with me and have a cup?"

"No, thanks very much. I'm due on at the Post at midnight. I'll take the opportunity to have a rest first."

Walking along the road with them, he gave Daisy a brief account of Elizabeth's day at the hospital.

"Such a nice man," Daisy sighed, as they watched him cross the road and let himself in at the house opposite.

"Yes, he is," Owen agreed.

There was nothing in his voice to show the warmth of his endorsement.

Henry thought about Owen at intervals throughout the rest of the night. The boy was in a queer frame of mind. He hoped that he had done him a little good, but it was impossible to tell how lasting the effect would be. Some careless or malicious person, or perhaps only something he had read, had planted a worm in his brain. Henry wondered what type of boy the cousin was. A lot would depend on that. All the same, he had not said a word that he did not honestly believe to be true. But of course there was always the possibility of arrested emotional development, a petrification of the age of adolescence. That was something which only time would show.

He wondered if he could discuss the matter with Elizabeth, but a deep-seated instinct of inter-sexual loyalty made him reject the idea. No doubt she would be sympathetic, but he didn't think that she would understand.

If Humphrey had been alive, he would have understood. The reflection brought him the first comfort on that score that he had ever known. Perhaps, after all, Humphrey's death had not been entirely futile and in vain.

CHAPTER XXI

"I've asked Anne up this evening, to play Rummy," Derek said. "I hope you don't mind a social evening?"

"No, I don't mind," Owen assured him.

But did he? He wasn't sure. He was getting rather bored with Anne. She seemed to have enrolled herself as welfare officer, responsible for the entertainment and morale of the injured hero. Apparently Derek liked it—though, to be just, he did his best to debunk the heroic angle. In his own view, he had committed a major black, and no amount of feminine sympathy could alter the facts of the case.

Secretly, Owen agreed with him. Even more secretly, he was pretty sure that, when the time came, he wouldn't make any such blunder himself. Now that he had seen Derek, could be perfectly satisfied that no great harm had befallen him, the incident took on a different aspect. For the first time since he had known him, Derek had failed to clear a hurdle. He had shown himself as fallible as other men. It didn't make him any the less lovable; perhaps it made him more so; but it reduced him a little in stature and toned down the dazzling high-light of consistent success. Smug in his newly acquired security, released from immediate fear, Owen thought, "Poor old Derek," and did not realise the measure of his stride forward.

They were lying on the lawn. Although it was only the first week of May, the weather was like mid-summer, hot and sunny. Aunt Susan and Harriet were gardening nearby and the boys were aware that they ought to be helping them. But no, Aunt Susan said, they worked too hard, they must rest while they could. So they sprawled on the grass and stared up at the blue sky. A bomber droned overhead ("Short-nosed Blenheim," Derek interpolated) and a Brimstone butterfly hovered round a flower-bed.

"Remember when we had a craze for butterflies?" Derek asked lazily.

"Yes. That pair of Clouded Yellows in the wood—we were so excited that we mucked it up completely and they got away. But we caught the Red Admirals feeding on that stinking weasel strung up on a tree."

"You were sick as a dog," Derek reminded him.

"And if I was? It showed a more refined nature."

Derek yawned and stretched.

"Well, I'm one up on the butterflies now. I leave them far below—but they make better landings."

"More practice," Owen suggested.

"You've said it. But you know, Tudor, I'm not looking forward very much to my next hop. I wish I could have gone up right away. But passing out the way I did and all that flap about a possible fracture of the skull, I didn't get the chance. I shall be in a terrible sweat next time."

"You'll be all right," Owen said confidently. "Honestly, I mean it—I'm not just trying to jolly you along. Good Lord, you talk as though you'd made the first punk landing in history. Scores of chaps must be doing it every day, all over the world."

"It isn't only that," Derek confessed. "The C.O.'s going to tear me off a hell of a strip when I get back. I'd have had it on the spot if I hadn't conked out. And look at all the time I've lost! I'll never get my wings at this rate. They might even turn me down." But that was such a terrible conjecture that he hurried past it. "All the decent blokes I know will go ahead and I'll have to start the next course with a bunch of newcomers."

"Yes, that's bad luck," Owen admitted. "But don't take such a dim view of things. It isn't like you. You've got a pretty good record up to date—that'll count in your favour with the C.O."

"All right, let's forget it," Derek said, cheering up now that he had unburdened himself. "I'll be a care-free Brewery Boy, thinking of nothing but wine, women and song. I'll gamble recklessly at Rummy and pawn the family jewels to pay my debts."

Anne came to dinner that night dressed with more sophistication than Owen had ever seen her. He supposed that she was really quite a pretty girl, though the only woman whose looks he could admire whole-heartedly was Cynthia, a feminine counterpart of her brother. Anne was dark, with fine, cloudy hair, a pale complexion and brown eyes. This evening she had put on a little lipstick, which would not have pleased her parents but which definitely improved her appearance. She seemed more animated, too—over-excited, Owen called it—and the three women complimented her. Derek did not compliment her, but he looked surprised and faintly self-conscious, as though he suspected that the lipstick and the dressing-up were both for him. There was an atmosphere of celebration about the evening, a rather pathetic attempt to make a riotous occasion out of wartime rations and a family card-game. Would Derek want to spend his leaves at home when he was a full-blown Fighter Pilot, taut with the strain of operational flights? Owen, pondering the matter dispassionately, thought that he probably would. He had strong loyalties and simple tastes. But there would be more merit in it than his mother or his sisters (except Cynthia) would realise.

After a while they stopped playing Rummy and danced to the gramophone—the two young men with Anne and Lorna. Harriet would not dance. It was Derek who mostly danced with Anne. They had been practising together, it seemed—there was always some new step that must be tried out.

"Never mind, Owen," Lorna said. "We'll just trundle round together in our old-fashioned way."

She gave his arm a squeeze, and there was something about the pressure, a suggestion of sympathy and consolation, which disturbed him. What was she trying to say? It was naturally more amusing for Derek to dance with Anne than with his eldest sister. He wasn't going to feel jealous about that, he told himself. What was it Elizabeth's father had said? "Jealousy's only another name for insecurity." He took comfort from the recollection, for why should he feel insecure?

One day, perhaps, he would want to dance with a girl himself, just for the sake of holding her, and she would be a nicer girl than Anne. He would probably meet a lot of girls when he was in the R.A.F. It was a popular uniform. But he didn't want just any girl. And he didn't want to make the running in public, either. He would keep very quiet about it and surprise everyone. "You're a damned dark horse," Derek would say. "Where on earth did you find her?" And it would be obvious that she adored him. Her eyes would follow him round the room when he danced with other women, just to be polite, and he would smile at her over his partner's shoulder, a secret, sharing smile.

"Darling, that was my foot," Lorna said. "Wake up!"

"Sorry, Lorna."

It was the last record to be played. Anne said she ought to go now—it was terribly late.

"The boys will see you home; of course," Aunt Susan said.

Owen was looking at Anne. He saw her face cloud. Quickly, he glanced at Derek. His expression did not change, but he hesitated for a moment before echoing his mother. They don't want me, Owen thought bitterly, entirely forgetting his own hypothetical romance. They want to go alone. He had a perfectly clear picture of them in his mind, kissing good night rather shyly in the vicarage porch. Then he heard his own voice saying amiably:

"Derek, you're the host. I'll leave you to do the gentlemanly thing. You'll excuse me, Anne, won't you? Dancing with Lorna has exhausted me."

"Owen, how dare you!" Lorna exclaimed.

The party broke up with good-humoured bickering. Anne went to fetch her coat and Derek and Owen were alone.

"Tact?" Derek asked with a grin.

"You might call it that."

"Quite the man-of-the-world, aren't you?" But he was a little sheepish in spite of his flippancy.

From his bedroom window Owen watched them walking down the lane in the moonlight, saw Derek tuck Anne's arm in his, possessively. He leant his forehead against the cool glass pane and a number of conflicting emotions fought a battle in his mind—pain, scorn, self-pity, self-congratulation. None of them won outright, but from their conflict was born a quite different emotion, a tolerant tenderness for Derek and even for dull little Anne. I don't mind, he told himself. If it makes old Derek happy, I don't mind. And suddenly he was possessed of a feeling of extraordinary peace and detachment. It was like waking from a natural sleep after a long period of fever and delirium, to the awareness of a cool body, cool sheets. "I don't mind!" he told himself with astonishment. "I don't *mind!*"

The ghost that Elizabeth Simpson had raised so unwittingly grew insubstantial, paled, disintegrated without protest. Limp and exorcised, Owen threw himself down on his bed and lay staring at the ceiling. Every now and then he smiled, for no especial reason. It was so amusing, and surprising, not to mind.

In the morning he left Lampton to go home. Derek came with him to the station; he was getting a lift back to the Training School himself that afternoon. The train was late and they paced up and down the platform for nearly half an hour, wheeling neatly either end, keeping in step. They did not discuss the events of the night before at all. There were so many things which they did not need to discuss. Lionel's prosecution, for instance. None of the Hammonds had mentioned that once, and yet their reticence had not seemed obvious or embarrassed. So now Derek talked about his training, already, in his mind, back on the job again, and crammed Owen with useful advice on how to overcome initial problems. He felt anxious about him, not having lost the habit of mind which had grown on him in their school-days. Tudor was such a funny, sensitive cuss and not a very good mixer.

In the rather rustic waiting-room a woman was sitting. Derek saluted her as he went by and Owen asked who she was.

"Oh, just an evacuee. Mrs. Foster. Lives at Downside. She's quite nice. It was her husband who came to borrow the car-chains last time you were here."

"I remember."

Owen was more interested than he sounded. He had wondered when he first arrived whether he would come across Elizabeth's boss this visit. Since the night when he had seen them together and guessed their relationship, he had felt curious about the man. And his wife—what was she like? Several times he saw the children out with their governess and once Aunt Susan mentioned the family. Mr. Foster hadn't been down last weekend. She thought he should have come, for Mrs. Foster wasn't very well just now. Afterwards Owen had forgotten about them, but now his curiosity revived. When the train came in he deliberately got into the same carriage with Mrs. Foster. Derek was surprised at this evidence of unusual sociability.

Naomi seated herself in the far corner and Owen stayed by the near door, leaning out of the window.

"Write and tell me what bones you fracture next time you try any funny stuff," he said cheerfully. "That'll be something else I'll remember to avoid."

"You are a low swine! I hate to think the same blood runs in our veins. I don't suppose I shall write now, just to learn you."

The train began to move.

"Give my love to Aunt Daisy," Derek called out.

"Give my love to Anne," Owen grinned.

Still smiling, he dropped back in his seat. Derek, too, was smiling as he walked away. Tudor had been rather decent about Anne. He hadn't been quite sure how he would take it. At school, he had sometimes been very queer and touchy about other chaps who wanted to tag on. There was time to go and see Anne now, before the car arrived to pick him up. The sun shone and life seemed good this 9th of May, in spite of the C.O.

When Owen glanced round, Naomi caught his eye and smiled.

"Have you been staying with the Hammonds?" she asked.

"Yes. They're relations of mine. I came down to spend Derek's leave with him."

"I think they're such nice people," Naomi said effusively. "Of course we're just dirt—miserable evacuees. But Mrs. Hammond and her daughters never make us feel like that. They've been much more friendly than anyone else in the place."

"I'm glad," Owen muttered.

He was beginning to feel embarrassed and to realise that he was going to pay a high price for his curiosity.

"Do you live in London?"

"In one of the London suburbs—Saffron Park."

He was absurdly afraid that she would immediately connect him with Elizabeth, but apparently she was not interested in where her husband's secretary resided.

"And you've been there all through the raids?"

"Yes."

"I do think that's so brave of you! Not that I wanted to leave myself, but naturally, with two children, I had no choice. My husband has been there all the time, except for occasional week-ends. His business is there and it isn't the kind you can evacuate."

"The raids haven't been so bad lately—" Owen persevered. "Not so frequent, anyhow. We're bringing down too many of their 'planes."

"I think the Night Fighters are wonderful! Has Derek Hammond done any night fighting?"

"He hasn't got as far as that yet. He's only training still."

"Oh." She looked vague. "And what about yourself? Are you going to join the R.A.F.?"

"When I'm called up," Owen admitted, wishing he could say that he was a Conscientious Objector, just to startle her.

"How splendid!"

Owen smiled weakly.

"Are you coming up to stay?" he asked, taking the offensive.

"Oh no. Just to do a little shopping. And then I mean to kidnap my husband from the office and bring him back with me for the week-end."

"Is it a surprise, then?"

He was aware of being rather impertinently pressing, but his interest was overpowering. Fortunately Naomi did not readily diagnose impertinence in good-looking young men.

"Yes." She smiled archly. "I'm just going to take him by storm. The weather's lovely and he works far too hard."

"You feel he'd be doing more good working in the garden, I suppose," Owen suggested, thus changing the conversation with more adroitness than he had believed himself to possess.

On and off, he had to talk to her all the way to Paddington and committed himself finally to calling at Downside the very next time he went to Lampton.

The moment he had seen her into a taxi, he looked round for a call-box. He had a wild idea of telephoning Elizabeth and warning her—perhaps, even, as an anonymous voice. But he was brought to his senses firstly by the recollection that he didn't know the name of her firm and secondly by an ashamed realisation that he had been thinking of the situation in terms of a strip cartoon—a drawing of a blonde stenographer sitting on the knee of a gentleman in pin-striped trousers, with the caption: "Caught by the boss's wife." It wasn't like that—he was certain it wasn't. But he wished, all the same, that he could just prepare her. And he wished, almost more, that he could be an invisible witness at the meeting of those three. In fact, the interest of imagining what might happen so engrossed him that he forgot to think about his own affairs for half an hour.

CHAPTER XXII

NAOMI SMILED at Miss Lewis, seated at the switchboard in the reception room, and asked her:

"Is my husband engaged?"

"Oh no, Mrs, Foster! There's no one with him except Miss Simpson,"

She flicked down a key and spoke into the mouthpiece.

"Mrs. Foster's here to see you, Mr. Foster."

Her trained, metallic voice sounded clearly inside the room. Elizabeth, sitting facing Alex across the desk, heard the words quite distinctly. She was watching Alex and she saw his face change. He looked surprised; but more than that, he looked afraid.

"Ask her to come in," he said harshly.

His eyes met Elizabeth's with an expression of uneasy apology. Unconsciously, he shrugged his shoulders.

Naomi came in with her arms full of parcels. It was a hot day and Elizabeth thought her looking white and tired, less pretty than usual. But she said quite briskly:

"It's all right—there's nothing wrong at home. I just had a sudden impulse to come up for the day and do some shopping. So I thought I'd look in and surprise you, and carry you back with me for the week-end. Good afternoon, Miss Simpson."

"Good afternoon, Mrs. Foster."

She had picked up her notebook and was half-way across the room.

"But, Naomi," Alex said impatiently, "I told you I couldn't get away this week-end. I'm up to my eyes in work."

Elizabeth did not hear any more. She was outside the door, exposed to Miss Lewis's pleased curiosity.

"Fancy Mrs. Foster coming up to London! Is she going to stop?"

"I think she's only here for the day."

She escaped into her own room and sat down hurriedly, feeling absurdly shaken. It had been rather a shock. Supposing Naomi had turned up tonight, at the flat? Supposing, even now, she were to go there? She tried to remember if she had left anything behind last time and hated herself, Alex, all three of them for having to do so. It was exactly the sort of thing she most detested—it made it all seem trivial, sordid, cheap. Powder and hairpins on the dressing-table, the knowing smirk on the face of a service apartment valet—the conventional trappings of sexual intrigue. Was it going to be like that always?

Naomi looked ill. Perhaps she had something seriously the matter with her and they would have to feel ashamed of being happy and deceiving her, a sick woman. In theory it wouldn't make any difference, but in practice it would. Oh, God damn everything.

Suddenly, jarringly, her buzzer rang. Alex was summoning her by buzzer! It was years now since he had done that; it sounded so rude and peremptory, he had said; he preferred to ask for her civilly, over the telephone. This was to show off to Naomi, she supposed—to impress her with the strictly official relationship existing between employer and secretary. It seemed an unnecessary insult. With deliberate, angry leisure she picked up her notebook and pencil. The buzzer rang again.

She walked into the room without knocking. Alex was alone—no, Naomi was there too. She was lying on the floor beneath the open window.

"She's fainted," Alex said helplessly. "My God, you took your time!"

Not bothering to answer him, she dropped on her knees beside Naomi and began automatically to loosen her clothing. The sight of her greenish pallor and the clammy touch of her forehead reminded her of the hospital, the air-raid victims, things she had been trying to forget.

"Make a couch with the chairs," she commanded Alex. "And help me lift her—"

She was surprisingly heavy and Alex was rather clumsy. Elizabeth felt impatient with his uselessness.

"Now fetch some water," she told him peremptorily. "And ask Miss Lewis for her smelling salts—she always carries them."

Flicking Naomi's face with a wet handkerchief, she questioned him:

"What happened exactly?"

"She said she felt giddy and asked me to open the window at the bottom. While I was raising it I heard a thud. I turned round and she was lying on the floor. It all happened very quickly."

"She looked pale when she arrived. Give me the salts. I think she's coming round."

"She'll probably be sick," he said anxiously.

"You'd better clear out, then. I'll manage."

But Naomi was not sick. She opened her eyes and looked at Elizabeth with a puzzled expression, then recognised her, tried to smile, and closed her eyes again.

"How silly of me," she murmured. "It was so hot . . . and I was tired."

"Don't try to talk." Elizabeth was surprised at the gentleness in her own voice. "You'll be all right in a minute. You only fainted."

She took Alex's overcoat off the stand and wrapped it round her.

"You're very kind," Naomi sighed, opening her eyes again. "Where's Alex?"

"I told him to keep out of the way." They exchanged a friendly, faintly conspiratorial smile. "Here, drink a little of this water." She slipped a hand under her head to raise it. But Naomi's hair was dry and clean and scented. There was no sticky, evil-smelling blood to stain her fingers. "Do you feel all right now? Shall I fetch Mr. Foster?"

"I'd rather you stayed with me a little, if you don't mind. I suppose you've guessed what's the matter with me?"

Elizabeth shook her head, but even as she made the gesture of denial it became a falsehood.

"I'm going to have a baby."

There was a pause which seemed to lengthen to a silence, significant and revealing. I must say something, Elizabeth thought frantically—I must say something or she'll realise. Her voice sounded strange and far away in her own ears.

"How nice. You don't show it yet."

"Oh, it isn't for ages—not till October. I ought to be pleased, I know, but I'm afraid I'm not very. I don't think people ought to have babies in wartime."

"You'll be pleased when it comes."

"I suppose so." She sounded more normal now; the familiar note of petulance was back in her voice. "But I'm an awful coward. And having that miscarriage has made me extra nervous."

"I didn't know you'd had one. I'm sorry."

"Yes. About a year ago—when we were first at Lampton. I had a fall."

"You must be very careful this time."

"That's what my husband says. I think he was rather cross with me for coming up today. But it's so boring in the country and not a bit satisfactory having to order everything by post. I'm sure the shops all cheat you."

Now she was no longer a patient and Elizabeth was no longer her nurse. Now the situation had become intolerable, the room was stifling and Elizabeth envied her her brief unconsciousness.

"I think I'd better let Mr. Foster know you're better," she said quickly. "He'll be worrying."

As she came out into the hall, Alex ran up the stairs, carrying a tumbler.

"I've fetched her some brandy," he said. "They let me have some in the office below."

"She's all right now. But make her sip it."

She turned her back on him and on the situation and went into her own room, shutting the door behind her. I mustn't think about this yet, she told herself—not till they've gone; it wouldn't be safe. Automatically, she put paper and carbon into her typewriter and looked at the shorthand in her notebook. But none of it made sense—she could not read a single outline or remember the context of one word. A telephone call came through and she answered completely at random, forgetting a moment after what it had been about. Someone had tied an iron band round her forehead and another round her throat.

Presently she heard sounds coming from the reception room. Carter had returned from doing an errand and was being sent to fetch a taxi. They were going away—Alex would probably take her all the way home, she thought. Then the door opened and Naomi stood there, leaning on Alex's arm. She looked pale but quite recovered.

"I've come to say good-bye," she said pleasantly. "Thank you, Miss Simpson—you were very kind. My husband tells me that you've had quite a lot of nursing experience, so I think I chose my moment very well."

Smiling, she held out her hand and Elizabeth shook it. She had an hysterical impulse to laugh. Alex looked so silly—so silly and so anguished. He did not meet her eyes.

"I'll sign those letters in the morning," he said curtly. "I won't be back tonight."

"Aren't you going to say thank-you too?" Naomi scolded him playfully. She was beginning to enjoy the commotion she had caused.

"Of course. Thank you, Miss Simpson." But he could not smile. "Come, Naomi. You ought not to stand about too long."

They turned and went down the stairs, still arm in arm. Elizabeth stood looking after them, forgetting where she was, till Miss Lewis's voice recalled her.

"Quite an excitement, wasn't it? But you were wonderful, Miss Simpson."

"Yes, it was. Did you get your smelling salts back from Mr. Foster?"

"I told Mrs. Foster to keep them for the journey," Miss Lewis said proudly. "I think he ought to go with her, don't you? But I heard him say he'd be back here in the morning."

"Yes. He didn't sign his letters. I haven't done them yet—"

She turned away quickly and went back into her own room. Tomorrow he would come in expecting to find her. But she wouldn't be there. She would leave his letters ready on his desk, their envelopes, stamped and addressed, beside them. She would ring up Miss Lewis and tell her she was not feeling well. Perhaps, then, he would go down to Lampton after all. On Monday . . . But there was no need to think ahead as far as that. She opened her notebook again.

"Dear Sirs," she typed, "Replying to your letter of the 7th . . ."

Outside in the street there was the sound of a taxi-door slamming to.

The journey home in the Tube had a dream-like quality. Elizabeth had a curious impression that she was sitting opposite herself, seeing herself, apparently composed, well dressed, nursing her handbag and her gloves and a copy of the "Evening Standard". A peace treaty between Thailand and French Indochina had been signed in Tokyo. That was probably very important, but she could only read the headline over and over again. Because she was conscious of hiding so much behind her public mask, she wondered what the other travellers were thinking and if their hearts ached for a better or a worse reason. They all looked tired and some of them looked unhappy. When the man sitting beside her lit a cigarette, she lit one too, automatically. She would have liked to go home and get a little drunk, peacefully and privately, as her mother had done. Alex would undoubtedly get drunk tonight. Men had more sense and better technique.

But at home there was her father. Remembering him, she felt a far-away warmth of heart and the bands round her throat and forehead seemed to slacken. Her father loved her. He knew about Alex and he had not chidden her. Now, if she told him what had happened, he would understand and be kind. But she did not want to tell him the exact truth. He would be angry with Alex, and in some obscure way it still seemed necessary to shield Alex from criticism. Exposing him, she would humiliate herself. It would be enough to tell her father half the truth. He would not question her beyond that.

Henry was in the sitting-room, reading an evening paper. He did not look up when she came in but said pleasantly:

"You're back. Good. I was getting hungry."

She dropped into a chair beside his.

"Get me a drink, darling. I've had such a beastly day."

"Of course—" He put down his paper and looked at her with concern. "You certainly look tired. I'll fetch the sherry—"

He watched her anxiously while she drank.

"You don't think you're going to be ill? I feel responsible for you, with your mother away."

"No, I'm not going to be ill." But she leant back her head and closed her eyes. One glass of sherry seemed to have done the work of several. She supposed it must be because she had had a shock.

"It's the sudden heat, perhaps," Henry suggested.

That reminded her of Naomi and she laughed. Even to herself it sounded false and a little hysterical.

"Elizabeth, what is it?" His voice was suddenly sharp.

It occurred to her that he might be wondering if she were pregnant too and this seemed to her extraordinarily funny. But it would be dangerous to let herself be too amused. With an effort she checked her laughter.

"Don't pay any attention to me. I'll be better in a minute. I told you, I've had a beastly day . . . I'm not going back to the office."

"I see," he said slowly. "You mean, you've finished with Foster?"

"Yes. That's all over." She poured herself out another drink, without looking at him.

"I'm sorry that it had to happen like this, suddenly. But I can't be sorry otherwise. I should be lying if I said I were."

"Oh, don't *you* lie," she said wearily. "I'm sick of lies, my own included. I've told so many in the last three years, and mostly to myself."

He looked at her rather helplessly.

"Do you want to tell me about it?"

She shook her head. "Not the sordid details. Not now. But I wanted you to know. Say something. Tell me what a lucky girl I am to disentangle myself from a low intrigue."

"You mustn't be bitter," he said almost sternly. Then, with a gentleness that palliated his tone, he took her hand and held it tightly. "Poor child. My poor child. I'm sorry."

"Don't be too kind," she muttered. But she leant her head against his shoulder for a moment. "I'm a fool. I bought it. But it hurts just the same. I feel so . . . taken aback. Often and often I've imagined a break-up between us, but I never imagined it would happen as it has. We haven't even quarrelled—though I suppose we shall. I just found out I'd been a silly dupe for years. I've been in love with someone who doesn't exist, someone I've just made up. And the stupid thing is that I still feel as if I want to go to him for consolation. I want the Alex whom I've imagined to console me for the pain the other Alex has inflicted on me. Isn't it absurd? And he'll be feeling like that too. He'll hate himself and want to come to me to have the sting taken out—"

"You draw the picture of a very weak man," Henry said. "I don't know what has happened, but I see that clearly enough."

"I suppose he is weak. I know he is. But weak people seem to get more loved than strong ones, don't they? Especially men. A part of me has always known that he was rather selfish, but then, I'm nothing very wonderful myself. We were in it together. That took away the loneliness. We all lead such lonely lives."

"Needlessly lonely," Henry suggested.

"I dare say. But that's the way it works out."

"You say that you're not going back to the office. Does that mean that you won't be seeing him again?"

"I shall have to see him once. It's been left all up in the air."

"You won't change your mind?" he asked anxiously.

"No. I won't change my mind." She dropped her head on his shoulder again. "Oh dear. I feel so tired."

"You'd better go to bed. I'll bring you up some dinner on a tray."

"I should be sick if I tried to eat. But I'll go to bed. Have your own dinner and then come up and sit with me a little while. Pretend I've got measles again. Do you remember how you used to sit beside my bed and read to me, when I wasn't allowed to use my eyes?"

"Yes. Dreadful twopenny weeklies. They made me shudder to think what your standard of literature would turn out to be."

He smiled and was pleased to see her smile back at him. "Perhaps that's when I started to go wrong."

"Perhaps," he echoed lightly.

"Oh, Father, I do love you. You'd never let me down, would you?"

"I don't suppose so."

"You won't get bombed, will you? Promise me."

"I don't suppose that either. Go to bed."

Alone again, she lost her childhood and the security of dependence. The past retreated and there was only herself and Alex in the whole world. Lying with her room in darkness except for the reading-lamp behind her head, she found that she could not relax. Her body ached with the protest of muscles held unconsciously taut for hours, and her thoughts raced. Phrases that Alex had used in the past six months kept running through her brain—lies of omission and commission, but chiefly of omission. He must have known that they would only serve him for a little while, but he was a coward and they had postponed an evil hour. Perhaps there had been times when he had wanted to confess. That evening in the office when she had taxed him with having changed and he had muttered sulkily that he would like to cut his throat—perhaps he would have told her then, if he had dared. But he had called her hard, not joking, and had taken refuge in the usual easy way by making love to her. "Let's live by the day," he had said. And she had told him, truthfully, but fatally as far as any hope of honesty between them lay, that she would love him less if he were ever to appear less lovable. The moment had gone by.

There were so many things she understood now which before she had been too afraid to probe. Alex's attitude to Bob, for one. That was unaccountable no longer. In a curious, roundabout way, she had atoned for any wrong she might have done Bob. She had given Bob counterfeit coin, but it was Alex who had paid her back in it. There was something peculiarly ugly in the picture of Alex, uneasy in the knowledge of his own shortcomings, soothing his conscience by inciting her to encourage another man. Or had he only wanted to ensure that, if the worst came to the worst, she would not be too utterly alone? Perhaps she would never find out the answer to that question.

Well, Bob was clear of the mess, anyhow. And Naomi would never know that she had been in it. She had wronged Naomi, whom she despised. But that was only a wound to her vanity and would heal quicker than the wound to her heart. They were both in the same boat, both women whom Alex had made fools of. Odd to think that she had ever envied Naomi. She had never seemed less enviable than now—the victor, the possessor.

Downstairs in the hall, the telephone began to ring. Elizabeth heard the door of the dining-room open and her father's deliberate step. Then the ringing stopped. She jumped out of bed and opened her own door, to listen.

"Hello," Henry said. "Miss Simpson? Who is it speaking? . . . Oh. Well, I'm not sure that you can. She isn't feeling very fit. She's gone to bed." His voice was dry and neutral. Elizabeth knew perfectly well whom he was talking to.

Glancing up, he saw her leaning over the banisters and raised his eyebrows interrogatively. She shook her head.

"Tomorrow morning? I doubt if she'll be able to go to the office. Can I take a message?" He listened for a moment. "All right. I'll tell her." He rang off.

"What did he say?" Elizabeth asked rather breathlessly.

"He wants you to telephone him in the morning, at his flat. He'll be there till ten o'clock, he says."

"Oh. Thank you." She turned to go back to her room.

"I'm coming up in a few minutes," he called after her.

She felt a certain sardonic amusement at the thought of Alex's discomfiture. Circumstances which had been a hindrance in the past had become now a protection. He could not reach her through the wall of deception which they had built up so carefully. Well, it would do him no harm to pass the night uneasily, as she must pass it. There was nothing they could say now, on the telephone; no comfort they could give each other. The hours till morning would be long for both of them.

Henry came upstairs bearing a tray of tea-things and made her drink a cup with him and eat some biscuits. He was not a domesticated man and it touched her to see the odd collection of china he had assembled. She thought that he must have been just as laboriously assembling subjects which it would be safe to discuss. He talked resolutely and with little pause about himself—his childhood with his parents, his early life in London articled to an old-fashioned firm of solicitors, peculiar cases he had handled for eccentric clients. Elizabeth found that she could not give him her whole attention, but she did her best.

"How often did you fall in love before you married Mother?" she asked suddenly.

"Only once. Well, only once that counted."

"And what happened?"

"She married someone else."

"Poor Father. Were you very unhappy?"

"Yes, I was very unhappy, for quite a long time. But I got over it."

"How old were you?"

"Twenty-three, when I met her. A bad age. But you needn't imagine that it was a serious affair. I wore very peculiar clothes—high, stiff collars and stove-pipe trousers and a straw boater in the summer. It's well known that nobody could really suffer, dressed like that."

"You know I don't think that," she said with amused indignation. "I think you must have been very attractive, boater and all. That girl was a fool not to marry you."

"I'm afraid you're biased. I wasn't much catch."

By tacit agreement, neither of them mentioned Alice. Elizabeth had sometimes wondered how her parents had come to make such an obviously ill-matched pair. But she would never wonder it aloud.

"Do you think there's any chance of your going to sleep now?" Henry asked.

"I think perhaps I might. I do feel very tired."

"Well, I've done my best to bore you into somnolence."

"You've been sweet," she said sincerely.

He looked pleased and almost boyishly embarrassed, as if, having summoned up the image of his own youth, it lingered with him.

"Breakfast in bed in the morning," he commanded.

Nice men, Elizabeth reflected, always thought the quickest cure for feminine disabilities was breakfast in bed.

"Very well, darling," she agreed.

When the door closed behind him, she turned off her light, but she did not fall asleep. She had not expected to be able to. The same thoughts, arguments and questions recurred monotonously in her brain. It was like being lost in a labyrinth of underground passages. Each way led only to a blank wall, but a kind of desperation drove her to explore them over and over again. Sometimes she was overcome with sudden, hot tears; sometimes she tortured herself more subtly by re-creating periods of great happiness. But no light appeared in the darkness, and her extreme fatigue was like the bruising of her flesh against the imprisoning stones.

Between three and four o'clock she fell asleep at last and dreamed that she was in an air raid. All was confusion, and Alex, who had been with her, was missing. She ran along a dark road calling to him, stumbling over broken glass and debris. A child kept crying to her for a drink of water, but she would not stop. She woke up with her heart thudding and her skin wet with perspiration. Directly she dropped off again, the dream began exactly as before, but this time it was Naomi who called for water. She was pinned under masonry and there was a baby in her arms. She begged Elizabeth to take it, but when Elizabeth stooped to pick it up she saw that its skull was fractured. Its brains oozed out and covered her hands with a brown slime.

The second time she woke, she switched on the lamp and read a novel for an hour, not comprehending one word. When Henry brought her in a breakfast tray, he found the light still burning and the book dropped on the floor. Putting down the tray, he tiptoed out again.

It was past nine o'clock when Elizabeth woke finally. She poured out a cup of tea, but it was cold. The house seemed deathly quiet and rather lonely. Her father had left for the office and the daily maid had not yet arrived. She lit a cigarette and smoked it very slowly and deliberately to the end. Then she put on dressing-gown and slippers and went downstairs to telephone.

The bell rang for quite a long while before Alex answered it. She pictured him blear-eyed and unshaven, with a bad hangover. His voice sounded nervous, oddly unfamiliar. He said:

"You're not really ill, are you?"

"No, I'm not ill."

"I must see you. Where can we meet?"

"I'd better come to the flat, I suppose."

He hesitated, and she realised that he would have preferred more neutral ground.

"All right. At least we shan't be interrupted. When will you come?"

"You've got a lunch date, haven't you? And then that appointment at Claridge's with the American. I'll come at six o'clock."

"Thank you." He sounded almost humble. "Elizabeth . . ."

"Yes?"

"Nothing. I can't talk on the telephone. Good-bye."

They rang off simultaneously.

So that's that, Elizabeth told herself. Her mind would carry her no further. So that's that, she thought listlessly. So that's that.

CHAPTER XXIII

WHEN ELIZABETH ARRIVED at the flat at six o'clock, Alex was not yet there. She let herself in with her latchkey and automatically returned it to her handbag. Then, remembering, she took it out again and left it on the mantelpiece, pushed behind a candlestick. She did not want Alex to notice it till after she had gone, for this last meeting was to be conducted decently, she had determined, without melodrama or gesture. She was not going to cry and she was not going to make recriminations. It would not be difficult, she believed, for she was encased once more in a curious mood of detachment. Everything seemed dreamlike and unreal—it was another woman who had been happy in this flat, who had loved the man who owned it and shared his life so intimately. Already the present had become the past.

The sound of Alex's key in the door was like a sharp blow on the protective glass of her aloofness. For an instant it seemed to shiver, threatening to break. But it did not break, and she looked up when he came into the room and greeted him quite calmly.

"Hullo."

"I'm sorry I'm late. I couldn't get away from the man."

"Did you bring off the deal?" Her voice was polite, like a stranger's.

"Yes, thanks." He held out his cigarette-case. "Smoke?"

"Thank you."

When he lit the cigarette for her, she saw with surprise that his hand was unsteady. That might only be the hangover, of course. He was looking worse than she was, because she had the advantage of make-up, and there was a dab of iodine on his chin where he had cut himself shaving.

He sat down opposite her, with the width of the hearth between them. He ran his hand through his hair and she thought again how thin it was becoming.

"I don't know where to begin," he said.

"Do you expect me to help you?" That sounded bitter and she had not meant to be bitter.

"I suppose I ought not to, but I do rather. You always have, you see." His tone was frankly pleading. "Elizabeth, I have tried to tell you, more than once. But I've always felt so terrified of losing you. I've kept putting it off, hoping for a miracle, even hoping that I might get killed by a bomb one night and never need to tell you after all."

"Don't you mean that you were hoping that your wife might have another miscarriage?" she suggested dryly.

There was a long pause.

"So you know about that too," he said at last. His voice had changed. There was a note of defeat in it, and she realised that up till now he had still imagined that he might be able to explain it all away.

"Yes. She told me. Please don't bring her into it. It would be too indecent—"

"Elizabeth," he said rather desperately, "you must realise that it's you I love. I'm married to Naomi—and it's been diffi-cult—but I wouldn't care if I never saw her again. If you leave me now . . ." He got up and began to walk about the room, but he did not approach her. "You're the only thing in my life that really matters. I'm not worth much, God knows, but I wouldn't be anything at all without you. You do believe that, don't you? You do believe I love you?"

He stood in front of her, his hands held out, as if he longed to touch her but did not dare.

"Yes, I believe it, oddly enough. But it doesn't seem to matter any more," she said wearily. "I didn't mind the other things . . . No, that's not true. I did mind them very much, but they seemed worth it while I thought that they were things you couldn't help. I never expected you to leave Naomi and give up the children. But this is different. It makes our whole relationship . . . it makes our whole relationship a dirty farce."

"I'll leave her now if you'll stay with me," he said eagerly. "I'd do anything to prove to you how much you mean to me. If I ask Naomi to give me a divorce, will you try to forget what's happened and stay with me?"

"You can't ask a woman who is four months pregnant to divorce you," she said harshly. "It's too late now for that. And even if you did, I wouldn't marry you. Some lies one can't forgive."

There seemed nothing more to say and she stood up to go, but this time he seized her hands and would not free them. There were tears in his eyes and he had flushed up to his forehead. He looked like Donald when Miss Glover had rebuked him.

"You can't leave me like this—I won't let you. We haven't said anything yet—we haven't settled anything. I won't believe that all these years can go for nothing. I've tried to make you understand how much I love you, but you haven't said you love me. But you do love me—I know you do. Whatever I've done, you'll go on loving me. I've made you unhappy, but you'll be much more unhappy if you leave me."

They stood facing each other, her hands limp in his grasp. His fingers were bruising her, but she did not feel any pain.

"I couldn't be more unhappy than I am now," she said in a steady voice.

Suddenly she began to cry and found she could not stop. It was the one thing she had been determined not to do, but circumstances were too much for her. Unresistingly, she let Alex push her gently back into the chair. He knelt down beside her, with his arms round her waist and his head resting on her lap, so that she could not move. His head felt heavy and inconsolable. He had trapped her and she no longer had the energy to struggle.

"That's better," he murmured. "That's better. You don't really hate me, whatever I've done."

"Hating you or loving you has nothing to do with it," she said through her tears. "Oh, Alex, can't you see? Everything's changed—it's all gone rotten. You've made it cheap and dirty. We could never forget what has happened, either of us—whatever you said or promised. I couldn't believe you about anything, after this."

His voice came to her muffled and forlorn.

"I'm not asking you to forget. I'm asking you to take what's second-best. We'll be so lonely without each other. If we were married and I'd been unfaithful to you with another woman, with Naomi, you'd forgive me, wouldn't you?"

He raised his head to look at her, trying to read her face.

"But isn't that the whole point?" she asked him very sadly. "I'm not married to you. I haven't any of the things that Naomi has—your children or your home or the right to live with you openly. I only had one thing and now I've lost that too. There's nothing left."

He took hold of her hands again and began kissing them, deliberately, soberly, backs and palms and wrists, as if it were a task to be accomplished and the time were short.

"My poor love. It was a bad day for you when you met me, wasn't it? Do you wish you never had?"

"No, I don't wish that. We've had our good moments." Her tears were over and had left her calmer and relaxed. The glass wall of detachment had been shattered and she found herself less vulnerable without it.

"They were the best moments I've ever had," he said sincerely. "You must believe that—you know it's true. Whatever harm I've done you, you've brought me nothing but happiness."

"I'm glad."

For a moment she surrendered herself to a feeling of tenderness, moved by the sight of his bent head and the touch of his lips on her hands. He sensed the alteration in her mood immediately.

"Elizabeth, don't go away just yet." He looked at her pleadingly. "I promise I won't try to make you change your mind, if only you'll stay with me now. Don't let's part with bitterness— we'll have a long time to remember. Couldn't we pretend, just once more, that everything's the same as it used to be? Have dinner together and spend the evening here? I swear I wouldn't try to make love to you. You could go whenever you liked and I'd accept the fact."

"I don't think you would," she told him ruefully. "You mean it now, but afterwards it might seem different. What's the use of torturing ourselves deliberately? It won't change anything. And everything we said or did would have an undertone—'This is the last time'."

"Please, Elizabeth!"

He was too wise to repeat his argument. It was enough that she would tell herself, without his prompting, that very soon he would not be there to plead with her, nor she to yield.

"I think it would be madness, from every point of view," she said.

But he knew that she consented.

"I'll get you a drink." He jumped to his feet. "I think we both need one."

He left the room and Elizabeth took out her mirror. She looked tired and plain and old, she decided soberly; if Alex loved her now, it was not for her appearance. The effect was a little better when she had re-applied her make-up, but the last twenty-four hours had left a mark which would not be easily erased. She thought about Monday and the office. She would have to find Alex another secretary. I can leave it to him to find another mistress, she told herself bitterly.

When Alex came back, carrying a tray, she said matter-of-factly:

"Miss Patterson could be your secretary again when I'm gone. She rang me up the other day. Her husband's been called up and she'd like to take a job."

"I don't want another secretary, ever," he said crossly. "I certainly don't want Miss Patterson."

"You were quite pleased with her until she left to marry and I came along. You'd far better have someone who understands the job already."

He put down the tray and looked at her with a kind of angry admiration.

"My God, you're hard, aren't you? I always said you were."

"Yes, you always did." She took the glass he handed her. "I always said so too. I never pretended."

"You're not much good at pretending, are you? You're fundamentally too honest. I wonder why you fell in love with me?"

"Attraction of opposites, I suppose."

"Darling, you actually smiled!"

His spirits rose almost visibly. Elizabeth thought, He still doesn't believe that I'm going through with this. He's quite stupid in some ways, but he can be so charming that one doesn't notice it. It was her brain that spoke, and not for the first time, but her heart did not ache the less because of it.

"Where shall we have dinner?" he went on.

"Anywhere. I don't mind."

"Prunier's?"

"If you like."

"I'll ring up and book a table, before you change your mind." He put down his glass with alacrity and went out into the hall to telephone. "I've made it half-past seven," he said when he came back.

"This is turning into quite a celebration, isn't it?" she commented dryly.

"Oh darling, don't be *too* hard!" He bent down and laid his cheek against hers in a momentary, almost timid caress. "Let's not quarrel any more. Give me something pleasant to remember."

"I don't think this is an evening in our lives that we shall want particularly to remember," she said evenly, too evenly. "But I don't want a scene, any more than you. What did you do last night?"

"I got extremely drunk, if you must know."

"I thought you would. Sensible of you. You don't ask me what I did," she added after a moment.

"That's cowardice. You know I'm a coward. What did you do?"

"I talked to my father. I told him about us."

"Good Lord. Did he know already when I spoke to him on the 'phone?"

"Yes."

"He sounded a bit curt, but I thought I must be imagining it. What made you tell him?"

"I wanted a little consolation. He's always kind."

"I suppose he thinks I'm an unmitigated cad?"

"I didn't give him any details. He's rather upset about it all, of course."

"I'm glad you've told him," Alex said reflectively. "I'm glad you've got that, anyway. But it makes me feel jealous, in an odd sort of way. I never meant you to have to go to someone else to be consoled for anything I'd done. That rankles. I know I've deserved it, but it rankles."

"Yes. I can understand that. I should feel like that if the positions were reversed."

"We do understand each other, don't we?" he said gently. "In spite of all our disagreements. We speak the same language. That's all it is, really. That's why people fall in love. It's like suddenly meeting a fellow countryman in a strange land."

She stood up abruptly.

"I want to tidy myself before we leave. Don't come with me."

Not looking at him, she walked into the bedroom and closed the door behind her. She was going to have to cry again and she was afraid—afraid of herself, afraid of him. Lying across the bed, her head on Alex's pillow with its faint familiar smell of hair-oil and the cigarettes he smoked, it was easy enough to cry. She wept for both of them, quietly, in case he should hear her and come in. She had been a fool to say that she would spend the evening with him. It was going to make it all much worse.

Presently she stopped crying and lay with her lids closed over eyes that ached and smarted. She would have liked to fall asleep—to sleep and wake up to find Alex beside her and the last twenty-four hours no more than the bad dream they still seemed. But instead she got up and washed her face with cold water, using Alex's sponge. The blue tooth-brush in the rack above the basin was hers. She put it in her hand-bag, to save Alex a stupid pang.

While she was making up her face again, he knocked on the door.

"May I come in?"

"Come in. I've just finished." She stood up hastily.

"All right. Don't run away. I thought I'd put on a clean collar in honour of our last evening." He started at his reflection in the mirror, "I look horribly dissipated, don't I? Do you like this tie?"

"Not very much."

"I'll change that too. I'll put on one of the ones you gave me." He opened his cupboard and looked rather helplessly at the row of ties.

"You can't remember which they are," she said with a laugh that was dangerously near hysteria. "You know you're colour-blind. Here, wear this one."

She thrust it into his hand and turned away quickly.

"I'm going to use the telephone."

"We can leave when you're ready," he called after her.

It was Henry whom Elizabeth rang up. She told him that she would not be home to dinner.

"I'm not quite sure when I'll be back. Don't wait up for me. If I see your light on, I'll come in and say good night."

"Is this a good idea?" he asked anxiously.

"No, it's a very bad one. But don't worry, darling. Nothing's any different."

She rang off before he could comment.

"Finished?" Alex asked from the doorway of the bedroom.

"Yes. I'm ready."

"Then let's go."

Driving in the taxi to the restaurant, she reflected that he was working very hard. She would have been amused in different circumstances. They had never dined at Prunier's except on special occasions. The stage had been carefully set to obtain the maximum sentimental effect, and he was probably already calculating how much he could persuade her to drink. It was one of their oldest jokes that he had basely seduced her. Tonight it seemed as though he might be going to make the attempt in earnest.

"What are we going to talk about through dinner?" she asked when they had driven a little way in rather mournful silence.

"I've been wondering that myself," he confessed. "I keep thinking of things to say, but they all seem to lead to dangerous ground."

"We could talk about the war, I suppose."

"Do we have to depress ourselves still further? I imagine the news is just about as bloody as it could be—we've been driven out of Greece, we're being driven out of Libya and Liverpool's been bombed to hell."

"We brought down over twenty 'planes the other night."

"Yes. I'd rather like to get into the Air Force."

"You're over-age."

"I know I am. But I could probably get into something on the ground. Intelligence, perhaps."

"They wouldn't release you."

"We'll see. I'm not going to stay in Soho Square without you. Let Rowland earn the dollars."

"He'd make a lovely mess of it without you."

"Maybe, maybe not. I'm getting rather tired of being a reserved civilian. If nothing else turns up I'll get into the R.N.V.R. and sweep mines."

She wondered if he meant what he was saying, or whether it was all part of a campaign to weaken her resistance. It was odd that you could think that of a man, so coldly, and yet love him still.

"We're here."

He paid the taxi-driver and they entered the restaurant. What a lot of places I shall want to avoid for the rest of my life, Elizabeth thought wearily.

When the meal had been ordered, Alex began a game of "Do you remember?" He did it skilfully, reminding her only of brief, snatched holidays together, incidents in the early air raids, jokes at the office. It was a flattering performance and not without its effect. It gave Elizabeth a foretaste of the loneliness she would endure without him. But it did not alter her decision. More terrible than the image of separation was the thought of what it would be like to go on in the old way, burdened with a new knowledge.

After the coffee, Alex ordered liqueurs; she had been right about the drink.

"I'll give you a toast," he said. "To us."

"To you and to me," she qualified.

"That wasn't what I said."

"I know."

He shrugged his shoulders.

"All right. Have it your way." He emptied his glass in a gulp. "I suppose there isn't really such a thing as 'us'," he added moodily. "We pretend there is, but it's always a you and a me just fooling themselves. Shall we go?"

"Yes. Let's go—"

Characteristically, he managed to persuade the taxi-driver to drive them back by way of Hyde Park, a wide detour.

"I thought you'd like a little air," he told Elizabeth. "It's still quite warm. Do you remember that night we had dinner in the open air restaurant in Hyde Park, before the war?"

"I don't want to do any more remembering. I won't remember."

"Grand, easy words," he scoffed. "You might give me the recipe before you go."

They sat in opposite corners, leaning back. Looking away from him, out of the window, Elizabeth asked abruptly:

"Alex, why did you get us all three into such a mess? How could you do it? It didn't even seem to worry you until you thought I might be going to find out."

"I don't know," he said gloomily. "I suppose I just took the line of least resistance. I wanted you and I knew I couldn't get you on any other terms. So the obvious thing was simply to lie about it. I'm not really polygamous—not more than any other man—but Naomi would soon have grown suspicious if I'd changed my relations with her, and I didn't want her snooping round in search of evidence for a divorce. I wasn't going to risk losing the children. I guess what I really wanted was to have my cake and eat it too. The old, old dilemma."

"But didn't it occur to you that you were cheating both of us?" she asked incredulously. "Didn't it make you feel ashamed?"

"I felt ashamed about you. Not about Naomi. Oh, I know I ought to have done, but it's wonderful how much one will swallow when it's dished out by one's precious self. It's difficult to see oneself objectively. One's prejudiced from birth. You'd be surprised how many men would do the same."

"My father wouldn't."

He did not answer. They sat in silence until the taxi drew up.

The flat looked desolate and untidy, with their used glasses still on the table and the ash-trays full of cigarette ends.

"Rotten service you get in this place nowadays," Alex said disgustedly.

He was moody now, openly miserable, making no further attempt to beguile her with words or caresses. He sprawled in a chair and lit one cigarette from the other. It was the moment to leave him. But she found that she could not leave him while he seemed so utterly defeated.

Suddenly he stabbed out his cigarette and stood up.

"Come up on the roof."

"On the roof?"

"Yes. I want you to see the view from there. I often go up when I'm fire-watching."

Helping her on with her coat, his arms tightened round her and he kissed her, briefly but with a kind of desperation.

Neither of them spoke. Still in silence they mounted the stairs and emerged by a trap-door on to the flat surface of the top-floor apartment. A parapet of sandbags had been built round the edge and they walked across and looked down over it. It was hardly more than dusk yet, but the moon had risen and they could make out the outlines of buildings quite clearly. Vast and shadowy, London stretched around them, her scars concealed.

"It makes me feel very small," Alex said in a low voice. "Very small and trivial. I wonder why I'm here and what I'm meant to do. It makes me wish I were a better man. I could have been, if I had married you, Elizabeth! We could have lived together decently and honourably. It isn't any fun to be the kind of man I am now."

As he spoke, she seemed to see him as he would become without her. She imagined him middle-aged and prosperous, a conventional, bald-headed business man, fond of his children and outwardly on good terms with his wife. Probably there would always be another woman discreetly in the background. But sometimes he would remember her, Elizabeth, and with regret.

And she? She ran the risk of growing bitter and discontented, increasingly self-contained, increasing hard. If she married at all, she would make a poor wife, always aware that this was second-best. But very likely she would not marry. She would spend her life debating whether she had saved her soul or thrown away her one positive happiness.

For the first time she wavered in her decision; but only for a moment. She could visualise too well the days and weeks and months that stretched ahead for both of them if she were to capitulate now—suspicions, lies, recriminations; passion without innocence and shame of self, which was the worst shame of all. Beside that negation of the spirit, loneliness and dearth seemed almost sweet.

"Poor us." She sighed and slipped her arm through his. "We've made a mess of things, haven't we? Perhaps we're the kind that always will—in between sort of people. If you can't be a happy sinner, it's better not to sin at all. And that so difficult."

"Loving you isn't a sin," he protested.

"That wasn't what I meant," she said gently. "It isn't as simple as that."

He did not answer and she became aware again of where they stood. She felt the rough surface of the sandbags against her knees and the sensation of height was suddenly frightening. London, spread out below them in the moonlight, looked enormous. Beneath her roofs, her children occupied themselves by day in living and by night in countering death. The moon was her enemy and mercilessly etched her vulnerability. Elizabeth felt her heart twist in her body with compassion for that vulnerability. High above the houses, looking down, she ached with longing to protect her. The pain of that desire burned out the pain of leaving Alex. London's sorrows were too great to leave them space for theirs. Her bravery rebuked them.

"Alex, let's say good-bye up here. I'd rather."

He drew her away from the edge of the world and faced her. He understands, she thought; perhaps this was why he brought me here.

"I'd rather too," he said. "Good-bye, my darling."

They kissed very tenderly, without passion. Then Elizabeth turned and ran down the stairs, down flights and flights of stairs, out into the moon-drenched, shadowy streets.

By the time she reached home, the raid had started. The sky was rosy with the fires of London burning.

CHAPTER XXIV

HARDLY HAD THEY unlocked the garage and lit the stove than the All Clear sounded. It was a few minutes past ten o'clock and it seemed that there had been a false alarm.

"I expect there'll be another Alert presently," Elizabeth said, "but I suppose we might as well go home in between."

"I shall go for a stroll," Owen announced. "It's such a lovely moony night. I won't go any further than the Common and I can be back at once if anything happens."

"Would you mind if I came with you?" she asked hesitantly. "I feel terribly restless, for some reason."

"I'd like you to."

A month ago he would have said it with embarrassment, but now he was not thinking of himself. He was feeling concerned about Elizabeth. Her nervous tension was apparent in her voice, her gestures and the expression in her eyes. He might have thought her suffering from the effects of the raid the night before, if he had not known as much as he did about her private affairs. Elizabeth must be ten years older than he was, he reflected, and yet she did not seem any better equipped to handle her life. There was something touching and puzzling to him about that.

The Common was intersected into squares by roads, and because they could not risk going too far away from their post of duty, they contented themselves with walking round the first square only. Other couples strolled arm in arm along the same way, or stood in the shadows of the trees; but these were lovers. The bond which united him with Elizabeth seemed to Owen at once a slighter and a more enduring one. Here they were, two people who happened to live in houses opposite each other, whom circumstances (and not the incidents of war alone) had brought together in an odd kind of intimacy. He visualised their lives as parallel tracks, which every now and then swerved in to touch and then branched off again. But only he knew at how many points the contact had been made. Elizabeth would never know. There was a certain satisfaction to him in that. It was a secret source of power, power which would never be used and therefore never dissipated. To understand was to mount a little hill and see the landscape in a pattern.

"It seems to have been the worst raid ever last night," he said to break the silence between them.

"Yes. I went up to the West End today, just to make sure that the office was all right—and some friends of mine. A landmine fell in Soho, quite near the square. It killed a lot of people whom I knew in shops and restaurants round there."

"I'm sorry. Did you go along to see the damage to the Abbey and the Houses of Parliament?"

"No. I funked it. I mind about the Abbey much more than St. Paul's. I wish I'd been more recently."

"I wish I'd seen the Temple Church. I always meant to go with Derek in the holidays, but churches aren't much in his line."

"My father told me that he'd had a crash. Is he all right?"

"Yes, he's all right."

They had come too close to Lampton now and Mrs. Foster in the train. He changed the subject.

"I've had my calling-up papers."

"Oh, have you, Owen? Are you glad?"

"I think so. It's a bit of a plunge now the moment's come. But I've been awfully fed up hanging about and waiting."

"I think you'll make a good pilot. I don't think it's only hearty, unimaginative young men who do well in conditions of great nervous strain."

He was immensely gratified, but he did not know how to respond. He wanted more than ever to be kind to her, to show her sympathy without intrusion. But how? She would think him crazy if he were to take her hand, and yet that was what he would really have liked to do. Nor did this desire seem to him at all a strange thing or out of character with his own ideas about himself. An emotion he had never felt before, a kind of chivalric tenderness, possessed him. Someone of his own sex had hurt her and he wanted to redress the balance.

"You'll have to fire-watch with another bloke when I'm gone," was all he found to say.

"Not for very long." She stopped walking. "Shall we sit down for a little while? Do you think the grass is too wet?"

"I've got a newspaper in my pocket. We can sit on that." They propped themselves against a tree and Owen hugged his knees and looked sideways at her profile in the moonlight. "Why did you say, 'Not for long'?"

"Because I'm going to chuck my job and take up nursing full time. I'm tired of office work."

"Oh." He felt as if she had handed him another piece to fit into a jigsaw. "Did you choose nursing because of going to the hospital that Sunday, after the dance-hall incident?"

"I suppose so. I'll be more use at that than having to be trained from scratch in one of the women's services. Besides—I'd like to help to save people's lives. There was a child in hospital that day with a piece of shrapnel in her chest. She was suffering the torments of hell then, and she lived for two more days. I couldn't do anything for her, but I'd like to make amends to her the only way I can."

If I say that often enough I shall come to believe it, she told herself bitterly. She imagined Norah Jenkins' too-bright eyes regarding her accusingly and felt ashamed. For it was improbable that she would have given up her job, which meant proximity to Alex, if Alex himself had not forced her hand. She was using Norah's thin, light body as a shield. That would be another thing to make amends for.

"It's funny," Owen said in a carefully casual voice, "but all the time you're learning to heal people after raids, I shall be learning how to drop bombs and smash them up."

"But there's another difference," she said quickly. "I shall be safe, as safe as I am anywhere else, and you'll be risking being killed yourself."

"I suppose so. But I don't like the idea much, all the same. Only, I know that someone's got to do it and I've always felt it's rather mean to leave the dirty work to other people. I mean, if you're going to accept the fact that this war has to be fought, it's cowardly to choose the cushy bits that won't give you nightmares afterwards, if you come through. That's how I see it, anyway."

"Does Derek feel the same?"

"I don't think so. He's never said so. He's a much more straightforward sort of person than me."

"Perhaps you'll turn up as a patient in my hospital," she said lightly, to comfort him. "And then I'll bring you all the nicest things to eat and risk a wigging from the Sister to come and talk to you."

He laughed. "Good idea. I'd like that. I'll try and time my crash to land in your locality."

"Oh dear." She sighed. "What a bad moment we chose to be born! Or don't you think so?"

"No, I'm rather pleased about it. It's a peak moment, and that's sort of thrilling. People will remember our generation and be proud of us, I hope. And of course I want to live to have a hand in clearing up the ghastly mess afterwards. Something constructive—that's what we'll all want to do at the end of this peculiarly destructive war."

"You never have any doubt which way it will end?"

"No, never. Neither have you. The English are so gloriously smug."

"I'm afraid I had some bad moments last May and June."

"Yes, that was pretty scaring," he admitted. "I've never been as scared in any of the air raids since."

"Well, in an air raid you can always console yourself with the thought that even if you are killed, you aren't indispensable."

"Exactly. It sounds rather elevated, but it is how one feels."

"Have you noticed how much encouraged everybody is by a really heavy raid?" she asked.

"Yes, it's odd, isn't it? Particularly after a spell of bad news on other fronts, such as we've had lately. I suppose it's because one feels like a participant again. It's always more alarming to be a helpless onlooker. You get an idea that you're contributing something just by surviving and not letting yourself be demoralised."

"Yes." She shivered suddenly. "I'm getting cold. Let's walk on a bit."

They went some way in silence. Now she's remembering again, Owen thought. But he felt pleased with himself for distracting her mind for even a little while and he wondered what else they could discuss which would be personal enough to hold her attention and yet would not drive her back into herself. He even imagined for a moment that he might tell her how much he had hated her, and why; but that was too great a sacrifice to make. Instead he began again, rather haltingly:

"I suppose people in the future will picture our existence now, in London, as quite abnormal and pretty terrifying, and yet it hasn't been, has it? I mean, in between the sticky moments, we seem to have gone on much the same as usual—being pleased or miserable about the same things, worrying about money and what our neighbours think of us, and getting a devil of a kick out of any sort of promotion or achievement. It's all right to be heroic in spots, but human nature's really rather childish, isn't it? And a bit callous, too. We're little people, and the big things have to be reduced in size or we can't handle them. I don't think it's anything to be ashamed of. I think it's better like that."

"It keeps us sane, anyhow. And we shall need our sanity." She looked at him wonderingly. "You've changed a lot lately, haven't you, Owen? I don't think it's only because I know you better than I did. I think you've jumped ahead of me in some way. What is it?"

"I believe I'm happy," he answered her with surprise in his voice. "How strange—I hadn't noticed it before. Do you think it's wicked to be happy now?"

"Of course not."

Touched by his confession, grateful for his companionship, she felt almost tranquil herself as side by side they walked across the Common in the moonlight.

THE END

FURROWED MIDDLEBROW

FM1. *A Footman for the Peacock* (1940) . . . . RACHEL FERGUSON

FM2. *Evenfield* (1942) . . . . RACHEL FERGUSON

FM3. *A Harp in Lowndes Square* (1936) . . . . RACHEL FERGUSON

FM4. *A Chelsea Concerto* (1959) . . . . FRANCES FAVIELL

FM5. *The Dancing Bear* (1954) . . . . FRANCES FAVIELL

FM6. *A House on the Rhine* (1955) . . . . FRANCES FAVIELL

FM7. *Thalia* (1957) . . . . FRANCES FAVIELL

FM8. *The Fledgeling* (1958) . . . . FRANCES FAVIELL

FM9. *Bewildering Cares* (1940) . . . . WINIFRED PECK

FM10. *Tom Tiddler's Ground* (1941) . . . . URSULA ORANGE

FM11. *Begin Again* (1936) . . . . URSULA ORANGE

FM12. *Company in the Evening* (1944) . . . . URSULA ORANGE

FM13. *The Late Mrs. Prioleau* (1946) . . . . MONICA TINDALL

FM14. *Bramton Wick* (1952) . . . . ELIZABETH FAIR

FM15. *Landscape in Sunlight* (1953) . . . . ELIZABETH FAIR

FM16. *The Native Heath* (1954) . . . . ELIZABETH FAIR

FM17. *Seaview House* (1955) . . . . ELIZABETH FAIR

FM18. *A Winter Away* (1957) . . . . ELIZABETH FAIR

FM19. *The Mingham Air* (1960) . . . . ELIZABETH FAIR

FM20. *The Lark* (1922) . . . . E. NESBIT

FM21. *Smouldering Fire* (1935) . . . . D.E. STEVENSON

FM22. *Spring Magic* (1942) . . . . D.E. STEVENSON

FM23. *Mrs. Tim Carries On* (1941) . . . . D.E. STEVENSON

FM24. *Mrs. Tim Gets a Job* (1947) . . . . D.E. STEVENSON

FM25. *Mrs. Tim Flies Home* (1952) . . . . D.E. STEVENSON

FM26. *Alice* (1949) . . . . ELIZABETH ELIOT

FM27. *Henry* (1950) . . . . ELIZABETH ELIOT

FM28. *Mrs. Martell* (1953) . . . . ELIZABETH ELIOT

FM29. *Cecil* (1962) . . . . ELIZABETH ELIOT

FM30. *Nothing to Report* (1940) . . . . CAROLA OMAN

FM31. *Somewhere in England* (1943) . . . . CAROLA OMAN

FM32. *Spam Tomorrow* (1956) . . . . VERILY ANDERSON

FM33. *Peace, Perfect Peace* (1947) . . . . JOSEPHINE KAMM

FM34. *Beneath the Visiting Moon* (1940) . . . . ROMILLY CAVAN

FM35. *Table Two* (1942) . . . . MARJORIE WILENSKI

FM36. *The House Opposite* (1943) . . . . BARBARA NOBLE

FM37. *Miss Carter and the Ifrit* (1945) . . . . SUSAN ALICE KERBY

FM38. *Wine of Honour* (1945) . . . . BARBARA BEAUCHAMP

Made in the USA
Middletown, DE
23 January 2020